THE SOUND
OF HEAT

RENEE WOOD

Cover design by: David Moore and Renee Wood
Cover photographs by: Renee Wood

For Moeie

BOOKS IN THE SERIES

CONTENTS

ACKNOWLEDGMENTS

My love and deepest thanks to Hope Borgan, Joanna Frueh, Sally Hatton, Elizabeth Hykes, and Phoenix Keffer. Thanks for believing and for all the help along the way.

i

Book 1 - The Sound of Water

CHAPTER 1

Curran TaZarin, the *Defender's* first officer, read his new orders in disbelief.

They were sending him back to Thaetar. Along with Ryerson, Collins, and Takawa.

As a young ensign in the Planetary Alliance's Sixth Fleet, he had spent nearly two years on Thaetar. With his strong background in the natural sciences, TaZarin had been part of a team assigned to help the Thaetan government assess the potential ecological impact of a major land reclamation project.

To a Deniban like TaZarin, his senses tuned to life in the high desert grasslands of Deniba's interior, Thaetar had been a nightmare world. The Thaetan sky was continually overcast. The air was oppressively humid and rank with the smell of rotting vegetation. In the moist heat of the Thaetan climate, plants of every kind grew in profusion and with astonishing speed. They died and decayed with equal speed.

Unfortunately, many of the people who'd gone with him to Thaetar had also died, only not nearly so quickly. The horror of watching helplessly as a seemingly endless assortment of Thaetan fevers took the lives of one team member after another was something TaZarin had never been able to leave behind. He did not want to go back, especially now, with the planet poised on the edge of all-out civil war.

TaZarin read the orders again, thinking about the current political situation in the Thaetan sector and what the four of them were being asked to do.

Thaetar was located in a disputed border zone between the Planetary Alliance and the Karghan Federation. Both had pledged to respect Thaetar's neutrality and the rights of the non-aligned planets within the zone, and until recently, neither had interfered directly in the planet's internal affairs. Now, according to the documents he was reading, Thaetan government intelligence reports indicated that the Karghans had entered the war on the side of the rebels and were supporting them with arms and advisors.

If true, the Alliance would be compelled to act. It was critical to Alliance interests in the sector to prevent a Karghan sphere of influence from developing there that might endanger nearby planets under Alliance protection. Still, most Alliance members wanted a political solution to the Thaetan problem, not a military one, and they remained reluctant to intervene without absolute proof of Karghan intervention. The four of them were being sent to look for the evidence.

TaZarin called the mission team together for a meeting in the ship's briefing room. When he arrived, the others were already there, clustered at the far end of the narrow conference table with Ryerson seated on one side and Collins and Takawa on the other.

TaZarin took a seat beside Ryerson, explained the purpose of the mission in a few terse sentences, and watched as an ironic smile spread across Takawa's lips, but didn't touch his eyes. Collin's expression progressed from condescension to outrage. Ryerson listened in disbelief.

"They are absolutely out of their minds," she said quietly to no one in particular.

Katherine Ryerson was the *Defender's* language specialist and epigrapher. She was forty-five years old, a tall, willowy woman with auburn hair and grey eyes, married and the mother of two young children. She was also a former intelligence operative who'd been transferred to the *Defender* five years ago after a deployment with the Alliance Defense Intelligence Service. Before her assignment to the *Defender,* she'd spent three years on Thaetar, supposedly studying Thaetan language and culture.

Ryerson had been staring at her hands while TaZarin explained the mission. When he finished, he saw her look up and glance at Takawa. Takawa returned Katherine's glance and tried to give her a reassuring smile, but couldn't quite manage it.

Fleet Marine Captain Kumio Takawa had served on Thaetar for almost three years as part of the Alliance's Embassy Guard. Nothing in either of their files suggested that they'd served together on Thaetar, but TaZarin knew they had. They had both been involved in espionage there, and they were both refugees from the Alliance Defense Intelligence Service. As a reward for having accepted second and then third tours of duty on Thaetar, promises were made to both of them, and places on the *Defender* had been one of them. Nice safe work on a nice safe research and exploration ship, leading to nice quiet retirements.

Although Takawa was an experienced combat team leader and an expert in small unit tactics, his current duties included nothing more demanding than the command of the small marine detachment assigned to the *Defender* to provide security for ground-based research and exploration missions.

"Idiots," Takawa said.

Takawa's normal expression was open and candid. Now his eyes were angry and guarded.

In the seat next to him, Collins was getting over his initial shock and starting to protest. Collins was explaining, with growing exasperation at TaZarin's apparent inability to understand, that he was a member of the fleet admiral's staff and was in transit on an assignment for the admiral himself—one that had nothing to do with going to Thaetar. Once his new orders were verified, they would be found to be in error.

TaZarin accepted the fact that Collins was angry and afraid. They were all angry and afraid, but the man's arrogance and blatant disregard for everyone else repelled him. Collin's military record said he had six years in the fleet, but he'd served all of them behind a desk. TaZarin stayed silent, his face expressionless, letting Collins reveal himself, waiting for him to wear himself out.

"Mr. Collins," TaZarin said calmly once the lieutenant finally came to a stop, "you may be in transit on an assignment for the fleet admiral, but it should be as obvious to you as it is to the rest of us that *you*, as the intelligence analyst, are the reason the rest of us are here. Your area of specialization is Karghan weapons and tactics, is it not?"

"Yes," Collins replied, annoyed.

"Then your new orders supersede any previous orders, Mr. Collins. They are not in error, and they need no further verification."

The only possible reason anyone would send Ryerson, Takawa, and him back to Thaetar was because they and Collins were all in the same place at the same time, and that place was only three days from Thaetar.

"As for the details of the mission," TaZarin said, "we will be going in as a Deniban arms trader and his staff. We'll be taken to the surface by one of the *Defender's* survey ships modified to look like a Carthian supply vessel. The survey ship will remain in planetary orbit to wait for us. The *Defender* will be sent to the Frithian asteroid belt to pick up drilling reports and core samples from the mining facilities there. Hopefully, that will be enough to prevent us from being connected directly to either the *Defender* or the Alliance if things don't go well."

"Unless, of course, the survey ship gets boarded for some reason," Takawa added with an ironic smile.

TaZarin said nothing in reply, although he agreed with Takawa that it was a possibility. Not everyone was welcome in Thaetan space, and inspection boardings were not uncommon.

"We'll be dropped off near a rebel base camp in a meeting place known to be used by rebel supporters," he continued. "We'll wait there to be picked up by a patrol and taken into the camp.

"They've planned a diversion for the next morning during which we're expected to make our escape."

"In other words, we're going to let ourselves get captured," Collins said.

"The plan admittedly has some flaws," TaZarin continued. "For one thing, all three of us have served on Thaetar before as military representatives of the Alliance."

"What difference does that make?" Collins asked impatiently.

"The Thaetan secret police keep detailed records on all off-worlders working on Thaetar, Mr. Collins, especially those working for foreign governments. Considering the value of that kind of information, the rebels will certainly have found a way to access it. It's simply a matter of time before they know who we are."

"That's just great."

TaZarin understood that Collins was still trying to integrate what was happening to him with his ideas about how the world should operate, but enough was enough.

"Mr. Collins, you will keep any further comments of that nature to yourself. This team needs you to do your job. That is all that is required of you."

"Since we'll be arriving at this meeting place uninvited," Ryerson said, "they may be willing to listen to us for a while, but you know as well as I do that they'll assume we're enemy agents for as long as it takes them to decide we're not."

"Until they decide, we should be relatively safe," TaZarin said.

"Well, it won't take long for them to figure it out," Ryerson replied.

"What is this diversion we're counting on?" Takawa asked, moving on.

"The information is on a need to know basis, and they say we don't need to know."

Takawa and Ryerson accepted TaZarin's statement without comment. Collins didn't.

"Why not?"

"Because we can't reveal during interrogation what we don't know," TaZarin answered.

"And what if this diversion doesn't work? What then? Is there a back-up plan?"

"No, Mr. Collins, there is not."

"We can't afford not to escape," Takawa said, putting into words what the others already knew. "Alliance military personnel caught in the act of spying would be an extremely valuable propaganda weapon for the rebels, and it would give the Karghans the excuse they've been waiting for to become fully involved in the war. It would also destroy Alliance credibility in the region as a neutral party."

"Our capture and use by the insurgents would be a serious political problem for the Alliance," TaZarin said. "They would simply find a way to take us out of the equation."

"Do they still have the kill team there?" Ryerson asked Takawa.

"Still do. Two of them, now."

TaZarin watched Collins' face go white. As part of his intelligence work, Collins would have routinely analyzed the information gathered by people sent on the kind of reconnaissance mission he was being sent on now. Collins surely knew that some of those people never came back, but it had apparently never concerned him until now.

"Are there any further questions?" TaZarin asked.

There weren't.

"Study the briefing materials. Memorize the maps and the escape route.

"Captain Takawa, I'll meet with you here again in an hour. The two of us will draw up a list of weapons and equipment a

Deniban arms trader might presumably have for sale."

**

Three days later, the four of them were taken to Thaetar and left in a rocky upland glade where they expected to be met by a rebel patrol. The glade was studded with bedrock outcroppings and surrounded by dense forest. Overhead, the sky was a uniform gunmetal gray, and a fine misting rain was falling.

All four of them were dressed in the *raddic* wool clothing TaZarin had managed to have brought to the *Defender*. Raddic wool produced a tough hard cloth, and when treated with *hath* oil, it became exceptionally water repellant. The loose-fitting pants, light-weight shirts, over-tunics belted at the waist, and the thick woolen ponchos they all wore matched the colors that dominated the Thaetan landscape; blacks, grays, muted tans and browns, pale blues and greens.

Katherine was leaning against a large rock near the center of the glade, watching TaZarin. He was sitting by himself at the edge of the clearing.

Katherine had never thought of TaZarin as a handsome man. *Interesting* was perhaps a better word, she thought. There was a reserve reflected in his face, a kind of self-sufficiency she knew made many humans uncomfortable. The reserve was a normal part of the Deniban character, a result of the Mind Disciplines, the skills and techniques they'd developed in order to control and use their telepathic abilities. The psychic abilities were innate in all Denibans, but it took years of training to develop them fully, and there was a vast disparity between the acceptable level of skill needed to function in Deniban society and the skills of a Deniban Master. Katherine had always found TaZarin's reserve soothing. It was one of the reasons she liked him.

Katherine had also thought she knew TaZarin reasonably well. They shared an interest in music and the arts and often spent time together on shore leave. Now, despite her familiarity with him, Katherine could barely find the man she knew as Curran TaZarin in the man she was watching.

TaZarin had the typical high cheekbones, copper-colored skin, and green eyes of people from Deniba's interior deserts. Now, his coarse jet-black hair, which he usually kept brushed back away from his face, was unkempt and unwashed, and he'd shaved off the mustache and beard that marked him as desert-born and a follower of Charik. Three days worth of stubble covered his face.

The Curran TaZarin she knew was educated, cultured, and in spite of his reserve, caring. He spoke Alliance Standard fluently and with almost no Deniban accent, yet the few times she'd tried to talk to this new version of himself, he'd answered in such heavily accented, guttural Standard she'd been hard-pressed to understand him at all. His voice had become harsh, the tone sarcastic. His green Deniban eyes had turned shrewd and calculating. Even the way he carried himself had changed.

TaZarin wasn't a physically imposing man. He was lean and sinewy, but as with many Deniban men, there existed an underlying quality of pent-up, almost explosive physical power. Now his presence had become physically intimidating. The transformation was so complete and so bizarre Katherine couldn't take her eyes off him. She had to force herself to look away.

Near the center of the glade, Kumio and Collins were sitting by a small fire Kumio had built to drive away a little of the chill and dampness. As usual, Collins was in his own world, restlessly tapping his foot while he peeled the bark off a stick with his fingernail. Then she noticed Curran and Kumio exchange glances.

"Our escort is here at last," TaZarin announced loudly in harsh, sneering Standard. "Invite them in, Katherine," he said, getting to his feet as the small patrol left the woods, entered the clearing, and surrounded them.

***

Curran watched as four un-uniformed men, all carrying automatic weapons and neural pulsers, and led by a uniformed officer, walked out of the woods. The neural pulsers were clearly of Karghan design and would be especially effective in the Thaetan marshes and swamps. Because any potential target would probably be standing on wet ground or in water, the weapon could kill or disable at an even greater range than its specifications said it could. However, Karghan-designed neural pulsers could be purchased through any number of sources. Their presence wasn't conclusive evidence of Karghan intervention by any means.

"I wasn't expecting to see anyone here today," the officer said cordially.

"I have business with the camp commander," Curran answered after Katherine translated the young man's comment. "You will escort us to him."

It was clear the young man didn't care for Curran's tone, and by the time Katherine finished translating, his smile had vanished. He ordered two of his men to search them for weapons.

"You will follow me," he said when they didn't find any.

"Of course I will, idiot," TaZarin snarled impatiently.

The young officer waited for Katherine to translate. When she hesitated, Curran angrily ordered her to translate his insult word for word in both content and tone. The young man's jaw clenched, but he held his temper.

They left the glade and walked for two or three miles skirting the edge of a swamp. Huge trees draped with overhanging vines and creepers grew out of the shallow black water. With the unremitting rainfall and impervious soils on this part of Thaetar, the ground stayed saturated, and swamps formed in the low ground. Where the land rose slightly, the hillsides were kept wet by the constant supply of percolating groundwater, and instead of swamps, there were marshes covered with heavy growths of sedges and dense thickets of short, fast-growing thorn trees.

From the maps he'd studied on the ship, Curran knew this swamp was the eastern approach to the camp. As they came within sight of it, he saw that the low fan-shaped ridge it occupied had been a farm until recently. Most of the ridge was cleared, drained, and planted to the less coarse sedges the local farmers used for pasture, but on the once-forested high ground, nothing was left but stumps. All of the timber had been cut for building materials and firewood.

The farmhouse and outbuildings were located toward the west side of the ridge, overlooking the rest of the farm. Behind the outbuildings, at the base of the ridge, he knew a broad sedge-choked channel carried the drainage water away from the farm and into the undrained marshes and swamps.

As the patrol led them through the camp toward the house, Curran kept his eyes moving, trying to take in as much as he could, studying everything carefully. The base looked well-defended and well-supplied. A chain of gun positions with interlocking fields of fire was set up on the perimeter, and the fighters he saw all carried good-quality arms and equipment. He also made note of the large number of unremarkable tracked and amphibious vehicles in the camp.

They were escorted into the farmhouse and held in the main room while the young officer in charge of the patrol knocked on the door to their right and waited for permission to enter.

The main room was small and the three clerks working in it, along with their desks and equipment, took up most of the space. A wood-burning stove was fitted into the stone fireplace the farm family once used for heating and cooking, and a small fire was built in it. The room was pleasantly warm.

The young officer came out and motioned for Curran and the others to enter. He dismissed three of his men, then he and the remaining member of the patrol followed them into the room and stood guard on either side of the door.

A small, well-built man of about sixty sat behind the large wooden desk at the far side of the room. Three chairs were arranged in a shallow semicircle in front of it. Two file cabinets stood in the corner to the left of the desk. A cot was placed against the wall on the right. The only light in the room came from the window behind the desk. A vidcam hung on the wall above the window.

The man looked up from his work as they entered. He had the thick mane of white hair typical of Thaetan men and a pleasant rather grandfatherly face. The Thaetan leaned back in his chair and motioned for the group to be seated. Collins, TaZarin, and Ryerson sat. Takawa remained standing.

The man handed some papers to an aide who was waiting beside the desk, the vestigial webbing between their fingers evident as the papers passed from hand to hand. The aide left, and the man looked up, his blue-blue Thaetan eyes with their nictitating membranes coming to rest on Curran.

From the pictures and the description he'd read in the briefing materials, Curran recognized the man as Praith, one of the principal leaders of the rebellion. According to what he'd read, Praith was a well-known academic who had taught political history at the Hall of Advanced Studies in Sharphron for many years before becoming active in the rebellion.

The questions began simply enough.

"What is your name?" he asked, addressing Curran in clear, carefully enunciated Standard.

"Sklar," Curran answered.

It was an unusual way for a Deniban to refer to himself, using only his personal name and not his House and place names as well, and as intended, it drew Praith's attention.

"And your House?" Praith asked pleasantly.

"I have no House."

"No House?" the man inquired.

On Deniba, a man with no House was less than nothing.

"My family didn't approve of my profession," Sklar answered with a sardonic smile.

"And what might that be?"

Compared to Sklar's mangled pronunciation, Praith's excellent

Standard made Sklar appear all the more coarse.

"I sell arms."

"An unusual profession for someone who supposedly wishes to avoid violence and war," Praith said, referring to the influence Charik's book *The Warrior's Way* had exerted on Deniban society. *The Warrior's Way* was a Deniban classic translated into many languages, including Thaetan.

"Their thoughts exactly."

A man like Sklar would have few if any ties to his homeworld and none left to his family. He would have given up the practice of the Warrior's Way, and if he had any talent with the Mind Disciplines, he most likely abused them.

"And what were you doing in the glade?" Praith asked him.

"Waiting. Patiently," Sklar answered. "You have a war. I have weapons."

"Why should I be interested?"

"I've seen the junk your people are using. I know the kind of prices you paid for it. I can supply you with better weapons at a better price."

"Why haven't I heard of you before? I know most of the arms traders in this sector."

"I've been busy on Arriga."

The war on Arriga had been going on sporadically for over ten years. For most of that time, an arms embargo had been in effect. For an arms dealer to deliver goods there, he would, at least, have had to be resourceful.

"What do you have to offer other than words?"

Curran drew a sheaf of papers sealed in a heavy clear plastic envelope from the large inside pocket of his Thaetan poncho and threw it on the desk in front of Praith.

Praith opened it and looked over the list of weapons and equipment.

The pages contained a broad selection of small arms, as well as shoulder-fired missiles, infra-red scopes, laser range finders, bridging materials, body armor, and spare parts. Curran knew it was a good offering, but nothing about it that was unique or unusual.

"No Karghan-made weapons?"

Of the weapons Curran had seen on their way through the camp, better than half were Karghan surplus. Praith would need replacements and spare parts. Unfortunately, most of what he had on his list were items manufactured on Alliance worlds. Not even the power packs were compatible.

"I don't deal in inferior goods," he said.

Karghan weapons comparable to what Curran was offering were every bit as good as anything on his list and sometimes better. Curran knew it was a poor answer, but it might pass. Running down the competition was a time-honored sales technique, even on Deniba.

"You have nothing here I need," Praith answered, tapping the papers lightly with the butt of a lacquered swagger stick he'd picked up from his desk. "However, I *would* be interested in the updated targeting software for the GL-117."

Curran's knowledge of current Karghan ordnance was thin, but Kumio had told him about the GL-117, a shoulder-fired armor-piercing missile.

"Do you have the original targeting system?" Curran asked.

"Yes."

"Then it seems we may have something to talk about after all because I have access to the new interface box."

"Perhaps we do have something to talk about," Praith agreed. "We can continue with that later. In the meantime, tell me about your associates. Who is this?" Praith asked, looking at Takawa.

"My bodyguard."

Curran knew Takawa didn't look like much of a bodyguard. He was small and wiry and looked more like an aging schoolboy, but this was the first thing Sklar said that wasn't condescending or disrespectful.

"And him. The pretty one," Praith said, moving on, turning his attention to Collins.

"He keeps my accounts."

"And the woman. Yours?"

"Hardly. The woman is my property. She translates for me."

Praith left the desk and walked to Ryerson. He touched her hair. Then his hands went to her neck. Then to her shoulders, stroking her in a very suggestive way. Ryerson sat quietly, neither accepting nor rejecting his attention.

Curran knew Praith was an educated man. He would know that pairings between humans and Denibans were rare and that this probably wasn't one of them. What Praith was doing with Katherine was a probe, an attempt to find a weakness in the group he could exploit if he decided later they weren't who they said they were. This particular tactic was probably not one the Thaetan especially enjoyed. He was simply doing what he knew would be offensive to a human to elicit a response.

"Nothing more?"

"There are other services she performs," Curran said, letting Praith come to his own conclusions as to what the nature of those services might be.

Curran watched as the Thaetan tried, but was unable to completely hide his disgust. Prostitution was virtually unknown on Thaetar, as was the sexual abuse of women. Although a woman taken as a prisoner of war faced the same possibility of physical and psychological torture as a man, she was never degraded as a woman. Her womanhood was absolutely sacrosanct.

"I understand she's very good," Curran continued in case the point had been missed. "You can do whatever you like with her. Just make sure my property is returned to me undamaged."

***

A woman who sold her body, Praith thought. A woman who would sell the most sacred part of herself.

14

It made his skin crawl to touch her.

He looked around the room at the four of them, his hands still on the woman's shoulders. The bodyguard looked bored, but he sensed that the pretty one was becoming restless.

He slipped his hand under the woman's tunic and rested his hand on her breast. He was hoping for some reactions, either from her or from one of the men as his touch became more intimate, but he was getting nowhere. He was about to change tactics when the one who kept the accounts started to get up. Before he was half-way out of his chair, the Deniban had slammed his hand into the center of the pretty one's chest. The man crashed back into the chair, doubled over, wheezing.

"How many times do I have to explain to you the way things are with her?" Sklar sneered in exasperation. "Now sit there and behave yourself.

"Please excuse our little domestic difficulties," the Deniban said, turning to Praith. "The puppy isn't quite house-broken yet, but we're trying."

The pretty one looked up, having recovered himself, and glared at Sklar in unvarnished hatred.

"He does not appear to like you," Praith remarked evenly.

"How true," Sklar said, apparently pleased with the situation.

Praith continued to study the man. Something had happened. Something in the group's dynamic had just been given a sharp twist, and it hadn't quite returned to its original shape. The Deniban had tried to hide it, but it was there, adrift in the silence.

He had almost believed the Deniban before. Now he didn't. If they were here to sell arms at all, it was secondary. With a growing sense of excitement, he began to consider the possibility that the Alliance had sent these people. Perhaps they were on a reconnaissance mission to see for themselves what the insurgents and the Karghans were up to. If that were the case, these people could be valuable beyond measure.

He routinely had the vidcam recordings of this type of

interview matched against the files they had on all known arms dealers and mercenaries working in the sector. Now he would have it checked against all known Alliance personnel as well.

***

Katherine had accepted the Thaetan's hands on her body. Until Collins had gotten up, the Thaetan's touch had been sexually neutral and inoffensive, something she had been prepared for. Now there was something menacing in his touch.

Earlier she had deliberately leaned her head against Praith's arm and nuzzled him softly. The result was what she'd expected. She'd actually felt him flinch at the contact. Until Collins started to get up, there had been no question in her mind that Praith had accepted everything Curran had said about her and perhaps most of the rest of what Curran had said. Now the Thaetan knew. He knew something was wrong, and he would start trying to find out what.

Katherine couldn't believe it. She and Curran had told Collins exactly how to handle this kind of situation if it came up, and he hadn't listened to a word of it. Collins had just given away the small margin of safety they had. Now, none of them were safe. She watched as Praith walked back to his desk and sat down.

"We'll talk again later," he said, smiling pleasantly.

He instructed the two guards to show his guests to their quarters and had returned to his work before they were even out of the room.

CHAPTER 2

By the time the four of them were brought outside, the sun was setting. The evening was cold and raw, but the rain had stopped. The two guards took them to a row of small pens constructed of saplings bound together with vines that had initially been built to hold domesticated animals, probably the family's raddic bucks. The cages were roofed, but were otherwise open to the weather. They were so small a man Curran's size couldn't stand without stooping or lie without drawing up his legs.

Curran sat in the mud of his cage, covertly watching a man standing under the eaves of a nearby shed. The man was making a pretense of whittling, but he was watching them. He was also wearing an earpiece. Despite the growing darkness, Curran had been lucky enough to see it. Whatever they said or did that was of interest would be reported immediately to Praith.

About fifteen minutes after they'd been escorted from Praith's office, the young officer who'd led the patrol left the farmhouse and came for Ryerson. Two cages away from him, Collins was sitting with his back against the side of his cage, watching Ryerson as she was taken to the house. In the cage between them, Takawa lay curled up in the mud, apparently napping.

"The whittler is wearing an earpiece, Michael," Takawa whispered, his voice barely audible above the sound of the wind.

"Watch what you say."

A few minutes later, Takawa spoke again, this time to Curran.

"Did you notice the tracked vehicles when we came in?" Takawa whispered.

"Thaetan," Curran answered.

"Right. But not the tracks. The tracks are Karghan, and they're the latest design. They're supposed to last twice as long as the best previous models and they're almost impossible to throw."

Curran considered what finding the latest development in Karghan tracks here on Thaetar meant. Unlike the Karghan-designed neural pulsers and the other surplus he'd seen earlier, the tracks were not an item that was likely to have been traded to the Thaetan rebels by gun runners or even by licensed arms dealers. The tracks would only be available if they had been stolen and sold on the black market, traded through government authorized middle-men, or received as direct aid from one government to another.

"I don't think we're going to make a sale here, do you?" TaZarin said softly.

"Doesn't look like it," Takawa answered.

"We need to be thinking about leaving. Tell Collins."

Several minutes later, Takawa made a futile attempt to stretch, then rolled onto his right side facing Collins, and curled up again to nap.

"Michael…" he whispered.

***

Michael glared at Takawa in response, angry that the marine had recognized the Karghan tracks when he hadn't. He knew all about the new Karghan tracks. He just hadn't seen them. In fact, he hadn't been looking. He'd been waiting to get back to the ship so he could get on with what he was *really* supposed to be doing.

"Michael."

"I heard."

"Be ready. If an opportunity comes, we'll take it."

"What are you going to do about Ryerson?" Collins snapped.

Takawa glanced at the whittler and caught him watching Collins. Collins had spoken loudly enough that the man had probably heard him clearly.

In reply to Kumio's silence, Michael launched another attack.

"Maybe what happens to her doesn't matter to a man like you, but it does to me," he said, regretting it instantly. It was inappropriate and insulting, and worse, he realized that if he'd been overheard and Kumio replied in character, he had dug a hole for himself he might not be able to get out of.

"Listen to me, Michael," Kumio said loudly enough to be sure the whittler could hear him, "you're new around here, so maybe you don't get the picture yet. She belongs to Sklar. Not you. Not me. Sklar.

"What you and Katherine do on your own time is your business. What she does for him isn't. Just stay out of it before he decides to explain it to you again like he did in that guy's office.

"Besides that, Katherine is my friend. She's been through more kinds of hell than you can ever imagine, and I don't want any harm to come to her. Not from him and especially not from you."

Then softer, just for him, he whispered, "That man in there isn't interested in her, and he doesn't want her. All he wants is a way to get to us, and you've given it to him. If he hurts her, you'll answer to me."

Collins sat motionless in the corner of his cage, staring straight ahead as a bitter, ironic smile began to form on his lips. Takawa was right. He needed to answer to someone for something, but it wasn't Takawa, and it wasn't Katherine. He owed a debt to another woman that he would never be able to repay as long as he lived, and now his empty gesture of concern for Ryerson had finally made it real to him.

Michael knew what Thaetan law said about a man who raped a woman. The man was given to the woman's family to be drowned, his body left in the swamps to rot, his property forfeit.

Perhaps it was what he deserved for what he'd done to Anna.

Ever since he'd joined the service, everything he was supposed to want had come easily to him. He'd become arrogant with easy successes and accustomed to getting what he wanted when he wanted it. He'd known when he asked Anna out that she didn't want him. They were just friends. But her refusal hadn't fit in with his plans for the evening, and it didn't stop him.

Now he was on Thaetar, the wrong man at the wrong time doing the wrong job, all because his brother had died in a stupid, drunken accident ten years ago, and his father had never let him think for a minute that he could do or be anything other than his brother's replacement.

He had already achieved everything his father wanted for Brian and nothing he needed or wanted for himself, and he was drifting through the years, leading a comfortable, empty life. The work had always been easy for him, the sucking up tolerable, and he'd never been in a situation where anything he did seemed to matter much.

Now people could die because of him.

**

Katherine stood quietly in front of Praith's desk, waiting for him to look up at her.

"What is your name?" he asked kindly in Standard.

"*Tu hata Katerein,*" she answered in perfect Thaetan. She looked at him, suddenly appearing uncertain.

"Did you bring me here to spend the night?" she asked. "Would you like me to undress?"

She could feel his shock and revulsion from across the desk. It was the reaction she'd hoped for. Even though Praith had started to doubt everything else about them, he still didn't doubt that part of Curran's story.

"Please sit," Praith said graciously, recovering himself. "May I offer you some wine?"

"*Rhetta* wine?" she asked.

"Yes."

"No, thank you. It makes me break out in hives," she chuckled softly.

Rhetta wine did cause allergic reactions in some humans, but Katherine wasn't one of them. She refused because she didn't want to sample wine that Praith might have drugged.

He took the bottle from the corner of his desk and poured himself a small glass. Then he walked around the desk and sat down next to her, turning his chair to face her. He didn't move close enough to be intimidating, just close enough to be at a friendly conversational distance.

"I meant no insult," Katherine apologized after he'd seated himself. "I had to ask. Sklar doesn't understand how it is on Thaetar."

"He would hurt you if you didn't offer yourself?"

"Probably," she said with a small, self-effacing shrug.

"I'm sorry," he said.

His concern seemed genuine.

"How did you learn Thaetan?" he asked her. "You speak beautifully."

"I have a gift for languages. Thaetan, Deniban, Standard, Carthian, I know them all. I've been to Thaetar many times. I love it here. I even lived here for a while, but that was a long time ago," she said wistfully.

"Do you read in these languages as well?"

"Yes, except for Carthian."

"Do you know the work of Frathco?"

Frathco was a well-known Thaetan author whose work was studied widely, even off-world.

"Oh, yes. I read *Ananthia* twice. It was one of the funniest, truest books I've ever read."

She and Praith spent most of the next hour talking about Thaetan literature. Praith was charming and gracious, a courteous and attentive host.

Katherine hadn't had any illusions about what could happen to her when she was taken back to Praith's office. She'd been afraid, but at least somewhat prepared if he decided to use force to get the information he wanted. She hadn't been prepared for this, and the longer it went on, the more frightening it became.

What was going on? Why had he even brought her in here?

Praith set his wine glass down on the desk. He'd only taken a few sips in the entire hour they'd been together. He got up, took Katherine's hand in his, and led her to the door.

"I've enjoyed talking with you, Katherine," he said, smiling.

His left hand rested gently on her back, and he was about to show her out when he struck her in the face with his right.

Pain and anger flashed in her eyes, and it took a considerable effort not to strike back.

"I admire your spirit," the Thaetan said as he stepped back to look at her cheek.

He was still smiling at her, but the warmth had left his eyes. He was looking at her simply to determine what kind of impression his handiwork would make. If the bruise wasn't sufficient, she knew he would hit her again, but even then, it would only be enough to be sure the proper impression was made.

Katherine finally understood what was going on.

None of this had been about her. It was about Collins. It was about what Collins would think was happening in here. It was about what Collins would see and what he would feel when they brought her back to the cages. It was all going to come to rest on him.

Praith called in two men to escort her back to her cell, taking one of them aside to give him additional instructions. When they were within plain sight of the cages, the man drove the butt of his rifle into her belly. She doubled over and went down to her knees as the air rushed from her lungs. The guards dragged her the rest of the way to her pen and threw her in. Then they left, taking Collins with them. She lay on her side in the mud, her knees drawn up to her chest, gasping.

"Come here, woman," Sklar snarled.

TaZarin had spoken loudly enough that the man she'd seen wearing the earpiece would have heard him. An instant later, she could feel the whittler's eyes on them. Katherine groaned softly and struggled to crawl to him, collapsing against the saplings that separated them.

"Back so soon?" Sklar leered. "What did he want?"

"Nothing," she said. "Just to talk. I told you he wouldn't want me."

"Don't lie to me!"

"I'm not lying! We just talked," she said, seemingly desperate to appease him.

"Is that what I keep you for?"

Sklar's tone was ominous. He grabbed the front of her poncho and jerked her against the saplings. Then he reached through the saplings with his free hand and grabbed a handful of her hair at the base of her skull.

She felt his grip tighten on the back of her neck, accompanied by a sudden sensation of pressure inside her head. She was momentarily shocked, but when the sensation eased, she had a faint, but growing awareness of being in psychic contact with him. She felt Curran's gentle concern for her and his hesitation.

'Can you take my thoughts?' she asked silently, afraid, but curious as well. She knew Curran had undergone the *Arak'Kaz*, the advance training n the Mind Disciplines, but it had never occurred to her that he could share her thoughts. Only those of other Denibans.

'I'm sorry, Katherine. I'm sorry it has to be this way, but I don't know how else to do this. Are you willing?'

'Yes.'

Despite her agreement, she could still feel him hesitate, unable to overcome his uncertainty about touching someone who gave consent without fully understanding what was being consented to.

'I trust you, Curran. Do what you have to.'

She lay still against the barrier between them, appearing for the sake of the whittler to be submissive and accepting of Sklar's abuse.

'Show me what happened, Katherine,' he prompted gently. *'Try to visualize it for me.'*

As she started to visualize the interview, she could feel Curran sorting through her most recent memories. The memories included thoughts about her home on Seora, her two husbands, her children, fantasies of escape, and fragmented visualizations of the interview.

She had no idea how to protect herself or control what he saw. She was so open to him, so vulnerable, she knew he could have taken anything he wanted.

When he had what he needed, he asked for her conclusion.

'He didn't want anything from me, Curran. Nothing at all. He's after Collins.'

Curran started to take his hand from her neck and end the touch, but she stopped him with a thought.

'There's something else, Curran. There are Karghans in this camp.'

'How do you know? Did you see any faces?'

'I didn't have to. They carry themselves differently than Thaetan men. You've lived here long enough to know how Thaetan men walk. Look around. You'll see.'

He gave her warning, then pushed her roughly away.

The whole exchange couldn't have taken more than thirty seconds.

"Worthless bitch! Perhaps I should return you to your family and have them pay what they *really* owe me."

She dragged herself across the cage as far away from him as she could get.

A few minutes later, the whittler got up and walked to the house to report. As soon as he was gone, she heard Takawa ask

Curran what he'd found out.

"She wasn't questioned," Curran answered quietly. "It's Collins that Praith is after, not her."

Collins was returned to his cell about an hour later. He avoided her eyes as he was led past her cell, glanced at Kumio, then sat down in the corner of his cage with his back against Takawa's wall, his head down.

"Are you okay?" she heard Takawa ask.

"Fine," he answered irritably. "I just need to rest for a while."

"What happened?"

"Nothing happened."

She listened as Kumio tried again, but Michael refused to answer.

Suddenly a barrage of mortar fire erupted along the eastern perimeter of the camp. Incendiary rounds hit the two warehouses closest to the perimeter, and the buildings exploded into flame. A few minutes later, small arms fire broke out in the same area. The fighting continued sporadically for almost thirty minutes before the perimeter was finally secured, and the fires were brought under control.

***

In the morning, no one was watching them, and Collins was sick.

Kumio reached into Michael's cage and tugged on his poncho to wake him. When he didn't get any response, he grabbed Michael's belt and dragged Collins around to face him. In the process, he accidentally touched Collins' right hand, which had been hidden under his poncho.

Michael gasped in pain and pulled away, clutching his hand against his chest. The hand was swollen to nearly twice its normal size. His right forearm was almost as bad. His face was flushed, his eyes were dull with fever.

"What happened?"

"Nothing."

"Tell me what happened, Michael or I'll break your goddamned neck."

"Well, to sum up," Collins began angrily, "the man asked me if I'd like to see Katherine raped."

Collins' voice was thick with sarcasm, aimed mostly at himself.

"I said I'd seen better shows on Largent's Planet. Then he asked me if I'd like seeing Sklar beaten to death, and I said I'd like it fine. The man owned me, and I'd be pleased if Praith would do me the favor of returning my freedom. Then he suggested that perhaps my life would mean more to me than the lives of my associates.

"He wanted to know if I understood what even a small cut could do to me here. He took me outside, picked up a sharp stone, and cut my hand. 'We'll see how much the Alliance means to you tomorrow when you're burning with fever, and you know I'm the only one who can save your life.'

"I told him he could take the Alliance and shove it up his butt. They'd arrest me if I ever went back there again. He didn't seem pleased."

"Why couldn't you have told me this last night when I asked?"

"Just what could you have done about it if I had?" he asked bitterly.

There wasn't much any of them could have done to help with the fever. They had all been inoculated for everything possible, but it had only been for the most common Thaetan diseases. Many of the vaccines and medicines available for the less common Thaetan infections were almost as dangerous to humans as the infections themselves. They were only given if there was no other alternative.

"Did you take the antibiotics you had?" All of them had a few broad-spectrum antibiotic capsules sewn into the linings of their ponchos. Sometimes they helped.

"Yes."

"Take mine," he said, tearing the lining of his poncho open to get at the small plastic packet.

Michael took the capsules from his hand and swallowed them.

Curran and Katherine were watching helplessly, having overheard most of what Michael and Kumio said.

"What's the matter with the puppy?" Sklar snarled at Takawa, keeping up the pretense in case they were still under surveillance.

"How should I know?" Kumio snapped back. "He says he's sick."

"One night in the rain and the cold and he's sick," Sklar taunted.

Collins turned to look at TaZarin, his eyes gleaming with hatred. It was impossible to know whether the anger was real or feigned, but at least he was fighting.

Several minutes later, all of them were taken back to the house. Collins, TaZarin, and Ryerson sat as they had the day before. Kumio positioned himself behind Curran's chair with his side to the guard flanking the door. Another guard stood behind Ryerson.

"Yesterday we played games," Praith said. "Today, the games stop."

He looked directly at Takawa.

"We know who you are."

Praith looked down at a sheet of paper on his desk and began to read.

"Kumio Takawa, Ensign, Planetary Alliance Sixth Fleet, assigned to Alliance Embassy Guard, Thaetar. Dates of service.... Do you really want me to go on?" he asked, looking up from the report.

"Sure, be my guest. But you need to change that part about being an ensign. Actually, I made lieutenant before they cashiered me," Takawa smirked. "Joining the fleet turned out to be one of those youthful mistakes we all regret, but the Embassy Guard was a good posting. Selling secrets on the side made me a lot of money, although it ended my military career a little prematurely."

***

Curran saw the indecision in Praith's face. Takawa did well, possibly even well enough to buy them a little more time, but regardless of when the planned diversion was supposed to happen, they couldn't wait much longer.

"And how are you today, Michael?" Praith said with mock solicitude. "Not feeling so well? That's too bad."

He had a small vial in his hand and was rolling it between his fingers, playing with it. "You have only a few hours to live before even this serum won't save you. Just a few hours to decide whether to live or die. Or for your friends to decide for you."

Collins stood up, tore the vial from Praith's hand, and threw it against the wall.

"A very pretty gesture, but wasted, I'm afraid. There's more where that came from, and it's yours any time you decide to change your mind."

Curran measured their options. This might be their only opportunity to get out on their own. For one thing, it wouldn't be long before Collins was too sick to work or even to walk. For another, all four of them were together. It might be the last time they would be. Also, there were only three people in the room with them. Those three weren't expecting to be attacked, and no one was working in the outer office.

He rose from his chair and stood in front of the desk, confronting Praith.

"I believe I mentioned to you yesterday that I wanted my property kept undamaged," Sklar said, motioning toward Katherine and Collins. His voice was soft and filled with menace. "You haven't, so the four of us will be leaving."

On the word *leaving*, Ryerson stood up, turned, and struck the man behind her in the throat. As he stumbled away from her, she dropped him with a strike to the temple. She took his spare ammunition clips and two fragmentation grenades, slid them into the pocket of her poncho, and picked up his weapon.

In the instant Katherine attacked, Kumio whirled and drove his hand into the nose of the man guarding the door, then broke his neck as Curran reached across the desk for Praith and with one sharp blow to the center of the man's chest, stopped his heart.

Curran turned to Takawa.

"Destroy the camera and take the data stick."

Then he turned to Collins. "It's time for you to go to work, Michael."

During the fight, Collins had watched in stunned silence as Ryerson, Takawa, and TaZarin eliminated Praith and the two guards almost before he'd even understood what was happening. He was looking around, still slightly dazed, when he noticed that they were all watching him.

"Michael, can you work?" TaZarin asked.

"Yes, Sir."

"You and Katherine go through everything on the desk and in the file cabinets. If you aren't sure about something, take it. If you can't read it, ask Katherine."

"Quickly! We can't spend much time at this."

Curran took the automatic weapon that was resting in the corner behind Praith's desk and stood guard by the door while Katherine and Michael began looking through Praith's papers. They had barely started when incoming mortar rounds began exploding at the east end of the compound like the night before, only this time the rounds were being walked in toward them. Bursts of small arms fire all along the south and east sides of the camp followed. The fighting kept getting heavier, and it was coming closer.

"Maybe this is the help we're expecting," Takawa said. He handed the data stick he'd taken from the camera to Curran, picked up the rifle from the man he'd killed, and went to the window. "At least it's drawing men away from this side of the compound."

Katherine and Michael looked through everything in and on Praith's desk and a good part of what was in the files.

"Katherine?" TaZarin asked.

"Nothing here, Curran."

"Michael?"

"Nothing."

Despite not finding anything, Michael's earlier depression had lifted. He was excited and animated. In fact, he looked almost healthy, except Curran knew that depression followed by mild euphoria was a common symptom of Thaetan fevers in humans.

Curran sent Takawa to guard the front door of the house and took over at the window. He told Michael to get started on the files in the main room while Katherine finished looking through the file cabinets in Praith's office. Ten minutes later, Curran made his decision. With or without anything, they were leaving. The fighting was too close. If they waited any longer, they might not be able to reach the escape route without having to fight their way to it.

"Let's go. Everybody out the window in Praith's office. If we get separated, meet at the drainage channel at the edge of the perimeter. Kumio, you're rear guard."

Ryerson grabbed a fistful of papers she'd set aside and stuffed them into the inner pocket of her poncho. TaZarin led Collins into Praith's office while Kumio fell back to guard the office door.

TaZarin opened the window and exited first, crouching in the weeds outside, ready to provide covering fire. Katherine and Michael followed. Just as Michael left, he saw Takawa pull the pin on a grenade and lob it through the door into the center of the main room.

Outside, the camp was in flames. Mortar rounds were landing deep inside the compound, and it was clear that the eastern perimeter had been overrun. Dressed like the un-uniformed irregulars who fought with the rebels and carrying the same kinds of weapons, Curran and his team had almost reached the relative safety of the sedges that choked the edge of the drainage channel when a stray mortar round exploded behind them.

TaZarin and Collins were both thrown off their feet by the blast. Ryerson, who'd been on point, was still standing, but when she turned to look back, she saw that Kumio had taken the full force of the explosion. He'd been slammed into the side of a building and was lying face down in the mud, his body torn by shrapnel.

Collins got up and started toward him.

"No, Michael!" Katherine fought to hold him back while Curran, who'd been badly shaken up, got to his feet and came to help her.

"Let go of me! Let me help him!"

"He's dead, Michael! Get behind me and stay there," Curran yelled.

Michael obeyed.

Katherine knelt and sighted her rifle.

"What are you doing!?" Michael shouted as he started to realize what she about to do.

"God forgive me," Katherine said softly, then she squeezed the trigger and fired two rounds into the back of Kumio's head, not because she believed he might still be alive and would be captured, but because the exit wounds would obliterate his face. Without a face, there would be nothing left of Kumio that anyone could use to trace them back to the Alliance.

"What are you doing!?" Michael screamed at her.

"There's no time, Michael. Go with Curran," she said, her voice dull with shock.

"They can't identify the body now," Curran said as he pulled Michael away and hurried him toward the marsh. "They can't connect him to the Alliance."

Michael jerked away from Curran's grip, falling to his knees and bringing TaZarin down with him. He started to vomit, but nothing came up.

"The view from this side of things is a little different than the view from your office desk, isn't it?" TaZarin said as he pulled

Michael to his feet and led him toward the drainage channel.

Katherine, who was now the rear guard, crouched behind the corner of the last shed to provide covering fire as the others waded into the sedges. Then she turned away and ran to catch up before they disappeared into the marsh.

***

On the other side of the channel, a narrow path had been cleared for them through the razor wire, and the two listening posts they had to pass between were neutralized.

The three of them moved on, keeping to a narrow spit of land that stretched deep into the marsh. A dense ground fog rose off the water, shrouding everything in a thick swirling mist. All of them knew that rebel patrols constantly swept these woods and marshes. The whole area was a free-fire zone, and everything in it was a target.

About two miles from the camp, they struggled up a long ridge covered by thick brush and second-growth timber. Keeping a good interval between them, Curran led, followed by Michael and Katherine. As they began to cross a small glade near the top, a fragmentation grenade exploded to Curran's left.

Shrapnel sang in the air and hummed and snapped through the leaves and branches. He was spun around by the blast and went down as his left leg crumpled under him. A second round exploded in the center of the glade, showering the clearing with splintered wood and metal.

Curran screamed in pain as he tried to get his left leg under him so he could crawl into the relative safety of the brush at the edge of the glade. His pants had been torn open from his hip to his knee and were covered with blood. He looked around him for Michael, but the brush was so thick he couldn't see him.

"Michael, where are you? Are you all right?"

"Help me with Katherine."

Curran dragged himself toward the sound of Michael's voice.

Michael had pulled Katherine into the cover of some heavy

32

brush about thirty feet from where Curran had been hit. Frothy blood ran from her nose and mouth, and the front of her poncho was soaked with blood, but she was conscious. Michael was kneeling beside her, unhurt, holding her hand.

Curran started to push aside Katherine's poncho and unbelt her tunic. She put her hand over his to stop him.

"Don't bother, Curran," she said, having trouble catching her breath. "I won't be going any farther."

He had no doubt that what she'd said was true. He could feel her wounds in his own chest. There was still the resonance of her in his mind.

"Michael, how well do you remember this place from the maps?" he rasped, barely able to speak.

"Very well."

Michael was looking flushed and feverish again.

"I want you to do a quick reconnaissance of the next small glade, the one at the crown of this ridge where it narrows above the two ravines."

Curran knew the patrol would be closing in soon to finish them. They had to find a place to make a stand.

Michael hesitated, not wanting to leave Katherine.

"Do it, Michael. Don't waste Katherine's time."

Michael met Curran's eyes and realized for the first time that Katherine was dying and that nothing either of them could do would change it. He let go of Katherine's hand and crawled through the brush and into the woods.

Curran touched Katherine's face. He was trying very hard to maintain some detachment, but it was impossible. He had been intimate with few women, and he and Katherine had been intimate. He had touched her mind and shared her thoughts, and because she didn't know how to prevent it, he had touched her much more deeply than he had needed or intended to. She was also his friend. Losing her would have been painful in any case. Now it would be much worse.

"Katherine, I think I may be able to help with the pain. May I touch you again?"

She nodded, unable to speak.

Curran used the same healer's touch he'd used before, this time to create a kind of white noise that would mask Katherine's pain, at least temporarily.

"It's better. Thanks."

He waited beside her, holding her hand.

"They promised me, Curran. They promised. I got married. I had kids. And now I'm going to die in some godforsaken glade in the middle of nowhere for nothing."

Tears of helpless rage rolled down her cheeks at being cheated out of the rest of her life on someone's whim. She gathered herself to speak again, and when she did, her voice was calm, and she was very composed.

"Curran, I want you to do something for me," she said, without looking at him. "When you write, I want you to promise me you'll tell Gareth and Daniel how much I love them. And tell the children... tell them... Oh, God, what does it matter now?" she said as the tears started again. "I'll never see them again, or touch them."

Curran rested his hand gently on her shoulder. Then he laid his palm against her cheek and left it there. He couldn't help himself. The resonance of her he felt in his mind kept surfacing, and he was too stressed from his own wounds to suppress it. He felt it all, everything she was telling him.

She pulled the bundle of blood-soaked documents from her poncho and handed them to him. "I hope these are worth dying for. I didn't have time to read them, but the signatures were Karghan, for whatever that's worth."

Curran took them from her hand and was putting them in the pocket of his poncho when Collins returned.

"It's the perfect place," he reported, once again going through a period of elation induced by the fever cycle. "It's the highest ground on the ridge, it overlooks everything below it, there's a good field of fire, and it can't be flanked easily. If they want us, it'll cost them."

"Can it be held by one man?"

He looked at TaZarin and then at Katherine. One look was enough for him to understand what the plan was.

"Yes, for a while."

"Michael, you lead. Take our weapons. I'll carry Katherine."

Michael picked up their weapons with his good hand and slung them over his shoulder. Then he led them to the defensive position he had already prepared in the glade. Curran set Katherine down with her back against a tree and tried to make her as comfortable as possible. Collins gave her the rifle she'd used before, making sure there was a full clip in it. Curran laid out the two grenades she was carrying on the ground beside her where she could reach them easily, knowing she would save the second one for herself. Then he sent Collins into the woods along the escape route, telling him he would catch up in a few minutes. Behind him, the woods were quiet. The patrol hadn't moved up yet to follow them, but they were still there. The lack of bird song told him that much.

Curran knelt beside Katherine, unwilling to leave her and took her hand in his. "I will tell your family what you said, Katherine. Everything. I swear it."

She nodded, and their eyes met. "Thank you," she said quietly, and then looked away from him. "Go now, Curran."

***

Curran caught up with Michael near the bottom of the ridge where he was waiting. It wasn't what he'd told him to do, but Curran was glad to see him there. He couldn't have walked much farther without help. His hip and leg were numb and burning when he was still, but when he walked, the pain was breathtaking.

The two of them made it the rest of the way down the ridge to the next marsh. Behind them, they could hear the sound of rifle fire, the sharp dry crack muffled by the thick foliage and the heavy, still air. Then silence. Then an explosion, followed by more rifle fire and a second explosion.

Curran staggered and fell forward into the shallow water as he felt the second blast tear through his own flesh. His body jerked convulsively, and his breath came in ragged, irregular gasps as he started to follow Katherine into death.

It took a few seconds for Michael to realize that TaZarin was going into respiratory arrest and would die if he didn't do something. He punched the Deniban hard in the center of his chest, remembering something in his training about stopping muscle spasms in the Deniban chest by using a shocking blow to the nerve plexus.

TaZarin's breathing stopped entirely, then after a terrifying silence, it restarted and became rhythmic and steady. He hauled Curran to his feet and started him moving again.

An hour later, they had to stop while Michael went through a violent attack of chills and high fever. When the attack subsided, and Michael was able, they moved on again, and thirty minutes later, they broke through the sedges at the edge of the clearing Curran thought was the rendezvous point.

He lowered Michael to the ground, then collapsed in the mud beside him, retching. He'd carried Michael most of the last quarter mile when he'd lost consciousness after another attack of fever. He wasn't certain he was stopping at the right clearing, but he knew he wasn't going any farther. He couldn't.

During the afternoon, the agony of the deep wounds in his left thigh and hip had spread through his body until his whole left side throbbed and pulsed with pain. With the help of the Mind Disciplines, the pain had been manageable before the infections took hold. Now he was burning with fever, and the pain was excruciating.

Suddenly he came awake without any awareness of having

been unconscious. He struggled to pull himself from the grip of the thick mud under his body and sit up. The mud around his leg was red with blood. The leg itself was so swollen and inflamed that the cloth of what remained of his loose-fitting Thaetan pants was stretched tight. He fought to stay awake. As long as he was conscious, he could use the Mind Disciplines to control his bleeding. If he passed out again, he would bleed to death.

Beside him, Michael was saying something. It took him a moment to understand that Michael wasn't talking to *him*. Instead, he was carrying on a fragmentary conversation with some unseen person, reliving events in his past, his voice raw with emotion. Such deep feeling, actually spoken out loud, carried enormous weight for a Deniban. It made listening to Michael's words almost unbearably intense.

Curran lay beside Michael, telling himself he couldn't do anything more for him, but even as he rationalized his inaction, he knew he was evading the truth. There *was* something more. He just couldn't bring himself to do it. After what had happened to him with Katherine, he didn't want to touch minds with another human. He didn't want to experience another human so intimately or to live through the pain of their death. On the other hand, he didn't know how much longer he could stand listening to Michael's voice. He needed to quiet him, as much for his own sake as Michael's.

Despite his reluctance, Curran took Michael's hand and reached out to him, touching his mind lightly to see if some part of it might still be rational enough to understand him. He immediately felt himself drowning in a mindscape of random disordered thoughts and feelings, but he didn't withdraw. Instead, he listened, waiting for the fever to subside, waiting for a time when he could say what was necessary and know Michael would hear. When the time came, he was almost too drained to try.

'Michael, your father used you to fulfill his own needs, and he left *you with a legacy of anger and bitterness that's spilled over into everything you've touched since you started trying to lead your brother's life. You know this is true.'*

He felt Michael accept what he'd said.

'Your father will never be able to give you what you need from him, Michael. It's not there to give. You know this, too.'

He felt Michael's surprise. Michael knew it was useless to keep trying, but it had never occurred to him that his father was unable to give him what he needed, only that he wouldn't.

'It's time for you to let go of the anger and resentment, Michael. Forgive him for what he can't do or be and go on. Now that you know who you are, what happens next is up to you.'

Curran felt Michael's grip on his hand tighten.

"I know," he said softly, without opening his eyes, and then he smiled slightly.

"Good. Rest now. They'll be here for us soon."

Several minutes later, Michael woke again. The fever seemed to have subsided, and Michael was clear-headed, but very weak.

"Curran?"

"I'm right here. How are you feeling?"

"I'm fine. I feel good. Just tired. It doesn't hurt anymore."

"I'm glad, Michael."

Curran felt as though he'd just been kicked in the gut. He'd seen it too many times before not to know what was happening. Michael's sense of well-being was part of the last stage of the fever cycle.

"It's awfully cold, though."

"It is," Curran agreed.

It was hot and unpleasant.

"It's not like I thought," Michael said.

What wasn't? Death wasn't? The mission wasn't? Curran didn't ask.

"Tell Katherine I'm sorry."

"I will, Michael."

"Curran, I'm scared."

Curran rolled painfully onto his side and took Michael in his arms. Michael died quietly a few minutes later.

Curran held Michael's body close. Two wrenching sobs escaped him before he was able to regain control of himself. His mind suddenly went blank, and he had an odd feeling of dissociation, of watching himself from a great distance and thinking that he was acting very strangely. Then without warning, he was flooded with Michael's and Katherine's thoughts and feelings, and he no longer had the strength to force them out.

He pressed the heel of his hand into the tiny transponder implanted in his bicep and activated it. The transponder was only capable of sending a homing signal for about an hour, but it really didn't matter. If they didn't find him by then, he knew he'd probably be dead.

He let go of Michael's body and lay in the mud, listening to the sound of water dripping from leaves.

In his mind, he kept revisiting everything that had happened during the last few days, blaming himself for things he could not have foreseen, trying to find something he could have done differently that would have prevented all their deaths, then realizing with a shock that he was losing the most basic of the mind skills. He hadn't experienced that kind of constant uncontrolled rumination since he was a child and been taught not to do it. Dwelling on the past wouldn't change it, and fixing blame on himself or others for things that were beyond anyone's control was a useless, self-indulgent waste to time and energy.

He began having vivid half-waking fever dreams. He'd wake from them terrified, but without remembering anything that happened in them. When he was able, he would force his mind away from Thaetar, away from Michael and Katherine, by remembering the last time he'd been with Jenny Black Wolf, the woman he'd become mind-linked with. He thought about the last time they'd been together and how it would feel to be with her again. He felt her presence with him. It soothed and calmed him. It kept the terror at bay.

CHAPTER 3

Jenny had jokingly extorted a night on the town from him after their mission to Caldera. She'd promised to meet him at Starbase Fourteen, the *Defender's* home port, when she finished her work on Caracor, but she still hadn't arrived. The *Defender* was almost ready to leave the base repair bays and begin her next cruise, and he was facing the very real possibility that Jenny had reconsidered and decided not to see him again. Then two days before the ship was scheduled to leave port, she arrived.

They agreed to meet for dinner, and he went to Jenny's hotel room to pick her up. When she opened the door, he realized with amusement that he'd been expecting to see her dressed in her work clothes—faded jeans, a black T-shirt with a flannel shirt over it, a well-worn pair of hiking boots, and an old leather jacket. It was the only way he'd ever seen her dressed, and it was how he had pictured her during the months of absence, so he had dressed accordingly.

Instead, she was wearing a simple black dress, the short stand-up collar and neckline embroidered in a traditional Deniban pattern. The dress draped softly around her, outlining the contours of her trim, well-muscled body. The color highlighted her deeply tanned skin and dark brown eyes. Her light brown hair was cut short, and she had Caucasian facial features.

41

She was also wearing perfume. The scent was Deniban—the subtle scent of a desert orchid after a light rain—and it suited her perfectly. He wondered briefly if she'd worn the same scent for her husband. It didn't matter to him, but he was curious nevertheless.

"It's good to see you, Curran," she said softly, her voice warm and inviting. "I've missed you."

Their bond pulsed with life as he stood watching her.

"I hope I'm not dressed too informally," he said.

She smiled at him, aware that he was dressed as he was on her account.

"Want me to change?" she offered.

"Not unless you want to."

"I don't," she said, smiling. "This is fine with me."

They walked to a restaurant nearby where he knew a Deniban harper would be playing. Jenny enjoyed Deniban harp music, and he knew the harper was a good one.

"The music is so good the food doesn't matter," she said, laughing in delight a few minutes after they'd been seated.

"The food is good, too."

Now that they were together again, they were both reserved and tentative with each other. The bond they shared had made them intimate, but it hadn't been intentional. Under normal circumstances, Deniban partners had to know each other well before a linking bond even began to form, if it formed at all. Yet he and Jenny were still little more than strangers, having shared nothing other than their experiences on Caldera and a deep but accidental bond.

That night they spent only a few hours apart before meeting again at Jenny's hotel in the morning. After a leisurely breakfast, they went for a walk in the forest east of the base. They spoke only occasionally, but they didn't need to talk for him to understand the pleasure she felt in his company.

When Jenny was with him, she was free to be fully herself. He understood the Deniban part of her, the part she'd learned from her husband, Kristen. He didn't know how long she and Kristen had known each other before they'd become mind-linked, but he knew they had been married for seven years, until Kristen was killed in an accident almost three years ago.

Early in the afternoon, they stopped at a small lake. It was a warm sunny day, and after they'd eaten, they lay beside each other in the grass, enjoying the sun. After a time, he rolled lazily onto his side to look at her. Jenny reached up and caressed his cheek with her fingertips, then drew him into her arms and let him kiss her. It was the first kiss they'd shared, a soft, slow, languorous kiss, but he felt Jenny's passion rise almost immediately. She'd responded so quickly and so deeply he was shocked by her reaction and a little awed that he could engender such passion in a woman.

Even though Deniban women were mildly receptive all year long, except for the time of mating in fall, sexual contact was slow-paced, without urgency, and often infrequent. Jenny had acted like a woman in season, and he had responded in kind. But if her response was unexpected, his reaction to it was more so. An explosion of sexual heat had flashed through his body as he'd returned her kiss and allowed himself to be drawn deeper into the embrace. At one point, he'd been so out of control that his sexual scent had enveloped them.

It was impossible for a Deniban man to hide his desire once he became deeply aroused. Jenny knew, and she would always know when he wanted her. He didn't understand how he could have felt what he had. He had never imagined that such a thing was possible, but he'd never been with a human woman before, and he hadn't expected Jenny to be so quick to flame.

When the moment passed, they'd rested uneasily in each other's arms, a little dazed and very careful to put some emotional distance between themselves. He was almost holding his breath, waiting for the reproach he was sure would be coming.

Sexual contact of any kind was always at the woman's invitation. Jenny had invited him, and he had disgraced himself. Worse, he had insulted her. He was well-raised and knew how to treat a woman with respect and affection and with no expectation of exclusivity. A woman was always free to change sexual partners; to choose another man or men for the season. But it seemed to him that the embrace they had just shared had a possessiveness to it that he'd never experienced before.

Instead of a rebuke, Jenny apologized.

"I'm sorry, Curran. It's my fault this happened, not yours. You had no way of knowing what might happen. I, at least, should have guessed."

She took his hand in hers and kissed his palm.

A burst of sexual heat raced through him even though he didn't think she'd meant the gesture to be provocative, just tender.

"I'm sorry, Curran. I didn't think I would feel this way. I didn't think." There was a long pause as he watched her reconsider what she'd just said.

"That's not true. I *did* think about it," she said, starting over. "I was afraid if I told you, you would think I was *shal'tan*," she said, avoiding his eyes.

Shal'tan only came to couples who were mind-linked, and it came to all of them eventually if they stayed together after the season ended. Without the bond, Deniban couples had no interest in remaining together once the season was over. It was the linking bond that created the desire to be together, and sexual contact deepened it—the deeper the bond, the stronger the desire to stay together. It was the profound psychological changes created by the marriage ritual that allowed a mind-linked pair to stay together unharmed. Still, marriage was not a choice to be made lightly, and it was one many Denibans refused because the bond of marriage was exclusive, irrevocable, and for life.

Shal'tan created hormonal changes that sent the couple's metabolic systems into overdrive and their bodies began to burn themselves out. There was intense physical pleasure, along with the sustained urgency and need of the time of mating. Over time, both the pleasure and the need became more insistent and more powerful, and like a drug, they became addictive. The partners were eventually unable to satisfy each other either physically or emotionally, and the relationship would inevitably turn violent and abusive as the couple sought what neither could give the other.

The shal'tan experience was so overwhelming that when it stopped, the partners felt nothing. The need to fill that terrible emptiness was so compelling they were driven to continue, even knowing the often irreparable damage they were doing themselves. Even if they eventually recovered their health, they were rarely able to return to a normal life. The shal'tan experience drew them back to each other, or forced them to look for new partners, repeating the cycle until it either killed them or brought on permanent insanity.

"Curran, when we're together, my sexual feelings may not always be as intense as they were just now, but they will always be there, partly because I'm human and partly because it's the way I am.

"Don't misunderstand. I enjoyed what you did, and I wanted it, but I also know exactly what will happen to us if we ever mate outside of marriage.

"I give you my word that I will never use the mind techniques to hide my feelings from you or to make myself seem more acceptable to you. You may find that you don't like the way I am or that you can't find a way to deal with it, but it's better that you know now, before we become more involved with each other than we already are."

In answer, he took Jenny in his arms and kissed her again. The second kiss was very different from the first, and he realized that despite what she'd said, Jenny had been almost as shocked by their first kiss as he'd been. She was warm and welcoming now,

45

more physically responsive than a Deniban woman would have been and more emotionally open, but she'd drawn herself back from the line she'd crossed before. He could feel that he excited her, but this time she kept her excitement in check, and he felt pleasure, but didn't become so deeply aroused.

He was relieved that it could be that way. It felt more natural to him. He was also slightly disappointed, and he found that disturbing. He couldn't honestly say that he hadn't liked what had happened. It made him feel incredibly alive and potent, but they'd been close to crossing the borderline between the sexual play that took place most of the year and the beginning of madness.

***

Late in the afternoon, they returned to the base and decided to have dinner at a small intimate cafe he especially liked. When the cafe closed, they walked to a nearby park and talked until he had to return to his quarters and get ready to report to the ship. Jenny went with him.

"I wish you didn't have to go so soon, Curran," she said, watching him as he walked into the living area in uniform after taking a shower. "I'm sorry I wasn't able to get here sooner so we could have spent more time together."

"We both know we've had all the time we needed."

He knew they could part now and allow the bond to atrophy, but he also wanted a chance to know her better before he decided. He thought Jenny felt the same way, but he wasn't sure.

"When you get your next leave, Curran, I'd like you to come to Gavalon to visit me."

"Are you sure that's what you want, Jenny?"

"Yes, Curran. I'm very sure."

"I'm glad." Those two words were so weighted with feeling he could barely speak them. "I'll be there."

***

Curran felt a gentle hand on his forehead, brushing the damp hair away from his face. The touch was tender and caring, and he didn't want the contact broken.

"Jenny..."

He tried to raise his left hand to touch her, but wasn't able to move. Half-conscious and near panic at feeling himself restrained, Curran began to struggle.

"Rest easy, Curran, it's just me."

The voice belonged to David Rawlins, the *Defender's* doctor.

Curran opened his eyes and saw David standing beside him, a tall, rawboned man in his early forties with unruly light brown hair, hazel eyes, and an open, friendly face.

Curran was in a critical care bed in the *Defender's* sick bay. A surgical tent covered his left leg so he couldn't see it, but he could see the tubes leading away from it, draining the wounds, and he could feel it. The skin felt tight and drawn, and the leg throbbed painfully. His left arm was strapped down, and an IV line was taped to his forearm. Sensors on his chest ran to a vital signs monitor. He was weak, and his whole body ached, but his mind was clear.

"It's good to see you awake, Curran. You had me worried for a while there. How are you feeling?"

"Tired."

Just saying the word left him exhausted.

"That's understandable. You've had a pretty rough time for the last three days, but you're going to be fine now. The fever finally broke last night."

"I've been here for three days?"

"Almost four."

"David, do you know what happened to the documents and the data stick I had with me?"

"I found them in your poncho and gave them to the captain. A couple of men from the Alliance Defense Intelligence Service came for them two days ago."

"It went that high up?"

"Apparently."

"Are they still here?"

"No. They wanted to question you, but I told them they couldn't. They went away."

"People from the Alliance Defense Intelligence Service don't just go away."

"Well, I didn't say they went away *happy*."

"Did they find Ryerson and Collins?"

"Just Collins."

Curran turned away from him and closed his eyes, gathering the energy to ask his next question.

"Will I walk again, David?"

"Sure. It's going to take a while, but you'll be as good as new. You need to rest now, though. We can talk again later."

David walked to the other side of Curran's bed, adjusted the drip rate on one of the drugs entering the IV line, and Curran drifted back to sleep.

***

Curran's first two days back on the *Defender* had been touch and go, and David was rarely farther away from his patient than his office. During the times when the fever was in subsidence, Curran would sleep quietly, but each time it began to rise, he would become more agitated, sometimes calling out in his delirium for Michael and Katherine, sometimes thrashing so violently that he had to be physically restrained. At the same time, his brain wave patterns would show a high output of *brecia* waves. Brecia waves occurred only in Denibans and were indicative of serious emotional or psychic trauma.

None of the more commonly prescribed Deniban sedatives were to be administered to quiet a patient in brecia—only drugs that allowed the body to rest without altering brainwave activity. The deep unconsciousness of the brecia state had to remain uninterrupted for as long as the patterns continued for complete healing to take place. Any interruption, either through the use of inappropriate drugs or by trying to bring the patient out of brecia prematurely, could result in permanent emotional damage.

On the survey ship, when Curran was being returned to the *Defender*, he had become violent. The Carthian medic onboard administered a commonly used Deniban sedative to quiet him. A Deniban healer would have known immediately through mind touch that there was brecia activity, but they didn't have a Deniban healer on the ship, and the Carthian had done the best he could, given the limited resources available to him. However, Curran had been back on the *Defender* for almost two hours before the sedative wore off, and David saw the first brecia waves appear on the monitor.

Also, each new attack of fever left Curran weaker than the one before, and David hadn't been able to find anything effective against the two remaining organisms that were still sustaining it. Finally, in desperation, he decided to wait until the fever spiked again to give Curran a drug that would elevate his body temperature further, and when the fever dropped, keep it higher than the organisms themselves did. The danger was that the sustained high fever could cause brain damage, but Curran was losing ground fast, and it was a risk David felt was justified.

Finally, after three cycles of the new treatment, the environment in Curran's body became inhospitable enough that the organisms couldn't survive in it any longer, and the fever broke. However, Curran had exhausted all of his body's reserves fighting the infections. It would be a long time before he fully regained his strength. Also, the leg wounds were serious, and they were going to take a long time to heal.

David was still furious with the two men the Alliance Defense Intelligence Service sent. The two of them had flown to a rendezvous with the *Defender* to get the documents and interview the members of the mission team and were very displeased when they learned that the only survivor was in Sick Bay in no condition to talk to anyone.

When David told them it might be a week or more before they

could talk to TaZarin, they insisted that he drug Curran into consciousness immediately so they could interrogate him then, at their convenience. David flatly refused. He tried to explain calmly about Curran's physical condition, which was very uncertain, and about the nature and significance of brecia waves, but they kept insisting.

"He's half-dead already," David had snapped, barely able to control his temper. "I can't allow him to be interrogated, and even if I could, I doubt that you could get a coherent answer out of him. He's been delusional most of the time he's been back here. You've already got the documents. What more do you want?"

"We can go over your head, Doctor," they'd threatened. "We can have you removed from the case. Stand in our way, and we can have you removed from this ship and brought before a board of inquiry."

David wasn't intimidated. Even if they didn't know the regulations, he did. His commitment was always to his patient, and his medical decisions could not be overruled, even by two men from the Alliance Defense Intelligence Service. Still, four months ago, David would have gone toe to toe with them, slugging it out verbally until somebody lost. Now he tried another tack.

"I'm sorry I blew up just now," he said. "I'm just tired. I've been up with this patient for three days now, and he's probably not going to make it anyway. I've seen it like this before with these Thaetan fevers. Even if he does survive, he'll probably be brain damaged.

"I know both of you probably have more important things to do than hang around here indefinitely waiting to talk to a vegetable, but if those are your orders, be my guest," he said, smiling graciously. "In the meantime, you'll have to excuse me. I've got sick call in ten minutes."

The two of them left the ward a few minutes later and were off the ship within the hour. He guessed that once he'd stopped resisting and invited them to stay, they didn't feel any further need to waste their time on him or his patient.

***

Four days after the men from the Alliance Defense Intelligence Service left, Captain Eriksson stopped by the sick bay to look in on his first officer and found him sitting up in bed reading.

"It's good to see you awake, Curran. You're looking a lot better than you were a few days ago."

"I'm feeling much better."

"The doctor tells me you'll be out of here soon and fit for limited duty. It will be good to have you back at work."

"Thank you, Captain. It will be good to be working."

"I don't know if the doctor told you yet, but the two of us got the Alliance Defense Intelligence people to agree to accept a written statement from you about the mission instead of remaining on board to interview you personally. You'll need to start on that as soon as you're feeling up to it."

"I'll do it tomorrow."

"Good."

"Captain, have the families been notified yet?" Curran asked.

"Yes, except for Captain Takawa. There's no next of kin listed in his personnel file."

"Have you written to the others yet?"

"I thought you might want to."

"Yes, Sir. I do."

"Good. Well, I'd better be leaving. The doctor said I could only stay for a few minutes."

"Thank you for coming, Captain."

***

The next morning Curran wrote his after-action report. That afternoon after a long nap, he began the letter to Katherine's family. He'd met both of her husbands and their two children the last time the ship had been to Seora for resupply.

Dear Gareth and Daniel,

By now, you have received the official notification of the death of your wife. I am not at liberty to tell you anything more about the circumstances of her death other than what you already know. However, I was the unit commander, and I was with her before she died.

Although she was gravely wounded, Katherine fought a rear-guard action that made it possible for me and another man to escape an enemy patrol and complete our mission. Before she died, Katherine asked me to tell you both how much she loved you and the children and that she was thinking of you.

I cannot tell you how sorry I am. I grieve with you. Katherine was my friend. She was also a woman of extraordinary spirit and courage, and it was an honor to have known her.

Katherine gave me my life, and I owe her a debt I can never repay, except to offer you and the children whatever assistance I can now and in the years to come.

Respectfully,
Curran TaZarin Shirraz'At

Curran thought for a long time before beginning the letter to Michael's father. He wanted Michael's father to understand the man his son had become before he'd died. Even though he wasn't sure the man would understand, he felt he needed to make the effort. A Deniban family would want to know.

Dear Mr. Collins,

By now, you have received the official notification of the death of your son. I regret that I cannot tell you anything further about the circumstances of his death other than that he gave his life to gain information that may be vital to Alliance interests, and that I am still alive because of him.

I was Michael's commanding officer, and I was with him when he died. Although Michael and I only worked together for a short time, I came to know and respect him. Beyond the physical courage it took for him to carry out his part of the mission, Michael found the courage to face himself honestly and make changes in his life. Perhaps there is no greater courage in life than that.

Sincerely,
Curran TaZarin Shirraz'At
First Officer
Planetary Alliance Starship *Defender*

When he finished, he asked David to read the letters to be sure he hadn't inadvertently said something that might hurt or offend a human family in some way.

"The letters are good, Curran. They'll be appreciated."

***

David was struck by the tone and quality of the letters, especially the one to Katherine's family. An offer of assistance such as the one Curran had made them was not made lightly. It was the offer of a place in his family's Household and the lifelong help that obligated if they were ever in need.

What had happened between Katherine and Curran that would have led him to make an offer like that? He knew Curran and Katherine were friends, but he had never known them to be especially close.

"David, since it looks like I may be here for a few more days, how would you like to continue your lessons to help pass the time?"

". . "I'd like that. I've got some time right now if you're interested."

***

He and Curran had been friends for a long time, but it had never been an easy friendship. When they first met, he'd been drawn by Curran's coolness and self-possession. Considering his own quick-tempered, volatile nature, he'd seen them as admirable traits. He also enjoyed the way Curran made connections between seemingly unrelated facts and ideas. His perspective was often unique and fresh, and David found their conversations intellectually involving and sometimes challenging.

On the other hand, that same coolness and self-possession often made trying to talk to the man on a personal level a real trial. He'd always felt that Curran probably experienced some of the same ambivalence toward him, but he also thought that the fact that they were so different was a large part of why they were still friends.

David had met Jenny Black Wolf at the same time Curran had, when she'd come aboard the *Defender* for the Caldera mission. When he found out she'd learned the Mind Disciplines, he asked Curran if Curran thought he could teach them to *him*.

Curran answered that he honestly didn't know. He wasn't sure if he had the skills to teach a human. Jenny was the only human he'd ever met who knew them. He also questioned David's seriousness, asking him if he understood the commitment in time and effort that it would take to learn. David replied angrily that he had his reasons, and he intended to learn. Period.

They'd been sitting in the crew lounge having a cup of coffee together when Curran decided to start teaching. The first thing he'd said was, "The mind is a reservoir of information and a means for solving problems, David, but the emotions are the true source of a person's knowledge about the physical world, the world as sensed and experienced. They reside in the body, not the mind. They're to be experienced directly and immediately, then dealt with and discharged.

"The first of the thinking skills is observation. You learn to observe your mind, watching the thoughts and emotions that pass through it, allowing them to leave without judgment or attachment. Non-reaction is a choice. So are your habitual reactions. Observation allows you to change your choices. Reaction is learned. It can be unlearned."

With that, the lessons had begun. Further, Curran wrote to Jenny to ask her specifically what concepts and techniques had worked best for her. Then Curran tried them on him. His progress was painfully slow at first, but he stayed with it, and gradually the thinking skills and the meditations became easier and more natural to him. He began to be attentive to his patterned behaviors and not be trapped by them. He began to learn a new way of understanding the world, his relationship to it, and to other people. As he progressed, he found himself becoming calmer and less volatile.

An additional and unexpected benefit was that the lessons became the bridge between their cultures that finally allowed the two of them to understand each other.

**

Curran's lesson for the day was an exercise in visualization. Visualization was a subject that had been especially difficult for both of them, and David wasn't making much progress. However, this time Curran had thought of another way to present it, and David understood. For the first time, he was able to stay focused enough to receive a simple image; just a picture of a long, rugged chain of red cliffs on Deniba, David guessed, but he was able to hold it in his mind for several seconds before it faded.

"You did well today, David."

"Yeah, I did, didn't I?" he beamed in self-mocking pride.

"We can try again tomorrow."

"Good. Now rest."

**

Two days later, Curran woke up from a nap, thirsty. When he

reached for his cup to get a drink of water, he saw a small velvet-lined box on the side table that hadn't been there before. The box was open, and inside, the Alliance Tri-Star, an award given for valor in combat, rested on the black velvet. The citation lay beside the case. He picked up the citation and without reading it, tore it into pieces, and put them in the box. Then he closed the box and quietly threw it away.

He was suddenly exhausted, and after a few minutes of unproductive and useless rumination, he tried to go back to sleep. In his dreams, a choking red mist drifted up off the Thaetan forest floor, enshrouding him, drawing him down into its depths to be buried alive. He could hear Katherine's voice but couldn't see her. Then he was suddenly lying beside her. He tried to move, but their bodies had fused into one flesh, and he couldn't. Katherine was dying. The body they shared was dying, but he was alive. When Katherine died, he would be alone, trapped somewhere between life and death for all eternity. The thought of being so alone terrified him.

A scream caught in his throat, and he woke with a start, his heart pounding, not knowing for a moment where he was. Then he remembered the mist, and his stomach turned. He sank back into the bed and closed his eyes, trying to calm himself by holding the familiar meditation image of the still pool of water in his mind.

In a few minutes, he was in a safe and timeless place where he was able, at least for the moment, to partition himself emotionally from everything that had happened on Thaetar.

***

The wardmaster called David as soon as he heard Curran's scream, but by the time David got there, Curran was sleeping quietly. David had disconnected the sensor leads to the monitor days ago when Curran's brain wave activity returned to normal, but he knew what he would see if they were still connected. There would be brecia pulses.

From what he'd read, outbursts like this weren't unusual in cases of severe trauma, but they weren't a good sign. If another episode occurred, it would be a sure indication that the psychic healing process had not been completed, and David would have to have Curran returned to his homeworld for treatment.

Curran's wounds were drained and closed, and he was walking a little further each day, but David decided to keep him in Sick Bay and under observation a few more days until he felt confident that Curran was all right.

***

Curran was released four days later, two weeks after being returned to the ship. He returned to his duties a week later. Except for the one outburst, he knew his recovery appeared normal. He gradually regained much of the weight he'd lost, and with continued rehabilitation, his leg improved steadily. However, for the first month after he was released, every time he tried to sleep, the mist returned, and the dreams and the images of Thaetar. When he woke, they were still with him, like aftershocks from an earthquake.

To the Deniban mind, fear was the result of a lack of knowledge, or it was a warning and necessary for survival. This fear was different. It wasn't caused by something outside himself that he could understand and intellectualize. It came from deep inside. When he opened himself to it, thinking he would be able to deal with it if he faced it head-on, the fear became so overwhelming he had to stop. When direct confrontation failed, he used his intellect to rationalize it. That failed as well. Finally, he began resorting to the Mind Disciplines to force the images away, altering his meditation, censoring specific thoughts and emotions, not allowing them to surface and be worked through.

Meanwhile, he learned to bury his feelings under constant work, and as he became more skillful at using the Mind Disciplines to control the fear, he felt it less. Eventually, the dreams stopped. When he thought about Thaetar at all, which he rarely did, he could control the images that came with the thoughts, and he could control his reactions to them.

Three months later, when the *Defender* returned to her home port, Curran left to spend his leave with Jenny.

As far as anyone knew, he was fine.

Book 2 - The Sound of Wind

CHAPTER 4

Curran stepped down from the cab of the freight barge, walked past the drive unit, and began helping Frank unload. The cab, drive unit, and the five big cargo sleds hovered a foot off the ground in front of Jenny's horse barn.

"Guess she's not home," Frank said when Jenny didn't come out to help.

He and Frank unloaded fifteen salt and mineral blocks, a box of veterinary supplies, several boxes of household goods and some tractor parts, and left it all just inside the barn door.

Jenny's ranch was the last place on the outbound part of the freight run, and Curran was the only passenger left by the time they got there.

"I'm glad I got to meet you, Curran," Frank said as he shook Curran's hand and climbed back into the cab. "You've been good company and good help. See you next time around."

The motors wound to a soft, high-pitched whine, and the whole train lifted three feet off the ground and moved off to the west.

Curran had been on Gavalon for three days. It had taken one of them to get from the spaceport to Medicine Rock and two more to get to Jenny's.

Jenny had told him to check in at Frank Ryan's freight service in Medicine Rock as soon as he got to town—that they would be expecting him there. When he introduced himself to the two men working behind the counter, they greeted him like a long-awaited friend and told him to be back at sun-up to help load.

He spent the evening walking around town and was back at first light to help Frank and four other people pack pallets of freight and load the cargo sleds. Until they left on the route, he didn't know that two of the four people he was working with were also passengers. Passengers got to ride for free if they worked.

By mid-morning, they'd made five deliveries, dropped off two passengers, and picked up six more. The freight included everything from machine parts, furniture, and feed grains, to a full sled of rough-cut lumber, three cages of domesticated birds, four saddle horses, and a pickup truck.

Two of the horses belonged to a Deniban woman who'd flagged down the barge on the prairie about fifteen miles from town. She'd loaded the horses on a half-empty sled, joined the rest of the passengers for a few miles, and then gotten off in the middle of nowhere and ridden away.

After only a few stops, Curran realized that besides his informal passenger service Frank was also running a neighborhood news and information exchange and that people expected him and whoever was with him to stop and visit for a while.

In those first few stops, Curran began to understand how physically isolated these people were from each other and how valuable Frank's free commuter and information service was to them. The country was rough and broken, and except for the few poorly maintained dirt roads or trails on each ranch, and sometimes between them, there were no other roads. After snow or heavy rain or during the spring thaw, the country would be almost impassable except on horseback.

That night he and Frank and two other people stayed at the

ranch of a Thaetan kinship group. Phath, one of its members, had ridden out from Medicine Rock with them.

From talking to the other passengers and visiting with the people at the ranches where they'd already made deliveries, Curran was learning about current range conditions, the prospects for a good hay crop, the severity of the last winter and of every other winter for the last twenty years as well.

He learned that Jack Larsson was living with a Thaetan woman, that Fiona Fitzhugh just had a baby, and that George Red Deer was building a new hay barn. By the end of the second morning, Curran was passing along bits of information about people he'd never met but had heard about four or five times during the day before.

He was also certain that by the end of the week, there wouldn't be anyone within a two hundred mile radius of Medicine Rock who didn't know that Curran TaZarin, an officer in the Alliance Sixth Fleet who served on the research ship *Defender*, was living at Jenny Black Wolf's. This information would be accompanied by a detailed physical description of him as well as any insights into his character the teller might have, along with whatever embellishments might make for a more interesting story.

Curran stood by himself in front of Jenny's barn and looked around. Jenny's house and outbuildings were sheltered at the head of a small valley, surrounded by miles of steep rolling grassland. In the distance about ten miles to the north, he could see a range of low, heavily wooded mountains.

For the first time in three days, Curran was alone, and the vastness of the country was beginning to sink in. There was just grass and wind and sky. Jenny's house and outbuildings were reduced to insignificance against the immensity of the landscape.

Even in the remotest interior deserts of Deniba when he was on foot and alone, Curran had never felt the same sense of aloneness he felt here. His land held thousands of years of history— cities long fallen into ruin, sites of ancient battles, trade routes unused for centuries. He was always surrounded by the roots of his culture and its history and aware of his connection to them. Gavalon had been settled for less than seventy years. Those things barely existed here.

From the maps Frank had shown him, Curran knew that Jenny's ranch joined a large section of the Medicine Rock Territorial Rangeland and Forest Management Area on the north and east. To the west, a large grant of land was held in common by the Lakota Sioux. The land to Jenny's south was extremely rough and subject to erosion and had never been opened to settlement. Jenny paid for the grazing rights to some of it, Frank said, but she never used it. She paid for the permit every year to keep someone else from using the land too hard and damaging the watershed.

Curran walked around the outside of the horse barn. A hayloft ran its full length, and on the west side, the side furthest from the house, there was a lean-to that was used as a machine shed. A hay barn stood to the west of the horse barn.

Behind the horse barn, a log corral opened up onto a fenced pasture. Two big bay draft horses and three saddle horses grazed in the pasture near a fenced-off bank of solar panels.

He continued his walk, exploring.

Behind Jenny's house, he discovered a large vegetable garden. The front half of the garden had been planted and tended; the rest was in a cover crop. A small tool shed with woodsheds built on either side stood between the house and garden. The woodsheds were nearly empty, but there was a considerable pile of firewood outside that needed to be split and stacked. A wind turbine sat on a knoll behind the house. All of the ranch buildings and the house itself were built with rough-sawn lumber, squared logs, or some combination of the two. They were well-constructed, well-maintained, and pleasing to the eye.

He walked back to the horse barn, picked up one of the boxes of household supplies, and carried it to the house where he set it down on the front porch. He made two more trips for the rest of the household supplies and a third for his sea bag. At the house, he opened the door, set the boxes and his things down just inside, but didn't go in. It wasn't his house, and he had not been asked in. He *did* look around.

The central part of the house was a single large room with a kitchen and dining area at the back and the living area in front. The walls and floors of the house were all made of planed planks. The wood was beautiful; a warm, golden-yellow color with reddish-brown highlights.

Four chairs were drawn up around the kitchen table. A coffee cup and a printed book rested on it. A wood-burning stove with a stone flue stood to his left between the living room and kitchen. Immediately to his right, there was a small alcove for coats and equipment. A couple of jackets hung from the coat rack's wooden pegs, along with a worn pair of chaps, some work spurs, and two hats.

To his left under the window, he saw Jenny's desk, flanked on both sides by floor to ceiling bookshelves. Around the corner, a flat-screen viewer and more shelves. Across from that, on the other side of the room, a comfortable couch, a rocking chair, and two easy chairs. A braided rug lay on the floor in front of the couch. On either side of it, doors led to the two bedrooms.

Jenny had told him a little about her house, and he'd tried to imagine what it might look like, but he could never have imagined the feeling he would have as he stood in the doorway looking in. In contrast to the cool simplicity of his parents' home, Jenny's house was warm and intimate, but the feeling he had as he looked in was the same. It was a place of rest and comfort, a center of spiritual calm and beauty.

To a Deniban, the simplest, most basic acts of everyday life — planting a garden, building a house, killing for meat, cooking — joined the individual to the rest of creation and made that person a part of the whole. Each of those acts required the individual to be fully conscious of that relationship and to show the appropriate care and respect. He felt that care and respect in Jenny's house. He understood her house.

Curran closed the door. He stood on the front porch and, for the first time, noticed the wind; the sound, and the feel of it. At home on Deniba, the wind never stopped. It tore at his clothes. It roared past his ears. It was hot and dry and desiccating. Here it was gentle and caressing, like Jenny's touch. It ruffled his hair and played with his shirt. It cooled him. In the distance, the spring-green grass on the hills rippled and flowed in the breeze like waves on an ocean, subtly perfuming the air.

It was late afternoon, but he had plenty of daylight left, and he wanted to work. He walked to the woodshed, found the splitting maul and some steel wedges, and started in.

***

Jenny's horse waited patiently while she took off her chaps and spurs and got ready to wade into the mud hole after the calf. Her native dog Jake stood guard in front of the calf's mother, keeping her away from Jenny while she worked. The calf was only a few days old. It had wandered away from its mother, and now it stood with its head down, hopelessly mired, too worn out to struggle.

Jenny picked up her rope, slipped the loop over her saddle horn, and was in mud over her knees by the time she got to the calf. She sank to her thighs as she worked to get the rope around it and was beginning to regret not taking off her boots before she started. She wasn't anxious to lose a good pair of boots in the mud.

Once she had the calf firmly tied, she gave the rope a tug, and the little gray gelding she was riding started backing up and pulled them out. She untied the little bull calf, stood him up, and watched him wobble over to his mother, and begin to nurse.

He wasn't even one of hers. From the brand on his mother, she knew the two of them belonged to the McGuires, and that meant she had another hole in her line fence that needed mending. She sat down in the grass and scraped the worst of the mud off of her boots with her bare hands. Then she cleaned her hands in the grass, coiled the rope, and mounted up.

Since early winter, Jenny had been working without a hired hand. Except for the month her brother Hawk had sent one of his boys to help, she'd done all the winter feeding by herself. It had been one of the longest winters she could remember, and she'd almost run out of hay.

Gavalon had four seasons, each about equal in length, and each about equally violent. The violence and changeability of the weather was something Jenny had learned to respect early. She'd seen spring hail storms so extreme that when they were over, there wasn't a leaf left on the trees. The trees survived by putting out new leaves from secondary and, in some years, even tertiary buds. Winter blizzards were often followed by sunny, bitterly cold, windless days. In summer, the land baked in the sun as dust-devils danced above the grasslands. When fall came, it could rain so hard it hurt to be out in it.

She rode home tired and hungry, filled with the rhythms of the steep grass-covered hills. Jenny knew every nuance and contour of her land as well as she'd known the curves and contours of her husband's body, and she loved them as passionately.

When she got to the top of the hill west of the ranch, she heard the ring of steel on steel—the sound of the splitting maul striking a wedge. She was surprised and pleased. She hadn't been expecting anyone. It was probably just some rider working for his dinner and a place to spend the night, but she was glad she'd have company and maybe some fresh news.

As she rode past the hay barn, she was finally able to see the person working at the woodshed. It was Curran. She laughed out loud with pleasure and watched as he pounded the wedge again and the piece he was working on split in half. She could see almost half a rank of freshly split wood stacked in the shed and another half rank lying on the ground.

She reined her horse to a stop near the woodshed and dismounted. Jake stood stiff-legged beside her, growling at the stranger.

"Jake, stay here."

The dog obeyed, but the fur on the back of his neck still bristled.

She walked toward Curran, leading the horse. He was about to pick up one of the pieces he'd just split when he saw her. Their eyes met, and it was as if an uncontrolled surge of electrical energy had just arced between them. They both stood motionless, stunned into silence by the sudden unexpected release of energy as their bond renewed itself.

"It's good to see you, Curran," she managed finally.

The gray reached out and brushed his muzzle against Curran's chest.

***

Curran rubbed the horse's muzzle, buying himself a few seconds to recover.

"I hope you don't mind that I'm early," he said. "There was a last-minute place on a military flight, and I took it."

"I'm so glad you're here, Curran."

The warmth in her voice left him momentarily without words.

Jenny turned to the dog.

"Come here, Jake."

The animal came forward slowly and stopped beside Jenny.

"Jake, this is Curran. Curran, meet Jake."

Curran offered his hand and let the animal sniff. Then he rested his hand on Jake's head and waited. When the dog didn't protest, he began scratching him behind the ears and along the throat. Then he looked away from Jake and back to Jenny, and another surge of energy passed between them as their eyes met again.

She dropped the reins and came into his arms.

"Sorry about the mud," she said.

In answer, he drew her closer.

"I'm so glad you're here, Curran," she said again softly. "How long can you stay?"

"Three months," he answered his voice thick with emotion.

"Are you hungry?" she asked, and they both began to laugh. Yes, they were both hungry; for each other.

"Very," he said, still laughing.

"I'll take care of the chores at the barn," she said, stepping away from him. "Then we can go to the house and get something to eat."

***

"I'll finish up here," he said, surprised by the sudden emptiness he felt at being physically apart from her.

Jenny walked to the barn leading the horse, and Jake followed her. Curran watched, wondering at the power of the feelings between them and, at the same time, cautioned by it.

How could he feel what he was feeling? How could he feel these things with a woman he hardly knew and had never even slept with?

When she disappeared into the barn, he went back to work. By the time she came out, he had finished stacking the wood. He felt Jenny's eyes on him as he put away the tools. He was tired and moving stiffly, favoring his left leg.

"Did you hurt your leg?" she asked.

"A few weeks ago, but I'm fine now." Then he quickly changed the subject. "It was my understanding that human women only applied mud to the face," he said, his eyes shining as he teased her.

"This is the latest thing. Very beneficial. You watch, all the best people will be doing it."

"I have my doubts," he said as they started to the house.

Jenny sat down on the porch swing and pulled off her muddy boots. She set them down just inside the door and saw the boxes of household supplies on the floor and Curran's sea bag beside them.

"Thanks for bringing everything in."

"My pleasure."

All the words they'd spoken seemed so ordinary, yet he was breathless.

"Let me show you where to put your things," she said, showing him into the bedroom nearest the front door.

"Make yourself comfortable. I'm going to take a shower, and then we'll fix something for dinner."

***

Jenny dumped her mud-encrusted clothing into the washing machine in the bathroom and showered. While she put together a quick dinner, Curran showered.

During the meal, Curran entertained her with all the latest news and gossip. When he finally ran out of things to tell her about, they cleared the table, washed the dishes, then sat quietly at the table together with Jake stretched out on the floor next to Jenny's chair.

"Curran, I hope you don't mind me asking, but I need your help around here. I'm behind on just about everything, and right now, I can't leave the calving grounds."

"I came here to share your life, Jenny. I want to work, but I know it can take more time to teach someone how to do an unfamiliar job than it can to do it yourself. I want to learn, but I don't want to be a burden to you."

"You won't be," she smiled.

She held his hand gently for a moment, then walked to her room.

CHAPTER 5

Curran woke the next morning to the smell of fresh-brewed coffee. The sun was just coming up when he walked into the kitchen.

"There's a fresh pot of coffee on, or would you like something else?" Jenny asked.

"Coffee is fine."

"There's bread on the table and meat and fruit in the refrigerator. Help yourself."

He poured a cup of coffee, sat down at the table with her, and cut a piece of Jenny's home-baked bread for himself.

"There isn't anything in the house that you can't use, or that isn't clearly marked as unsafe for Denibans. I took care of that this morning. I also ordered some Deniban staples that should be here by next week. I'll show you the list later. If there's anything else you'd like to have, we can order it tonight."

He thanked her and asked if he could help with the cooking. "I like to cook, but don't get to very often."

"That will be fun. We can do the cooking together, so you learn where things are in the kitchen and how to fix what grows locally."

"I'd like that."

"Have you had a chance to do any studying about this part of

Gavalon?" Jenny asked.

"Some. I wanted to understand what I'd be seeing when I got here."

"Something you need to know that you probably wouldn't have read about is that the most dangerous animals around here are wild dogs like Jake. People steal the pups from the den when the mother is out hunting and try to keep them for pets. Later they realize they can't handle the animals, or they just lose interest in them and turn them loose.

"Dogs that have been beaten and kicked around or just left to go wild again can be dangerous. The wild ones have some fear of people. The feral ones don't. Normally they hunt deer and small game, but a pack led by a feral dog will go after cattle and horses, and they won't hesitate to attack a person.

"Don't ever leave the ranch without a rifle. You may never need to use it, but you should have it with you just in case. You can use the one in the gun rack by the door. We'll take a few shots before we get started this morning, and I'll show you how to take it apart and clean it this evening."

"No disruptors?" he asked, only half-joking.

"No disruptors," she laughed. "Even the military surplus ones are too expensive, and besides, if I had one and it broke, I wouldn't be able to fix it myself or get it repaired locally."

After breakfast, when Jenny felt confident that he could use the rifle well enough to protect himself, they went to the barn. He told her that he'd done some riding when he and David had gone on leave together on Earth and packed into the Montana backcountry near David's home, so while Jenny saddled a small buckskin mare, he saddled the gray.

They left the barn and rode north toward where Jenny told him she was still holding the cattle on the winter feeding grounds. The country offered a good mix of open rangeland and wooded draws that provided shelter from the wind in winter and protected places for the cattle to calve in spring and for the deer Jenny raised to fawn. The two of them rode all day, Jenny teaching him about the weather, the landscape, the animals, and the relationships between them.

Each time they found a new calf paired up with its mother, Jenny would take out her tally book and make notes. Her saddlebags were packed with veterinary supplies in case she needed to doctor a sick or injured calf or its mother.

She began showing him how to watch the cattle for signs of illness or injury; what the medicines she was carrying were for and how to use them; how to use the tally book to note what they'd observed or done and to which cow or calf. Then she handed it to him.

Jenny explained that the deer she raised fawned in very early spring and had already been worked, and now, according to her tally, she had only two more cows to calve. So far this season, she told him, she'd already lost a yearling heifer, two calves, and a cow. She couldn't afford to lose many more.

"What happened to the animals that died?" he asked.

"See those small trees in the brush over there?" she answered, pointing to a scraggly clump of brush.

"That's buckthorn. The deer eat the leaves all year long, but in the spring, the leaves are poisonous to cattle. Normally cattle won't touch them, but this year after the grass had already greened up, it snowed again. The buckthorn was already leafed out, and the cow I lost ate a lot of it and died."

"And the others?"

"The yearling fell through some rotten ice on a waterhole and drowned. The first calf got crushed when a tree fell on it during a windstorm. I don't know what happened to the second one. I never found it."

They stopped for a while to watch a small bunch of cattle in the distance. One of the cows looked like it was being pushed around by the others.

"What's going on over there?" he asked.

"She's probably a stray. Sometimes it takes a while before a newcomer starts to fit in. When you see one like her, try to make a note of the brand and the cow's markings. When we make the spring gather, we'll cut them out and let the owners know we have them. They'll be doing the same for us."

He made note of her use of the word "us," but not in the tally book.

The second day they found the last two calves paired up with their mothers. Both looked well-fed and healthy.

He liked seeing the mother cows grazing belly deep in the sweet new grass with the sun shining on their scruffy, half-shed winter coats. He liked watching the young calves playing. He liked the work.

That evening after dinner, he sat on the front porch with Jake while Jenny baked bread. A light breeze carried the sounds of the horses in the corral behind the barn up to the house. Insects chirped and buzzed, and several night birds were calling back and forth.

With the bread in the oven, Jenny came out on the porch to sit with him. As they watched, a starhawk swept low over the hills to the south, looking for unwary rodents. In the distance, they heard the low, sonorous moan of a Blake's owl. As night fell, the owl was joined by a *chucka*, a ground-nesting bird Jenny said lived in the brush behind her garden. A few minutes later, from far away, there came a long series of screams so eerily human, it sounded as if a woman was being murdered. The sound sent chills through him.

"What *is* that?" he asked.

"It's a Woodson's cat. A Woody for short. They're common, but you almost never see them. They hunt mostly at night. The females are very territorial and will defend about twenty-five miles around their dens. The males have a bigger range but usually don't defend it, and they never go back to the same place at night. I always feel like the one that lives in the bluffs above the river is my own personal cat. She's lived there almost as long as I've lived here. We're neighbors."

"Perhaps she thinks of you as her own personal human."

"She might."

When the bread was done, Jenny brought a loaf out to the porch. They ate half of it as soon as it had cooled a little. Afterward, they decided to go inside and watch a broadcast of the latest planet-wide news, which was followed by a discussion of some of the current political issues affecting the Alliance as a whole. The situation on Thaetar was one of them.

He'd watched the local news with interest, asking Jenny questions and making comments. Then the debate about Thaetar started. The report began with pictures of the fighting and progressed to a discussion of Alliance options in light of the new evidence of substantial Karghan intervention. He got up, and without a word to Jenny, went to his room and quietly closed the door, leaving her to watch the rest of the report by herself.

***

The next morning they walked to the barn together to do the morning chores. Curran saddled the gray, and together they packed the supplies he needed for the day on one of the pack horses. When they finished, he followed her into the machine shed.

The day before, he'd noticed her two tractors. They were both contemporary machines, but like her pickup truck, they looked like antiques. They operated on internal combustion engines of a very simple design, and both ran on methane. When he'd asked her about them, Jenny explained that she couldn't afford more modern machines.

"Even used, those tractors are expensive. The parts are expensive too, and I'd need a whole new set of tools to work on them. At least with these, I can usually fix them myself when they break down, and I can make the methane they run on. Two of the biggest factors in keeping this ranch solvent, Curran, are that I do almost everything myself and that I'm not in debt."

Jenny opened one of the cabinets above the workbench to get the maintenance manual for the solar-electric water pumps she used to pump water into her stock tanks and handed it to him. She'd already given him a topographical map marked with the locations of all of the tanks. Now he looked through the manual and assured her that he felt comfortable about doing the maintenance on them and about being out on the land alone. He went back to the barn for the gray and his packhorse and rode out to work, thinking about what Jenny had said about her financial situation the day before and what it meant.

He knew Jenny owned over nine thousand acres of good rangeland and timber. Grassland like what Jenny had would represent enormous wealth on Deniba, yet she was concerned about going into debt to pay for improvements or to buy better equipment. She worried about hiring extra help or buying extra hay to get through a hard winter, and she lived very simply. If she worried about such small sums, the margin by which she held and operated the ranch had to be very small. Clearly, Jenny wasn't a wealthy woman.

***

It took him a good part of the day to locate and tinker with the four units she'd thought he could get to in one day. Jenny had explained that she used the stock tanks to control the movement of her cattle by controlling their access to water. It helped prevent overgrazing. She needed to be sure the pumps were working by the time the two of them moved the cattle to their summer range.

He was finished by mid-afternoon, but instead of starting back to the house, he wanted to ride out toward a landmark Jenny called the Castle, a massive outcropping of rock that was the remains of an ancient volcano. It could be seen for miles from almost any high ground, and he'd been using it, along with the topographical map, to stay oriented.

He went through a gate that left the north section of Jenny's home range, crossed Lost Camp Creek, and rode for about three miles before dismounting to water his horses at a small spring he'd seen on the topo map. He picketed the horses and walked out of the draw to the top of the nearest hill, a tiny life caught between an immensity of earth and sky. The grass rippled softly in the breeze, a sea of greens and tans, dotted with wildflowers. The sight of it filled him with pleasure.

Curran sat down and carefully studied a single blade of grass, then the whole plant, then the other plants growing around it. There was such diversity, such excess here, even in this tiny area. The earliest records on Deniba showed that *cacholo* and *camaranth* forests had once covered the rough hills around Shirraz'At. There had also been thick stands of short drought-resistant grasses on the plains and good agricultural land along the rivers. Overgrazing, careless agricultural practices, and prolonged drought had devastated what had once been dry but productive land.

Curran couldn't even begin to guess at the thousands of trees he and his brother had planted and the acres of grass and forbs they'd reseeded. Some years, half the trees he and Ri'kar planted died. The rains didn't come in time, or they were damaged by wind or hail. Other years the grasses never even germinated, or they dried up in the summer heat before they'd had a chance to establish an adequate root system. Those years were a disappointment, but when he and Ri'kar were successful, when he would go back into the desert and see their work added to the work of earlier generations of TaZarin and to the legacy of his House, the feeling was beyond words. He had a deep and enduring attachment to that land, an almost mystical bond with it. Perhaps in another five or six generations, there would be good grass growing on all of TaZarin's land, but in the meantime, he had this. He felt at home here, at one with himself and with Jenny's land.

***

Jenny spent the day working on the pickup truck and the two tractors. She had the truck and the small tractor finished, but the heavier one was still running rough. She left it idling in the machine shed and was looking in the barn for some parts she'd misplaced when Curran rode in.

"How is everything?" she asked, her hands and arms streaked with grease and oil, a grimy rag stuffed in her back pocket.

"I got to all four of them and did the maintenance. I'll get the others done tomorrow."

"I'm still working on the big tractor," she said. "I'll be lucky to have it finished before dark."

"I'll cook tonight, then," he volunteered.

She was about to thank him when three loud explosions rang out from the machine shed.

Curran threw her to the floor and covered her body with his own.

"Curran, what in hell are you doing?" she yelled, struggling to get up.

He wouldn't let her.

"Stay down!" he said hoarsely.

"Curran, we're not being shelled or rocketed! It's just the damned tractor backfiring!"

His eyes were anguished, and she couldn't tell if he'd heard her or not.

***

Before his eyes, Jenny's face had become Katherine's. Frothy blood ran from her nose and mouth. Her chest was torn open by shrapnel. Her clothes were blood-soaked.

He closed his eyes, trying to force the image away, and pulled Jenny into his arms, unconsciously hoping that the feel of her body against his would make it stop.

She didn't return the embrace. She lay under him, not resisting, but he could feel her anger rising. He released her and opened his eyes.

76

Jenny's face was her own again.

He rolled onto his back, his heart pounding, breathing hard and lay staring up at the loft floor.

***

Jenny was stunned. She had *felt* his horror, not just seen it in his face. She had felt it with him, and she had almost seen what he'd seen.

Two more explosions followed. Curran's body jerked involuntarily at each.

"You bastard." Jenny's voice was soft but intensely emotional. "You *lied* to me."

"I haven't."

"Well, you didn't exactly tell me the truth, did you? 'I'm fine,' you said. Well, screw that! You were wounded, and you're not fine! You son of a bitch! Why didn't you just tell me?!"

"I didn't want your pity."

"Well, you don't have it!" she snapped. "Just what did you think, that I would fall all over myself trying to take care of you if I found out what happened? Well, I don't have the time, even if I had the inclination.

"Did you honestly think I would have tried to take your independence from you? Or maybe you were afraid you might let me try, is that it?"

They sat facing each other as the tractor backfired again.

"Do you want to talk about what happened to your leg?"

"No!" he said, more sharply than he'd intended. "I mean, no, I'd really rather not."

"I see," she said coolly. "Well, at least get out of the way so I can turn off the damned tractor before it blows itself up."

She left to turn off the tractor and put things away, and by the time she got back to the horse barn, she'd calmed down, and Curran had finished the chores.

"I guess the tractor can wait until tomorrow," she said. "Let's make dinner."

***

After dinner, Curran showered while Jenny sat at the kitchen table, studying one of the latest government bulletins on rangeland management. When she heard the bathroom door open, she looked up. Curran was wearing nothing but a T-shirt and his shorts.

He walked into the kitchen and poured himself a glass of water, then walked to the table and looked over her shoulder to see what she was reading, deliberately standing with his left side nearest to her.

If he didn't want to talk about what had happened to him, he couldn't have found a better way to be open with her about the extent of his injuries. Long white scars ran the length of his thigh and up his hip, disappearing under his shorts. She traced them with her fingertips. With modern medical techniques, wounds like Curran's usually healed cleanly, without scarring, unless they had been terribly infected. Curran's scars would be with him for the rest of his life.

With a flash of insight, the few things she'd seen began to come together. She was certain now that Curran had been to Thaetar, and from the age of the scars, it would have been right around the time the first reports of Karghan intervention started to appear.

He put his hands lightly on her shoulders. "Would you like to read together on the porch?" he asked.

"I would."

He kissed her on the back of the neck and went to his room to get dressed.

CHAPTER 6

Sometime during his fourth week at Jenny's, Curran realized that he had become a part of the ranch work and its rhythms. Morning chores at the barn, working the cattle, tending the garden, maintaining buildings and equipment, checking the deer feeders Jenny used to supplement their natural browse and attract them to specific areas—all of it had become familiar.

The evening after they finished mending some of the fence on Jenny's west line, Jenny did the dinner dishes while Curran sat at the kitchen table reading the rangeland management bulletins Jenny had finished several weeks earlier. He was puzzled by a lot of what he read.

"Jenny, why do they say here that it's not a good idea to run cattle and deer on the same range? Why are you doing it if it isn't profitable?"

"They're coming at the problem from a different point of view than I am, that's all."

"I don't understand."

"The people who write these are looking for the fastest, most efficient way for a rancher to make money. I'm looking for the best way to make a reasonable profit and maintain my range in the best condition I possibly can.

"The economics of the thing are simple; deer take more time

and effort and are harder to work with than cattle, and since they don't bring as much money on the market, most ranchers would rather not bother with them."

"I still don't understand. The bulletin implies that the deer population needs to be suppressed, but from everything I've seen, you encourage them."

"I've seen what happens when you suppress the deer population. It's taken me almost ten years to undo the damage."

"Did your parents raise deer when they lived here?" he asked, looking to find a window into her past by asking. He knew she had a brother, but she never spoke about him. He also knew that when she was seventeen, her parents had decided to leave Gavalon. She'd been staying with a Lakota family who lived on tribal land about twenty miles from her parents' ranch and had refused to leave with them.

"Actually, they didn't live *here*. The original house burned in a grass fire almost eight years ago. The house was located about five miles from here on the other side of Dry Creek. When I finally decided to live on this land, John Standing Bear and his son Hawk helped me build this house and the barn. And no, my parents did not raise deer."

The bitterness in her voice made him hesitate to ask anything further, but to his surprise, Jenny continued on her own.

"When my father saw a doe, he'd trail it back to its fawning place and kill it. The fawns, too. Then he'd tear up the fawning place so no deer would ever be attracted to it again. He just left the bodies there to rot. We never even took them home to eat."

"You saw this?"

"More times than I care to think about."

She was so angry there were tears in her eyes, but the anger passed quickly, and she continued.

"It's true, what they say in the bulletins, that the deer eat grass that could be used to feed cattle, but most of what they eat are forbs—the weeds and wildflowers and brush that come up in the grasses. The forbs don't make very good cattle feed, but their roots and tops help feed the soil organisms that keep the grasses healthy.

"Without an adequate population of deer, there's nothing to control the growth of the forbs. Once the forbs grow to maturity, even the deer won't eat them.

"At the same time, if cattle are allowed to overgraze, the grass can't reproduce the way it should, and the forbs reseed themselves or send out new runners, and they begin to take over. The damage from overgrazing can happen pretty fast if the cattle aren't moved and the grass given time to recover, but fences are expensive.

"The only other natural control that can maintain grassland without the deer is fire. People use controlled burns as a management tool sometimes, but they're not always a very practical solution. That's how my parents' house burned."

Curran sensed that what she'd said was true; that her parent's house had burned in a grass fire, but he also sensed that perhaps she hadn't tried very hard to save it, that she hadn't wanted to.

"My father about ruined this land. By the time they left, it wouldn't support a third of the cattle it had carried when he'd started the ranch. The land was paid for, but they couldn't make a living off it anymore. They sold the cattle to pay their way off Gavalon, and when I wouldn't leave with them, they gave me the land, or what was left of it.

"I worked away from here to earn a living, and when I finally came back to stay, I lived with John Standing Bear and his family. They're my family, Curran.

"I couldn't make myself live in my parents' house, but I still worked on the land whenever I had the money. I rebuilt the deer habitat. I did controlled burns. I even bush hogged some of the pastures to control the brush so the grass had a chance to recover. My neighbors had a good laugh over that one. They all thought I was crazy, and maybe I was, but it worked."

"Who taught you to *see*?"

"John did. He taught me how to watch until I understood the connections. He's the reason I became a botanist. He tried to teach me to watch my life the same way, but I wasn't ready to learn any of that until I met Kristen.

"Most of the ranchers around me carry a lot of debt, Curran. They borrow to build a house and outbuildings and they buy enough cattle to stock their range as heavily as they can in order to stay solvent."

"But as their range deteriorates, so does its carrying capacity and the condition of their stock. The cattle would become less profitable."

"Of course."

"But can't they see what's happening? Don't they understand the cost?" The cost on Deniba had been enormous, and it was still being paid.

"Some of them do, but they're trapped by their debts; others by denial or their unwillingness to change. Some of them never go onto the prairie and really look. I've even known people who were terrified to leave the sight of their buildings and fences. I guess they feel overwhelmed by the vastness of this country. I never have. I've always thought it was exhilarating. I've never minded knowing how insignificant I am compared to all this. Anyway, they don't actually understand what healthy range looks like, and while their land is changing all around them, they justify it with all sorts of reasonable-sounding excuses."

She thought for a minute and then looked at him squarely.

"Curran, maybe you don't understand yet how little I really have here. I know that to you, all this good grassland looks like it should be worth something, but it's not. I live very modestly by choice, but even if I wanted to live differently, I couldn't afford to. My fences are worth more than the land, the house, and the buildings put together.

"Some years, I do better than others, but I never make a lot; just a living. I work off-world for Dalt-Ex Survey and Exploration or take search and rescue jobs for the fleet because I enjoy practicing my profession for one thing, but I also take them because the research project I'm working on on Caracor takes a lot of money and if I want to continue with it, I have to. The ranch doesn't earn enough to support it.

"When I'm away, my brother, his boys and his wife work the place for me. My brother is my partner here, not an employee. He doesn't own any of the place, but we share what we make here. If I marry and I die before my husband, my brother will become my husband's partner."

"Jenny, you don't have to do this."

"Yes, I do, Curran. These are things you need to know. You need to understand that I have nothing to bring to a marriage other than what you see around you here and who I am."

"Jenny, I appreciate your honesty, but I will never measure your worth in terms of money, nor will my family. My family does have land. It's rich in history and tradition, but little else. My father is a sculptor. He's just becoming well-known. My mother is a weaver. My own earnings are more than enough to meet my needs, and I have some savings."

"It wasn't my intention to push you into talking about this, Curran. I'm sorry if I did."

"You didn't," he said. "You need to know, too."

Then changing the subject, he asked her what she'd like to do with the rest of the evening.

"I'm tired. I think I'll just finish that book I've been telling you about and go to bed. How about you?"

"I'll read with you."

They sat at opposite ends of the couch, their backs against the arms, their legs entangled together in the middle. It was a warm sultry night, and as they sat reading, the wind began to pick up, followed by dull flashes of lightning and distant thunder. Although the worst of the storm missed them, within an hour, it was raining hard. With the storm continuing outside, the house felt especially warm and intimate, and the two of them were enjoying it.

Jenny closed her book and yawned, put her feet against Curran's legs, and stretched.

"Finished?"

"Uh-huh."

"How was the book?"

"It was good. I think you'd like it."

Curran lay down next to her and took her in his arms. With a sigh of contentment, Jenny curled up against him, and in a few minutes, she was asleep.

***

When she woke in the middle of the night, it was still raining. She became aware of the gentle rise and fall of Curran's chest against her arm and felt a surge of tenderness for him—a surge of tenderness colored by need. Not the blatant need she would feel with him at the time of mating, but need of *him*; his touch, his voice, his ideas, his friendship, his sharing of her life.

She liked him, and she was beginning to believe she loved him, but mixed into it all, there was a constant and growing undercurrent of eroticism that touched everything she did, whether they were together or not. Caring for the garden, working with the horses, cooking, eating, everything she touched, everything she saw, everything she did, colored by it, deepened by it, everything a source of pleasure and wonder and of sensual involvement with the world around her.

At the same time, she knew they were living on a knife's edge. If they mated outside of marriage, fall or not, they would become shal'tan together. She might have doubts about loving him, but she hadn't the slightest doubt about that.

How was she to distinguish love from the feelings created by her displaced need and the beauty they added to her life? She loved the feelings she was experiencing because of him. She was honest with herself about that. But sexual need wasn't a relationship, and mistaking it for one with a Deniban man and marrying because of it would be a lifelong catastrophe for both of them.

She got up slowly, careful not to wake him, picked the book up off the floor, and went into her room. She took the quilt from the foot of her bed and gently covered Curran with it. Then she kissed him goodnight and went to bed.

CHAPTER 7

The next morning when he got up, it was still raining. He and Jenny did the morning chores and decided to take the rest of the day off.

After eating a leisurely breakfast and watching the planet-wide news together, Jenny played a recording of a Deniban harp recital by the master harper, Hakar. Later, Curran turned on the extended agricultural and livestock market report, which was followed by the Zone Seventeen long-range agricultural weather forecast. In the meantime, Jenny wanted to do some baking.

When the weather report was over, he walked into the kitchen to ask Jenny where the book she'd finished the night before was.

"It's on the nightstand in my room."

Curran had never been in Jenny's room. He had never been asked in, had never gone in on his own, and this was the first time he had been given permission, albeit implied permission, to enter.

He went to the nightstand, picked up the book, and was about to leave when he was caught by several photographs on the wall, all landscapes, and especially by the one on the nightstand — a photo of Jenny and Kristen.

He hadn't intended to stay in the room and risk violating Jenny's privacy, but he couldn't help himself. He picked up the photograph.

In the photograph it was summer, and Jenny and Kristen were standing together on the back of an empty hay wagon with their arms around each other. Kristen was smiling down at her. The photographer had caught the two of them by surprise and captured a small moment of intimacy between them.

Curran sat down on the bed, still holding the photograph in his hands, considering what he saw there. He was sitting on what had been Jenny and Kristen's marriage bed, and he thought about that as well. He looked at the man in the photograph again and knew that man had loved her.

Jenny came to the door and looked in. Her hands were powdered with flour, and she was wiping them on a kitchen towel.

"Curran?"

"I'm not like he was, Jenny."

"No. You're not. Had you expected him to be more like you?"

"I don't know."

He looked back at the photograph again.

"He loved you, didn't he?"

"Yes. I think he did."

"Jenny, I can never love you. I have no understanding of what that means."

She sat down beside him on the bed and looked at the photograph of her and Kristen in his hands.

"Curran, I don't know if I know what it means either. I just know that neither of the human men who wanted to marry me could give me the freedom and acceptance I felt with Kristen.

"All Kristen ever wanted from me was to share my life. Other than that, he simply wanted me to be myself, and he enjoyed seeing me grow and change. It didn't intimidate or frighten him. He accepted me as I was, and he cared for me in a way I'd never experienced before. Kristen never told me he loved me, but I felt loved."

Curran set the photograph back on the nightstand.

"Jenny, there are things I'd like to know. Things I have no right to ask or expect answers to, but…"

"You have every right, Curran."

"I keep remembering what you said when we were at the lake—that you knew exactly what would happen to us if we mated outside of marriage."

He hesitated, uncertain how to continue, then just said it.

"Did you and Kristen bed before you married?"

"We did. And we were fine. For a while. We were idiots and thought because I was human, everything would be alright. Well, it wasn't. It was worse."

"When the two of you bedded, were you already mind-linked?"

"No, but I was in love with him, and I knew I wanted to live with him. Then the bonding link began to form, and as it got stronger, it began to feel like a giant feedback loop with each of us feeding off the sexual need of the other.

"I think he was experiencing a lot of the same things you are. The sudden unexpected arousal, the emotional emptiness afterward, the uneasiness, wondering if he would become shal'tan because of me. I didn't understand much of it then. I just knew that the longer we were together, the worse it got and that he wanted me as much as I wanted him. We talked ourselves into believing we would be alright."

"What happened?"

"Well, for one thing, we didn't have to wait for fall. One day we went to bed together, and it just started. The violence of the feelings between us was terrifying. The few times I was able to leave the bed, the emptiness I felt was so devastating I had to go back to him. When we were apart for even a few minutes, I felt as though everything inside me was being emptied out, and there would be nothing left of me without him. Even though I knew I was going crazy, I couldn't tear myself away from him."

"Then how were you able to save yourself?"

"I had nothing to do with it. I was finally so exhausted I

couldn't stay awake any longer. Somehow Kristen found the strength to leave. I didn't see him again for months, but the aftermath of the madness didn't stop. It was as though a part of my own flesh had been torn away. There were times when I thought I was literally going to die. It took weeks before it stopped. When he finally came back, he asked me if I wanted to marry him and I said yes.

He accepted her explanation without question, knowing the choice she and Kristen had made was the only choice they had. It was the same choice he and Jenny would have to make. They could enact the marriage ritual together, or they could part. There was no other way. They couldn't even see each other as seasonal partners or friends. The bond was too deep. The feedback loop she was talking about was always just a misstep away, and he needed her. It was summer, and he needed her.

"Jenny, are you interested in me because I am who I am, or is it just that I'm Deniban? We bonded by accident. It wasn't a choice either of us made."

"I *am* interested in you because you're Deniban. It's part of what makes you the person you are, but it's also because from the beginning I knew you understood me. I didn't have to explain myself to you or try to be someone I wasn't. And I felt something from you, too, Curran. I felt that you were interested in *me*, or maybe *intrigued* is the better word."

"I checked yesterday, Jenny, and there's a flight off Gavalon in three days. Are you sure you want me to stay with you for the rest of my leave?"

"I'm sure, Curran. I know how difficult this relationship is for you, and I know that until you decide what you want, it will only get harder. If you want or need to leave, I'll understand."

He knew what she'd said was true—she would understand—but he'd also felt the ache of loneliness, almost of despair that shot through her when she'd said it.

He looked at the photograph again, then at her. The softness

89

and concern in her eyes filled him with feeling. And along with her concern, he felt her hurt and sadness that he might leave her, and he felt her desire. It was always present, like a small fire burning inside him, uniting and separating them at the same time. And in the back of his mind, there was the constant and growing fear of his own feelings.

He took her hand in his and held it for a moment, then left her room without the book he'd come for in the first place.

Jenny heard the screen door slam closed behind him, and a few minutes later, she heard him at the woodshed, splitting wood.

CHAPTER 8

Two days later, when they drove the tractors and haying machinery to the first of the two fields Jenny planned to mow, it was hot and sunny. The good weather held for the five days it took to work the first field and bring the hay up to the barn. The following day, they moved the machinery to the second field and started work.

When they were about half-finished, Jenny called the freight service office and asked to have two empty sleds brought to the field so she and Curran could load them and have them delivered to George Red Deer's place. Jenny had traded two years' worth of first-cutting hay from this field as payment for the team of draft horses George had raised and trained.

Frank arrived the next day with the sleds, both with retractable wheeled undercarriages so they could be pulled behind a tractor and loaded. Curran and Jenny were eating lunch under the shade of a tarp they'd stretched between the two tractors when he arrived. They invited him to stay and eat with them, and he sat down under the tarp, shared their food, and exchanged the latest news. His last piece of news, tossed out almost as an after-thought, was that the annual baseball game was going to be held at George Red Deer's at the end of the week.

"Really? It's this weekend?"

"Yeah, didn't you know?"

"No, I didn't. I've been so busy I haven't been checking the bulletin board."

When they'd finished eating, Frank got up to leave, and Curran and Jenny walked back to the barge with him.

"I'll be back for the first load this evening and for the second one late tomorrow," he said. "If I don't see you then, I'll see you at the game."

"Okay. And thanks again for reminding me, Frank. I really appreciate it."

Frank started up the drive unit, waved goodbye, and drove off.

"Curran, we've got two days to finish baling this field and loading George's hay. We are absolutely not going to miss that baseball game, even if we have to work all night."

"What's baseball?"

"You poor benighted soul, you mean you really don't know?"

"No."

"Well, let's get this field finished so you can find out, because you truly don't know what you've been missing."

"Well, that much is certain," he agreed.

By the time they got home that night, they'd finished baling about half of the field and loaded the first of George's sleds. Jenny steadfastly refused to tell him anything about baseball, insisting instead that it be a surprise. All she would say was that a game had been played every summer, rain or shine, for the last fifteen years and that it was the biggest neighborhood event of the year.

Jenny's excitement about the weekend was infectious. As she happily went around the house gathering up camping gear and hunting for baseball gloves and bats, Curran surreptitiously looked up baseball online and tried to get a basic understanding of the game.

By late afternoon the next day, they'd baled the last of the hay, filled the second sled, and hauled what was left to Jenny's hay barn. The following morning, they saddled their horses, loaded the camping gear and baseball equipment on a packhorse, and started for Red Deer's place with Curran leading a green-broke colt. The colt was the last part of the trade Jenny had made for the draft horses and Curran had been working with him for over a month.

The morning had been cool and sunny when they left the house, but it was hot by the time they stopped for lunch. After letting the horses drink their fill from a shady waterhole on Little Copperleaf Creek, they picketed them and sat down to eat. They had almost finished when the horses started to act up. Curran and Jenny both went to quiet them, but they wouldn't settle down. Curran drew his rifle from the scabbard.

Suddenly a buck crashed through the woods behind them, passing within just a few yards of where they'd been sitting. The buck's eyes were wild, its sides heaving and flecked with sweat. The animal stumbled down the steep draw, saw them, shied away, stumbling again, regained its footing, splashed across the creek, and disappeared just as four wild dogs burst from the woods, chasing it.

The dogs disappeared into the woods and their horses quieted, but Jenny had been startled, and her heart was racing. Further, she'd felt the same sense of horror and of almost seeing that she'd experienced the evening Curran had the flashback at the barn.

Before she could gather herself to say anything, Curran had returned his rifle to the scabbard, untied his horse and the colt, and ridden off without a word to her. She stood with the reins in her hand, her head against her horse's neck, trying to calm herself. Then she mounted up, untied the packhorse, and left the waterhole at a walk.

***

The two of them arrived together at the site of the game — George Red Deer's newly-mown two hundred acre hayfield — late in the afternoon. The field lay in a bend along the Middle Fork of the Redstone River, and at one end, Curran recognized the diamond-shaped playing area he'd seen online. A large wire cage was set up behind home plate. The dirt infield was freshly groomed. The rest of the playing field had been hayed, then gone over with a finish mower. From a distance, it looked like a lawn, but Curran knew how rough it would be, given the kinds of bunch grasses that were growing on it. Several hundred feet away, ropes had been stretched between tall posts to form the fan-shaped boundary of the outfield.

Temporary camps dotted the hayfield opposite the diamond, with picket lines for the horses and a parking area for trucks and wagons further out. Dozens of camps were already set up around the field, including a group of Sioux lodges.

"My parents are already here, Curran," Jenny said as they rode in. "That's their lodge over there, the one with the rising sun painted on it. We can eat with them tonight, and you can meet them and my brother and his family. Hawk's lodge is the one next to it with the lightning bolts on it."

Hawk was just walking back to his family's lodge from the river when he saw them. He greeted Jenny with hugs, treated Curran as if he was already a member of the family, and offered to take care of their horses while they set up their camp. "Mom and Dad are out visiting right now, but everyone is planning to be back this evening to eat together," he said when Jenny asked him where the rest of the family was.

"We'll see you then," Jenny said. "And, thanks."

Hawk left with their horses, and Curran and Jenny set up camp near her parents' lodge. When they finished, they went off to look around.

In part of the camp, a trade fair of sorts was going on. Curran and Jenny walked around the fair, looking at the items for sale—boots, hats, harness and saddles, clothing, moccasins and beadwork, children's' toys, furniture—all laid out on makeshift tables or the tailgates of wagons or pickup trucks. At one table, a tailor measured a man for a new jacket. At another, a boot maker was re-soling a pair of boots while the owner waited and visited. Further on, a gunsmith was working on a broken rifle. There was even a tailgate barbershop that was doing a brisk business.

When the two of them finished looking around at the fair, they took the time to visit at all of the camps where somebody was home. Curran understood that Jenny had known most of these people since childhood and only got to see many of them once a year, but he also knew that if they married, these would be his friends and neighbors too. They were visiting everyone she could find because she wanted him to have a chance to meet them before he decided.

He talked easily with most of the people they met and had become knowledgeable enough about local politics and ranching to be able to hold his own in almost any conversation. He was enjoying the visiting, especially with Phath and his wife, his friends from the Thaetan kinship group he'd stayed with on his way to Jenny's, but by the time they got to her parents' lodge for dinner, he was tired.

Jenny's family tried to make him feel at home. In fact, their informality and the immediate acceptance they offered him were so unexpected it was making him uncomfortable. Still, by the time the meal was over, he was beginning to relax. Then just after dark, the women and Hawk's two boys went out for a walk, leaving the men behind to talk together.

The three men talked politics. They talked about the weather. John and Hawk told stories, mostly about previous games and the people he was meeting. They asked him what he thought about Gavalon and whether or not he liked ranch life. They talked about everything but Jenny, and after nearly an hour, he'd become decidedly uneasy.

"Hawk, why don't you see to the horses for a few minutes," John suggested.

"Good idea," Hawk said, smiling as he left the lodge.

John's long silver hair was tied loosely behind his neck, and his sun-weathered face was lit with a soft smile. As soon as Hawk left, he said, "You may as well relax and enjoy yourself, Curran, because I have no intention of asking you about your relationship with my daughter.

"I've never interfered in Jenny's personal life," he continued. "I *have* tried to show her alternatives when I thought she might be headed in the wrong direction, but Jenny makes her own decisions about her life and always has. I know just by watching the two of you together how you feel about each other. If she comes to me and tells me she wants to marry you, she'll have my permission, although knowing Jenny, she would do what she wanted with or without it. Since you're an off-worlder and don't know our customs, I don't expect you to offer anything for her."

The women returned before he could ask John what he meant about not offering anything for Jenny, and a few minutes later, he and Jenny left to go back to their camp. It was late, and most of the camps had already turned in for the night. Curran commented on how quiet it was.

"Things will get started pretty early tomorrow morning," Jenny said as they rolled out their sleeping bags, "but the serious partying doesn't get going until tomorrow night."

He wondered about how serious "serious partying" might be, but didn't ask. He'd find out tomorrow.

***

By eight in the morning, sides had already been chosen, and the players' numbers handed out. Thirty-five players were starting on the Blue team and thirty-six on Red, although everyone knew more people would be trickling in all day to sign up. Players rotated into the game throughout the day, and the official scorers had to be notified before each substitution. The scorers and umpires, like the team managers, were chosen from the ranks of the players and served four-inning tours of duty.

Jenny told him that the first games had been played without scorers, but people had so much fun, and some of the things that happened were so outrageous that everyone wanted something to remember the games by, so the scorers were added. About a month after each game, an official scorecard complete with team rosters, batting averages, team stats, and highlights of the game was sent to everyone who'd played. Jenny had played in eleven of the fifteen games. Her scorecards were among her most treasured possessions.

She explained that the games were played according to official Terran major league standards, with certain local modifications to the ground rules. In addition, umpires patrolled the foul lines and the outfield on horseback to retrieve foul balls and home runs. The baseballs were expensive and not easily digestible by haying machinery.

By coincidence, both Curran and Jenny happened to be on the Blue team, although neither was scheduled to start until the twelfth inning. They sat behind the third-base line with Hawk, watching the game while she and Hawk tried to explain the rules and their local modifications to Curran. Later they joined some of the other players to play catch, take some batting practice, and play a little Bounce or Fly.

By the time they were substituted into the game, it was early afternoon, and the Red team already had a fifteen run lead. Curran commented to Hawk that he thought the situation looked close to hopeless.

"In a game this long, nothing is hopeless, just serious," Jenny said.

"Actually," her brother added, "in a game like this, *nothing* is serious."

Curran started at second base, and four innings later, was rotated to right field when another player left the game. Considering that he'd never played baseball until a few hours earlier, he was a reasonably good player, and he was enjoying himself immensely.

Jenny started out playing center field, but while Curran stayed in the game and went to the outfield, Jenny rode down to the river for a swim and to catch a fish for dinner before taking her turn as a scorer.

By late afternoon, the game had started winding down, but the Red team had the bases loaded, two-out, and one of their best hitters, Slzzz, was at-bat. The Thaetan worked the pitcher to a full count, then hit a long fly ball deep into the gap in right-center.

Curran and Phath's wife, who was in center, converged on the ball, but it was over their heads and on its way over the rope fence when Curran put his hands on Shar's waist and lifted her over his head. She extended her gloved hand and made a spectacular backhanded catch. The crowd and the players went wild, cheering and booing simultaneously, while the team managers converged on the hay wagon where the scorers worked, demanding a ruling.

After deliberating with the other scorers, Jenny announced the results over the PA system.

"The official scoring goes as follows: first, the play is totally illegal. However, the put-out goes to Shar Phath with an assist from Curran TaZarin. Being a newcomer to baseball, it's clear that Mr. TaZarin hasn't quite mastered some of the finer points of the game. Still, quick thinking, creativity, and sheer outrageousness should not go unrewarded, and besides, it's starting to get dark, and we're hungry. So, the batter is out, all three runs score, and Mr. Slzzz is credited with three RBI's."

Although the day's game was over, people continued to arrive, many of them coming just to visit with their neighbors for the evening and for the dance that would begin at dark.

As evening fell, several pickup trucks were pulled up along the first-base line with their headlights shining across the diamond to illuminate the dance floor. Three different bands were scheduled to play, each providing music from a different culture.

Curran and Jenny danced together for the first time, especially to the slower tunes later in the evening. The feel of her under his hands, her scent, the swaying of her body to the music were having a powerful effect on him. He was in a state of mild excitement all night, and there was no mistaking Jenny's excitement and desire for him. Jenny wasn't a drinker, but she'd been sharing from a bottle that was being passed around among the dancers. She'd stopped dancing altogether during one song, put her arms around his hips, and swaying slowly against him to the music, kissed him deeply. Despite the strong Deniban prohibitions against showing affection in public, he kissed her back—a long, slow, languorous kiss that left them both a little dazed.

It was very late when they left the dance floor and went back to their camp, but they stirred the fire, added a few more pieces of wood, and sat talking quietly for nearly an hour. When they were ready to turn in, Curran took his ground cloth and sleeping bag from the tent and slept outside.

***

The game started considerably later the next morning amid a lot of good-natured groaning about sore muscles and hangovers, but by noon, it was in full swing again. Curran and Jenny played quite a bit during the morning, then stopped to do some trading in the afternoon.

Curran located Phath, and the two of them decided to get in line for haircuts. When they were done, Curran went looking for Jenny. He found her with George Red Deer by the picketed horses.

George was pleased by how well the colt had been gentled and even paid Jenny a little extra for him in cash. As soon as George left with the colt, Jenny gave Curran the money. He tried to give it back to her but she wouldn't take it

"Keep it, Curran. You earned it. By the way, you look nice," she added as she ran her fingers through his hair and gave him a quick kiss on the cheek. "I like your hair cut. I think I'll get mine cut, too," she said and walked off to get in line at the barbershop.

The day before, he had seen Jenny looking at a handsome pair of work spurs, but he didn't have enough cash. Now he bought them for her. He bought a new belt for himself and pocketed the rest of the money.

He finished the afternoon playing the last few innings of the game. In the end, the Blue team had come from behind in the final three innings to beat the Red team by five runs.

After the game, he and Jenny spent the early part of the evening with Jenny's parents. At twilight, she invited him to ride out onto the hills to watch the moon rise. After picking up a ground cloth and the picket pins, they saddled up and rode away from the camp.

They rode for several miles before Jenny stopped them at a gentle fold in the hills where they picketed the horses and spread the ground cloth on the grass.

She took his hand and drew him down to the ground beside her. They lay together, watching the stars, listening to the night sounds. Then Jenny began softly stroking his cheek, brushing her fingers through his hair. He pulled her close. It was a warm night, but she was trembling in his arms.

"Are you cold, Jenny?"

"No. I'm fine. Just hold me."

He did as she asked and held her close. Then he kissed her. A slow, luxurious kiss, not playful, but not intended to be especially provocative either. Just one to give pleasure and to receive it.

She moaned softly as she returned the kiss and began to tremble again. Then the kiss ended, and the words came.

"I love you, Curran," she said softly.

Her words left him breathless even though he already knew she loved him. He'd known since the day he'd asked her if she wanted him to stay with her for the rest of his leave, but she had never said the words. Her words opened his heart and flooded him with feeling.

He was about to answer her words with another, deeper kiss, but she wouldn't let him. She touched her lips to his, just barely, again and again, not letting him kiss her in return. The sensation was so erotic he cried out softly. Then she allowed the kiss.

White heat shot through his body and settled in his groin as his sexual scent enveloped them.

He unbuttoned her shirt and slid his hand over her flank to her breasts, touching gently. Under his T-shirt, Jenny's hands caressed his back.

His hand moved to her waist and along her thigh. Her whole body bucked at his touch.

He began to unbuckle her belt.

"Curran, no!" she whispered.

"I want to, Jenny."

"I want it, too, but…"

"Let me pleasure you, Jenny."

"No, Curran, please, Not this time. Not tonight. I have no control tonight."

"I do," he said quietly, slowing himself down, kissing her gently.

"Do you?" she said. "Then tell me, Curran, what will you do when I beg you for the rest?"

"Beg me?" he said, not quite believing she'd said it. No woman would beg except during season.

"I would, Curran. And when you said no, I don't think it would stop me."

He gasped as she touched his groin and kissed him again.

"I would beg you tonight, Curran."

All it had taken was that touch to convince him that Jenny was right to stop them now. If she begged him, if she touched him that way again, he would do anything she asked, regardless of the consequences.

To Curran, everything they'd done to this point in their relationship had been in the nature of the sexual play between seasons, always close to the edge, but still play. This was different. He knew they were here tonight because he was leaving in two days, and this was where and how Jenny wanted to tell him she loved him, but they had just arrived at the edge and dared not step over it.

"We need to go back," he said quietly, getting to his knees.

Tears shone in her eyes.

"I think I'll sleep at my parents' lodge tonight," she said, laughing softly as she brushed them away.

He could feel her wanting to pull him down to the ground to lie beside her again.

"Good idea," he said, almost letting her.

***

The next morning they ate with Jenny's parents and later rode to the river to bathe and swim. When they got back to Red Deer's, the camp was breaking up. They helped her family break camp and said their goodbyes, with Jenny promising to see them in a month. The two of them arrived home near dark, tired, but content.

They both got up early the next day. Other than doing the chores and taking turns keeping an eye on a mare that was going to foal in the next day or so, they spent the time together. In the evening after dinner, Jenny brought in an old saddle, and Curran took in some of the work harness. They sat at the kitchen table with the leather-working tools, repairing the equipment.

Neither of them was looking forward to his leaving, and there wasn't much conversation.

After a while, Curran began asking Jenny questions about some Sioux customs he wanted to understand better. Most especially, he wanted to use the conversation to find out obliquely what Jenny's father had meant about not asking anything for her.

"Traditionally," she answered, "a man goes to the father of the woman he wants to marry and presents gifts for her. He can't buy a wife with the gifts, but he's showing his respect for the woman by the value of the gifts he's willing to offer and demonstrating his ability to support her. Still, it's always the woman's choice."

He was thinking that he would willingly offer Jenny's father everything he owned for her.

"He said I wouldn't have to offer gifts for you and that you make your own decisions and always have."

"True," she said, smiling to herself about what John had implied about her stubbornness.

A long pause followed as he waited at the edge of asking her to marry him. He got up from his work, walked around the table to her, and kissed her softly on the back of the neck. Then he went to the kitchen counter and poured a cup of coffee for himself.

"Curran…"

Her voice was shaking.

"There's something I have to tell you."

He stood at the counter, his back to her, pierced to the heart by the sound of her voice.

In spite of her Deniban training, Jenny was being completely human with him now. It wasn't that her mastery of the Mind Disciplines was a façade—she had mastered them, and she used them—yet the closer the two of them became, the more human she was with him. Her emotions were often very close to the surface, and he had come to understand that the more important it was to her to be understood, the more emotionally open and human she became. The raw emotion in her voice filled him with dread.

"There was another mission like the one to Caldera that I didn't take when it was offered," she said. "I didn't take it because I was pregnant at the time."

Hoping against hope, he tried to believe that her child was with Kristen's family. It was better than believing what he knew was coming. He felt flushed and sick.

"A month later, the baby was born prematurely. She died within a few hours. Six months later, I was pregnant again. I took all the latest drugs the doctors prescribed, I did everything they told me to do, but I lost that baby, too.

"Both of us wanted children. Kristen was perfectly capable of fathering normal, healthy children. I'm capable of bearing healthy children. Just not *his* children. We were genetically incompatible. With a man of another line, it might be different, but I don't know that it would be."

His coffee cup crashed down on the counter, and the coffee splashed out of the cup. As if in a trance, he reached for the sponge, dampened it, and mopped up the spilled coffee. He didn't turn to face her.

When he'd first come to accept their bond and decided that he wanted to see her again, he'd read what he could find on Deniban-human matings. From the available information, it was clear that the odds of her bearing children to him unaided by drugs were about sixty-five percent in favor.

Even knowing the statistics, he had always imagined that he and Jenny would have children together, and as a married man, he would have a chance to raise them with her. Those odds had seemed acceptable at the time, but now he knew she'd already failed twice with a Deniban man. He also knew that while the drugs improved the chances of a normal birth, they were still experimental and potentially life-threatening to the mother. He would never ask her to take them, and he was sure Kristen hadn't either.

How could he have allowed himself to become this deeply involved with an alien woman? Their lives were so entwined now he would never be free of her. When he wasn't with her, he felt a kind of spiritual and erotic impoverishment he could never have imagined before. When they were together, his feelings and awareness deepened, and he opened himself to the world around him in new ways, discovering himself anew in her. Their relationship had grown far beyond the pleasure he felt in her company, his physical need for her, even the bond itself. A bond of the spirit existed between them. She was the other half of himself, the *Kotaho*, the embodiment of The Woman-Who-Dwells-

Within-The-Man. Now he had to face the likelihood that she was barren, or at least would be with him. His whole body ached. He couldn't bring himself to look at her.

"I should have told you sooner. I have no excuse. In the beginning, I thought that even though we enjoyed each other so much at the base, you would think about the consequences of this relationship and decide not to involve yourself further. The bond could have been allowed to atrophy.

"Then, you came here. And it was all right, your not knowing, while I was still unsure of how I felt. But it's different now. Everything is different, and you have to know."

When she realized he had nothing to say to her, she crossed the room to the door and left. He turned slightly to watch her go, then turned back to the sink. He stood staring into his empty coffee cup as the world receded all around him, and his life shattered.

He turned around and stared at the door. He knew Jenny was alone somewhere, probably crying. She hadn't wanted to burden him with her grief, and she hadn't expected him to comfort her. That saddened him, but it was also a relief. He didn't know how to deal with his own grief, much less hers.

He sat down in Jenny's chair and picked up work on the saddle where she'd left off. When he'd regained some control, he began to regret that he hadn't stopped her from leaving. He should have taken her into his arms and let her spend her grief there, not alone, but he had been too hurt and angry, and so deeply shaken by the intensity of her emotion he couldn't think.

If at first he was afraid she was going to tell him it had all been a mistake, that she didn't love him, he knew now how wrong he had been. Her telling him this last secret about herself was a gift of love. She had risked everything to tell him the truth. When she returned, he would let her know he was sorry he hadn't given her comfort. He didn't want to ruin their last few hours together.

Soon he had lost himself in the work. It was repetitious and soothing, and he worked without thought, his mind empty and calm. When he finished and looked at the clock it was very late, but Jenny still hadn't come back. He knew that he had no right to look for her if she wanted to be alone, and he decided to go to bed. He would tell her in the morning.

That night the dreams of Thaetar returned, only much worse. More graphic yet more surreal. Katherine lay on the ground in the mist, blood pouring from her chest. It spattered the leaves beside her. It splashed him as he tried to help her. She was trying to speak to him, to tell him something he desperately needed to hear, yet no matter how hard he tried, he couldn't understand what it was. Each time he felt he was on the verge of knowing, she would fade into the mist calling to him. He had to force himself to wake to keep from following her. If he walked into the mist with Katherine, he knew he would die.

***

The next morning they met at the kitchen table. Jenny had made coffee and set out some bread and fruit, but the food went untouched.

So much emotion stood between them, and it was so close to the surface, neither of them could speak. They sat together silently at the table, waiting for Frank.

He broke a piece of bread from the loaf and offered Jenny half of it. She couldn't meet his eyes. She took the offering from his hand and looked down at the table, hiding her tears. She had accepted all the pain of the night before and still hadn't closed herself off from him.

Outside they heard the whine of the freight barge motors as Frank arrived. Jenny walked with him to the door. For a long moment, they embraced, and for that moment, it was as though nothing had happened. Then he picked up his things and was gone.

CHAPTER 9

Jenny raked the fire in the woodstove, laid some kindling on the coals, and waited for it to catch. She'd been gone all day. The fire was almost out, and the house was cold.

Although fall had started early, the long-range agricultural forecast wasn't calling for unseasonable cold or early snow. The days were cool and sunny, the evenings chilly with light frost most mornings.

With the coming of the cooler weather, the cattle were beginning to drift back toward the winter feeding grounds. Jenny had spent the day riding the east section of the summer range, looking for stragglers and driving them slowly toward the ranch.

While she waited for the house to warm, she poured herself a cup of coffee, took a pot of leftover deer stew out of the refrigerator, and put it on the cookstove to heat. She sipped the coffee slowly and absentmindedly stirred the stew to keep it from burning. Then she went back to the woodstove, tossed in a few larger pieces of wood, leaving the draft door and damper partially open until it caught. She was about to go back to the kitchen when she heard someone at the door.

"Hang on a minute, Jake. I'm coming."

When she opened the door to let Jake in, a man was standing motionless deep in the shadows of the porch roof, out of range of the light from the house. She couldn't see his face, but Jake was standing next to him, leaning against his leg.

"Come in, Curran," she said quietly. She hadn't seen or heard from him since he left her house three months earlier.

As she stepped aside to let him in, Jake rushed past her, circled three times, and flopped down by the stove. Curran stood in the alcove, hanging up his jacket while Jenny closed the door. When she turned around to look at him, she saw his face for the first time. Her shock was so obvious and unguarded she knew he'd seen it.

Curran looked as if he hadn't slept for weeks. His normal expression of quiet calm was gone. Instead, there was nothing at all, just a blankness that took the light from his eyes.

"The ship is here for provisioning," he said. "I have the captain's permission to be here until it's completed. May I stay?"

His inflection and body language were very formal.

"Of course, Curran. You're always welcome here. I've got some stew heating. Can I get you something to eat?"

"I need to rest."

Without another word, he walked into his room and shut the door.

Jenny stood in the living room, staring at the closed door. They had hardly spoken to each other, yet she felt estranged from him. She also felt uneasy and vaguely fearful. She went to the stove and threw in another piece of wood to drive away the chill.

After eating a little of the stew, she tried to read for a while, but after going over the same passage five times without remembering a word of it, she finally gave up and decided to go to bed. Even though several hours had passed since Curran's arrival, she still wasn't able to shake her feeling of uneasiness.

She left the couch and opened the door to Curran's room to let some of the heat from the woodstove in, and without thinking, began watching him. He seemed to be sleeping quietly, but she had the same sense of foreboding and horror she had already experienced through him twice before, and of hurt so deeply engrained he no longer had any conscious awareness of it.

She went to bed but didn't sleep well, waking with a start several times during the night, aware that Curran had cried out in his sleep. At first, she wasn't sure if his cries were what had awakened her or if she had come awake with him, somehow affected by his dreams.

Each time she woke, her heart would be racing, and she would remember vague images shrouded in a suffocating red mist. She knew something terrible happened inside the mist, but she couldn't see what it was. Yet with each dream, the images became clearer until she knew she was seeing part of what happened to Curran on Thaetar, only strangely altered and surreal. Her fear of what waited in the mist grew until she was afraid even to close her eyes. Sometime before dawn, she heard Curran get up and start restlessly prowling the house. A few minutes later, she finally fell into a deep, dreamless sleep.

When she got up, the house was already warm, and fresh coffee was brewing. She was momentarily confused until she remembered that Curran was home and had already been up for hours. She dressed and walked into the kitchen.

From the second she entered the room, she could feel the mental barriers he'd started to build between them. For the first time since they'd met, he was shielding himself from her. She felt the character of the bond begin to change, its resonance fading.

"Curran, please. Don't do this."

He was standing with his back to her, taking a plate from the cabinet beside the sink. He set the plate on the counter as Jenny crossed the room and put her arms around his waist.

'Don't touch me!' he snarled in Speech.

The effect of his words was more devastating than if he'd struck her.

"That's all you ever wanted from me, isn't it?" he lashed out, his voice cold and colored by an undercurrent of suppressed rage.

"Your desire disgusts me. *Ra'zan ja'hai haz raka'ar. Sha'tar pai'ee!*"

A stifled cry caught in her throat as she turned away from him to hide her tears of anger and humiliation. He had called her a woman in heat in the crudest possible terms and followed it with another obscenity. He could not have chosen words that would have hurt her more deeply.

"Shal'tan," he spat. "Shal'tan bitch!"

She stood motionless with shock, her back to him, waiting until she was sure she had enough control of herself to speak.

"If you want to work," she said coolly, "you can start at the north fence line and begin moving the cattle toward the feeding ground."

She walked stiffly to the alcove and picked up her chaps and jacket. Curran spoke again just as she was about to leave.

"Jenny, don't go, please," his voice a hoarse whisper. "I don't know why I said those things. I don't know what happened."

She thought he probably really didn't know what had happened, but it didn't matter. She couldn't have spoken to him even if she'd wanted to. She opened the door and walked out.

***

Curran was stunned. All Jenny had wanted to do was offer him comfort and show her concern for him, and he had savaged her for it. If he couldn't control himself, their bond would become nothing but a source of anguish for them both. It was bad enough that he hadn't been able to keep his dreams from touching her, but this was inexcusable.

He put the plate back in the cabinet, turned off the coffee pot, and went out to work.

***

It was warm and sunny when Jenny left the house, but the wind picked up gradually throughout the morning, and by mid-afternoon, the temperature was falling steadily. Jenny was hardly aware of it. She felt as though her heart had been frozen, and her feelings along with it. The character of the bond was changing, transformed from a source of pleasure and intimacy with a man she loved into a source of pain. It wasn't until late in the day that she was able to think clearly about what had happened during the night.

She realized that by using the psychic shields, Curran was trying to protect her from his dreams, not cut himself off from her. The dreams and flashbacks and the terror that went with them had stopped almost as soon as he'd done it. She understood that the shields protected *her*, but they also left *him* more isolated and alone than he was before.

By the time she got back to the house, she'd accepted what happened, although it didn't alleviate the pain or alter the fact the she didn't want to be hurt like that again.

Curran wasn't back from wherever he'd gone, so she tended the fire and started dinner. It was almost ready when he came in.

"The food smells good," he said, hanging up his jacket and chaps.

It was clear he was trying hard to make things seem as normal as possible.

"Do you want anything to eat?"

He went to the stove and served himself, sat down at the table, and didn't eat. Jenny served herself and joined him.

"There was a dead doe and a yearling heifer on the north range today," he said after a time. "Both kills were made by dogs."

"Was the deer one of mine?"

"No. It wasn't ear-tagged. The heifer was yours, though."

"Where was this?"

The conversation seemed ordinary, except for the tension between them and the lack of emotional openness.

"I found the doe about two miles south of the dry wash near Black Rock and the heifer further north, near the big waterhole on Old Woman Creek. The heifer was a recent kill, maybe two days old. I tracked them for about a mile."

"There've been some reports of a pack of dogs north of there. If they're starting to come onto my range to hunt, we'll have to go after them."

"I'll start tomorrow."

"I'll go with you. It's too dangerous to go alone."

"I'll go by myself."

She wanted to talk Curran out of it, but said nothing, knowing that anything she might say would only provoke an argument or make him more determined to go alone. Anyway, with the cattle drifting south toward the feeding ground and the pack apparently moving north, the dogs might move onto government land before making another kill. With any luck at all, they would be miles from their last kill, and Curran would never see them. He was in no condition to meet a pack of feral dogs by himself.

The talk about the dogs was the extent of the dinner conversation and most of the talk for the rest of the evening. Curran was unwilling or unable to allow any physical or psychic contact between them, and Jenny allowed him to keep his distance, hoping that if she gave him enough room, he would eventually come to her on his own.

The next morning he already had most of his gear together by the time she got up. She stood in the living room, watching him get ready to go.

"Curran, please, talk to me about what's happening to you. Talk to me about Thaetar. I know you came here because you wanted help. For God's sake, let me help you!"

"How can I ask *you* for help?" he said bitterly. "You're the cause of it all."

He picked up his rifle and bedroll and started for the door.

"That's enough, Curran!" Jenny said, blocking his way. "You're not the only one here who's hurt and angry. I understand that we have sexual problems. I understand that it hurts you that I may not be able to have your children. How do you think it makes *me* feel?

"How do you think it makes me feel that I can't be with the

man I love or that I don't even know how he feels about me anymore? I've got problems, too, Curran, but I will not accept blame for things I can't control, and I will not allow you or anyone else to punish me for them."

She moved out of Curran's way, but he didn't leave.

"Why in hell did you come back here anyway? So you could hurt me the way you think I've hurt you? All I did was tell you the truth, Curran. The rest of this is your doing."

He glared at her in reply, but still didn't try to leave.

"Tell me what happened on Thaetar, Curran," she said gently. "I've already seen some of it. Why not let me see the rest and have done with it?"

"What may or may not have happened there is my concern, not yours. I'm not about to touch you with it."

"You already have, and you know it!" she said in frustration. "For God's sake, Curran, it's eating you alive. Please. Let me help you!"

"We have nothing to discuss," he said and walked out.

***

Curran rode back to where he'd stopped tracking the day before. He felt none of the joy and freedom he'd felt during his first stay on Gavalon and no relief from his pain.

By late afternoon he was ten miles from the ranch, on government land near the Castle. He had tracked the dogs to the place where they'd rested after gorging on the heifer and from there into a rocky wooded draw where he'd lost them.

During the afternoon, a dense cloud cover rolled in from the west, and the sky began to take on a sickly greenish-yellow cast. The color was so intense the hills themselves began to take on the same coloration. It was the kind of sky Jenny had taught him to be wary of, and he always had been before. Now he was too self-absorbed to give it much attention and too close to the dogs to quit. He wanted to find them before dark.

He was trying to pick up the trail where he'd lost it in a rocky draw when the temperature started to drop. With astonishing suddenness, the clouds opened up, and the rain came down in torrents, mixed with a vicious, wind-driven hail. Within minutes the ground was covered with an inch of icy slush.

Curran struggled into his slicker, giving up whatever hope he'd had of finding the dogs. He needed to find shelter. He and his horse were taking a beating. He rode back to a rocky forested place he'd passed a little earlier, dismounted, and led his horse into the protection of the woods, out of the worst of the wind and the driving rain. About a hundred yards in, he spotted an old copperleaf tree, its huge trailing lower branches forming a cave-like enclosure large enough to shelter him and the horse.

He led the skittish, exhausted animal into the enclosure, tethered him to a branch, and cared for him. When the horse settled down, Curran gathered the driest wood he could find under the tree and built a small fire, using some of the tree's dry inner bark for tinder. Then he ate a cold meal of the meat and bread he'd brought with him.

In less than an hour, the rain stopped almost as suddenly as it had begun, but the temperature kept falling. Curran was wet and cold, and his back and shoulders ached from the pounding they'd taken.

He was very aware that the dogs could be nearby and possibly hungry. Now that the night had cleared, they could be out hunting again. The fact that the heavy damp air would carry his scent well did nothing to ease his mind.

He was so tired he could hardly keep his eyes open. He couldn't remember the last time he'd slept through a whole night. He drew his rifle from the scabbard and rested it across his knees. He was counting heavily on his horse to warn him if trouble came. He was too exhausted to stay alert, and he knew his mind was starting to play tricks on him.

Twice he thought he'd seen something moving in the woods — a mottled hide and the flashing yellow eyes of a dog watching him from behind a fallen tree—but both times, his horse continued calmly munching the leaves off the copperleaf tree, apparently unconcerned.

Curran dozed fitfully. He could see Katherine and Michael running toward him in the mist. Tendrils of ground fog curled around their legs as they raced across a rocky glade deep in the Thaetan woods. It was night, but the glade seemed to be lit by an unseen fire, and eerie shadows danced and flickered in the trees. A pack of yapping, snarling dogs almost entirely hidden by the fog was pacing them.

Suddenly he was surrounded by a blood-red mist so dense he couldn't see past his own hands. The mist drew him down into the mud and softly, painlessly began crushing the life out of him.

He woke screaming, gasping for breath.

He got up to calm his frightened horse and started pacing, trying to clear his head. He had to think. Then, with a jolt of recognition, he realized that all he had left was his thinking. He no longer knew what he felt about anything, only what he thought.

By denying his feelings, he had gradually felt less pain, but he felt less of everything else as well until he felt nothing at all except with Jenny. He had invested his entire emotional life in her, deadening himself to everything else, and it had all worked until she'd told him about herself and Kristen.

The truth was that he had come back to Gavalon to find escape from his anguish with her. It hadn't worked, and now he was blaming Jenny for his pain simply because she made him feel anything at all.

He knew he couldn't stay with her as he was. He had become a danger to her and to himself as well, and no matter how hard he tried not to, sooner or later, he would damage their bond beyond saving. He took a deep breath and allowed himself to experience the emptiness inside himself. It was like stepping off a cliff into an endless darkness.

By first light, he had reached a decision. He saddled up and rode slowly back to the ranch.

***

Curran arrived home after dinner. Jenny warmed some food for him and sat across the table while he ate.

"I'll be leaving tomorrow," Curran said without preface. "I'll call Frank later and leave a message for him to stop here and pick me up on his way through."

She accepted his statement quietly. It was clear that Curran had come to some kind of decision about himself. He was tense, but not hostile or potentially explosive as he had been before.

Curran showered and went to bed early, but Jenny stayed up for another hour, listening to a concert. When it ended, she added some wood to the stove, closed it down for the night, and went to Curran's room to open the door.

She stood in the open doorway for a long time watching him sleep. He was lying on his side, uncovered to the hips, the sheets and blanket twisted around him and partly on the floor.

She walked to the bed, knelt beside him, and laid her hand at the point of his hip. He was resting quietly on the edge between sleep and awareness.

'Curran, don't wake. Just listen to me,' she said softly in Speech.

He stirred slightly but didn't wake.

She moved her hand along his hip and down his thigh, running her fingers gently over the long scars. *'I want to understand about this, Curran. About all of it, or any part of it, or about anything else you may want to talk about. I want to know how you feel and what's happening to you.*

'I love you, Curran. There is nothing you can tell me about yourself or what you've done that can change the way I feel about you. Whatever this decision is that you've made, I will honor it, and for as long as I feel your presence with me, I'll stay with you.'

She untangled the covers and tenderly drew them around his body. Then she kissed him and left the room.

***

Curran was putting on his jacket, getting ready to go, when Jenny came in from doing the morning chores. The few things he'd brought with him were lying on the floor by the door.

"I'm going to wait outside," he said, barely having looked at her.

"I'll wait with you."

"No! Stay here until I'm gone," he said harshly.

"As you wish, Curran," she answered quietly.

Jenny took off her jacket, hung it up, and stepped aside. He stood with his back to her, his hand on the door latch, but he could feel her watching him.

He'd heard every word Jenny said to him the night before. Now he couldn't find words to tell her how much they meant to him.

He'd always thought that at some point he would be able to tell her how beautiful she was to him. That should have been no more difficult than saying that a particular sunset was beautiful. It was simply a fact of nature. It would be more difficult to tell her that her spirit was also beautiful, but he had never said that either. He couldn't even find a way to tell her how much he wanted her without making his physical need sound like the need of a rutting animal. How could he explain his caring? He couldn't even explain it to *himself* in words.

"Curran, what is it?" she asked gently.

He stepped back from the door and turned to face her. The tension in his body rippled and surged through his muscles in waves. He half carried, half pushed her against the wall behind them, and drove his leg between hers.

Jenny was aflame at his first touch, reaching under his jacket, tearing his shirt from his jeans, wanting to feel his flesh under her hands.

He tore open her shirt and kissed her hard. His hands were everywhere, taking in everything as if there would never be another chance. His touch wasn't gentle, and neither was hers.

117

He moved his hands down her back and under her jeans to her hips, pulling her to him as she began riding his thigh. He rammed his thigh against her, pacing her, driving her into the wall behind them, not stopping until she came.

"Mei kei'thara, Curran. Kei'thara ayala," she whispered, her arms around his hips, breathless and spent. *"Mei kei'thara."*

Outside, he heard the whine of the freight barge motors.

He held her hard against him, his fingers knotted in her hair, breathing in her scent, drawing it deep. Then he picked up his things and ran from her house. He only became aware of her tears on his cheek when the cold wind touched his face.

Book 3 - The Sound of Heat

CHAPTER 10

Jenny received David's urgent message eight days after Curran left Gavalon. David insisted that she come to Deniba immediately, gave her an address in Shirraz'At where he was staying, and told her a ticket was waiting for her on the next ship out. He offered no explanation.

Jenny arrived at Shirraz'At four days later. She was standing in the shade of the ramada at the western entrance to the old city's central plaza, the sun blazing down from an almost cloudless blue sky, searing everything it touched. Above her, the light was so harsh and glaring she could hardly stand to look up without sunglasses. It was late summer, and the heat was breathtaking.

She was dressed in her usual faded jeans and work boots, along with a loose-fitting, traditionally-styled *sandia* cloth shirt. The shirt had a short stand-up collar and was embroidered along the neck and placket.

At the bottom of the placket there was a heavy sewn-in tab of cloth where the shield of a person's House was pinned. Jenny wore the shield of House Kei'heila, Kristen's house, and would for the rest of her life, unless she remarried.

She had her shirt sleeves rolled up above her elbows and the shirt untucked. Even standing in the shade, she was sweating, but the air was so dry the sweat evaporated almost immediately. In the open, a human on Deniba could lose a quart of fluid in an hour. A human out in the open on the Deniban desert would die in a day without water.

She stepped out of the shade of the ramada and crossed the plaza to the well. Even wearing the heaviest sunscreen available for human use, she could still feel the sun burning her skin. She had arrived at midday, and the plaza was empty. Even Denibans avoided the full sun of midday.

Like most ancient Deniban cities, Shirraz'At was laid out around a central plaza and its well. The plaza was surrounded by a square of one and two-story buildings constructed of native stone or adobe. Wide ramadas roofed with brush or mats woven from thin strips of wood gave shade to sidewalks paved with stones. There were benches outside the doors of most of the businesses, and tables outside the restaurants and *cama*houses. All of the buildings were plastered and painted white or in soft earth tones. Some were decorated with traditional designs stenciled or hand-painted around the doors and windows.

The well was enclosed by a small open-sided pavilion framed with hand-hewn timbers. It had a tile roof and a stone floor. The walls were oriented to the four cardinal directions, as was the plaza itself. Outside the well house, flowers grew in the deep shade of the well house eaves.

Jenny walked to the south entrance and gently touched one of the rough-hewn posts with her fingertips. The wood was darkened and worn smooth by wind and weather and the touch of generations of other hands. She put down her duffel bag, raised the bucket from the well, set it on the stone wall that encircled it, and reached for the wooden dipper that hung on the post to her left. She filled the dipper with water and, holding the bowl in both hands, carried the water outside to make the offering.

"'This land is my body. This water, our blood. Thank you for the water that quenches our thirst,'" she said both aloud and in Speech. Then she knelt and poured the dipper full of water at the foot of a shrubby *anthiar* abloom with bright yellow flowers. *"'By this act, I give life. By this act, life is given to me.'"*

She went back inside, filled the dipper a second time, and drank. When she was sated, she gave the unused water to the anthiar and hung the dipper on its peg. She stood in the shade, looking out at the plaza, taking in everything. To her, Shirraz'At was rich beyond measure—rich in history and culture and tradition. Coming from a place like Gavalon, which had almost no history of its own and very little sense of itself other than of its potentials, Shirraz'At was a wonder. The city was over twenty-five hundred years old.

Shirraz'At was located in a bend of the Zuhar River in a broad basin between the Tappelin Mountains to the east and the Rodavin Mountains to the north and west. The town had begun as a small farming settlement in early historical time and eventually grew into an important trading and cultural center on the main route between Sadakia to the north and Sinolaira to the west. At its height, its population was almost twenty thousand.

The Zuhar carried snowmelt water from mountains far to the north and from several smaller tributary streams as well. It offered year 'round irrigation water for crops, and its location provided protection from the savage *shirraz* winds that tore across the grasslands during the dry season. After the Great Catastrophe, four hundred years earlier, the Zuhar continued to flow, but only intermittently below Broken Knife. The Bondas River, eighty miles to the west, where Sinolaira was located, continued to flow along its entire length, although the volume of water it carried was almost halved. The country between the two rivers emptied as drought forced people off their land. Most went west to Sinolaira and others to the towns further south along the Bondas.

Drought took a third of the city's population within ten years of the Great Catastrophe. Famine and disease, another third. Together, famine and disease all but broke the matrilineal system that had existed before the catastrophe. It had taken many years for it to be restored. Even after the recovery began, the old trade routes were never reestablished. Shirraz'At continued as a center of education and culture for some time, but even that eventually fell into decline as the city was literally left by the wayside, as intellectually isolated as it was physically. Then, at the beginning of the Restoration, a school for the study of agriculture, forestry, and wildlife management was started at Shirraz'At, and the town's fortunes changed again.

Jenny picked up her duffel bag and started across the square to a camahouse where she'd been watched by several people sitting at a long table under the ramada. She'd drawn a lot of interested looks as she said The Words of Blood and Water at the well and made the offering. Foreigners in Shirraz'At were a common sight because of the school of forestry, but off-worlders who knew the traditions and acted in accord for them were not.

Conversation all but stopped as she approached them. An old man rose to meet her. His eyes went to the shield of Kei'heila on her shirt, then to her face. His gaze was direct and open, and once their eyes met, his eyes never left hers. For most humans, this total focusing of the attention was disconcerting. To a Deniban, it was a simple courtesy. A person did not break eye contact during a first meeting. To do so was a sign of disrespect or deceit.

Jenny returned the man's gaze calmly and asked him in the fluent Sixtos-accented Deniban she'd learned from Kristen for directions to the Street of the *Tr'yan*. The man answered her in a formal, almost courtly manner, and without offering his name or asking hers, escorted her to the correct arcade, then directed her from there. She thanked him and continued on by herself.

Jenny was fascinated by the look and the feel of the city. The streets of Shirraz'At were clean and neat, the city seemingly bleached spotless by the sun and scoured clean by the wind. There was nothing superfluous, nothing wasted.

On the residential streets, most of the houses looked much alike from the outside except for the courtyard gates and the choice of flowers planted beside them. The wrought iron gates were sometimes very ornate in design, sometimes quite simple, but all of them were works of art. A native could walk down any street, look at the gate, and name the craftsman who'd made it and when he lived.

Following the man's directions, she arrived at the Street of the Tr'yan and followed it to its end. The house she was looking for was the second to the last on the right. Jenny stood outside the gate for a moment admiring the beautifully made, highly stylized desert orchid worked into the wrought iron, then she opened the gate and entered the courtyard.

To her left lay a food garden large enough to supply most of the fresh vegetables for the household. To her right, a separate garden for kitchen and medicinal herbs, and a small formal flower garden. The gardens were beautifully designed and well-kept.

Carefully spaced around the gardens, several dwarf *jahara* trees helped shade the more sensitive plants from the summer heat, and because they secreted a potent chemical toxin, they also helped discourage more than a few kinds of garden pests. Each tree was planted in a wind well. The three-foot-tall square of unmortared stones on the surface condensed moisture from the air as they cooled at night. The lower part, which was dug into the ground, funneled the water to the roots.

The jahara leaves were still green. Almost everything else except for some of the herbs was dormant. This time of year, only the toughest, most drought-resistant plants showed signs of life.

Jenny walked to the doorway to the right of the courtyard, took the small wooden mallet from its place in the alcove beside the door, and struck the chime four times. After a short wait, a middle-aged Deniban woman of about seventy came to the door. She had high cheekbones, almond-shaped eyes, and delicately arched eyebrows. Her long black hair was tied loosely behind her neck, and she was wearing a soft-yellow caftan, belted at the waist. The woman was Curran's mother. Jenny knew her from the pictures of his family that he'd shared with her.

"Lady Halaya," she said, meeting the woman's eyes.

"You are Jenny Black Wolf?"

"I am."

"'Enter and quench your thirst.'"

The words were a ritual greeting and were said to anyone who came to the door. No one, not even an enemy, was turned away from a Deniban home without the offer of water.

The woman stepped away from the door, and Jenny entered the house. It was pleasantly dark and cool inside. She took off her sunglasses and accepted the earthenware cup of water Halaya poured for her from the pitcher in the recess by the door. She savored the coolness of the house and the feel of the rough, hand-turned pottery in her hand. She drank the water and handed the cup back to Halaya.

"I received an urgent message from a friend to meet him here. Is David Rawlins within?"

"I am," David answered as he came to the door to greet her. He picked Jenny up in his arms and hugged her. She hugged him back, laughing with pleasure as he kissed her cheek.

"It's good to see you again, David. It's been a long time."

"It has."

"So what's all the rush about anyway? Why all the hurry to get me here? You couldn't have missed me *that* much."

"*I* asked David to bring you here," Halaya answered quietly.

"*You* did? Why?" Jenny was genuinely surprised.

"The doctor tells me that you are a skilled tracker."

"I am."

"I want you to recover the body of my son."

Jenny's face went white. The shock of Halaya's words cut through her chest like a knife, leaving her breathless. There was a long, uneasy silence before Jenny was able to trust herself to speak calmly.

Across from her, David looked stunned. He had no idea this

was coming and no way of knowing that what Halaya had implied wasn't true.

"Your son is alive," Jenny answered, having recovered herself. "You know this as well as I do. His presence lives inside you as it does in me."

Telling Jenny that Curran was dead was a quick but brutal way of uncovering the nature and depth of her relationship with Curran, one that didn't allow for thought or prevarication on Jenny's part.

"My son is dead."

Insisting a second time that he was dead when they both knew he wasn't was something else again.

"If he *were* dead, any tracker would do."

"Any tracker would *not* do."

"I don't understand."

"You've bedded him?"

This time Jenny was angry. Telling her that Curran was dead had been hurtful but had at least served some purpose. This was offensive, as if the responsibility for their sexual life lay with her alone.

"What we did or did not do is our concern, not yours. We're not shal'tan. That is all you need know."

"The doctor informs me that you were the cause of my son's problems."

David said nothing, and Jenny's eyes never left Halaya's.

"The doctor has told you nothing of the kind."

If she so much as looked at David for assurance, let alone asked him if he'd said it, it would have been the same to Halaya as if she'd called David a liar. The statement was a test of Jenny's self-control and David's, and of their mutual trust, because the only correct answer was no answer at all. The statement itself was unworthy.

"I want you to recover my son."

'Recover my son,' not 'recover my son's body,' Jenny thought.

There was a reason it was different this time. She just didn't know what it was.

"If I am to be a guest here, I will be treated as one. If not, if I'm here as an employee, tell me more about what you want done and what you'll pay me to do it, and I'll decide whether or not I want to take the work."

Jenny had no standing in this Household. She was mind-linked to Curran, not married to him. She hadn't borne him children, and even if she had, they would have belonged to her, not him, to be raised in her Household, not Halaya's, and by now, Halaya would certainly be well-aware of the shield of House Kei'heila on her shirt.

"You don't claim standing or guest-right?"

"I don't."

Even though Halaya, by her own admission, had been the reason Jenny was here now and was thus obligated to accept her as a guest and provide for her during her stay, Jenny refused. She had no intention of forcing Halaya to accept her, regardless of the obligation the woman had incurred.

"But there was trouble between you and my son?"

This was not another challenge, but the question of a concerned parent. Jenny's answer was open and without hesitation.

"There was trouble between us, and I was the cause of some of it."

"I believe my son has chosen well," Halaya said with a slight smile. "You are welcome here, Jenny Black Wolf."

Jenny was left wondering what would have happened if she'd given the wrong answers. Would Halaya have sent her away despite the need?

Halaya asked David to show Jenny to the living room while she went to the kitchen to get something for Jenny to eat. Once there, David crossed the room and stood in front of the thermal glass doors, staring out into the courtyard. Jenny looked around for a moment, then sat down on the couch, and David joined her there.

The walls of the large open room were painted a soft tan and were undecorated except for a rug of TaZarin design that hung in the center of the east wall above the couch. On the south wall, wooden shelves held several small sculptures by Curran's father, Kierst. Several neatly trimmed and shaped shrubs grew in wooden planters on the floor along the west wall. The plants weren't in bloom, but their foliage was pleasantly aromatic. The furniture, which consisted of the couch, two end tables, and several chairs, was all made from split camaranth branches bent to form a frame and caned with *tiantha* splints. The furniture was surprisingly light, almost indestructible, and like many items in a Deniban home, made by local craftsmen. Such items weren't cheap, but for the quality, they were reasonably priced. Denibans did not want and would not buy things designed to be thrown away later.

The room itself was typical of the Deniban use of interior space. Everything in it was placed to give an overall impression of spaciousness and tranquility. It was quieting just being in the room.

"All right, David, what's going on here? Why are you here? Why am *I* here, and better yet, where is Curran?"

"Why I'm here is the only part I can explain," he said, turning to face her. "The Fleet sent me to Deniba to take an advanced course for human physicians in Deniban medicine. It's part of my normal recertification. When I told Curran I'd been assigned to the hospital in Sinolaira, he asked his parents if I could stay with them. They agreed. I commute to the hospital every morning. I've been here for two months.

"As for why you're here, I'm not so sure anymore. I thought I knew, but now I'm not so sure."

"What about Curran?"

"He came here twelve days ago while I was at work, stayed a few hours, and told Halaya he was going to the family altar in the desert to meditate. He never came back. Halaya and I went there six days ago, but there was no sign of him.

"Two days after that, Halaya came to me as a friend—more than a friend—as a member of this Household, and she asked me about you."

"Okay," Jenny said, thinking it over. "So, where is her husband? And where is Curran's brother?"

"Kierst has been gone for almost two weeks. He's setting up a new show of his work in Canobar and will be there until it opens. He should be back in a few days. Ri'kar has taken a job in Fara'Kee and moved there temporarily. I've never met him, and as far as I know, he isn't a married man. Does it make any difference that they're not here?"

"Maybe, but I'm not sure. I'm sorry I interrupted you. What else did she say?"

"She said she's known for almost a year that Curran had bonded with someone, but it was obvious from the questions she was asking that he'd never told her anything about it. She asked me if I knew who the woman was and if she was the woman in the photograph."

"What photograph?"

"There's a photograph of the two of you in his room. He brought it with him."

Jenny wondered where Curran had gotten a photograph of them. She couldn't remember one ever being taken.

"I told her the woman was you. She wanted to know about you, what kind of person you were, how deep your commitment to Curran was, if you knew the Warrior's Way and the Mind Disciplines.

"After I'd answered, she gave me the money to buy your passage and asked me to get you here any way I could. When I asked her what was going on, she said she couldn't explain."

"How did Curran get leave to come here?"

"He didn't. I checked. He's absent without leave."

"Curran? I don't believe it."

"Well, believe it. It's true. He's been AWOL for almost a month."

"Okay. So let me get this straight," she said. "He's been gone for twelve days?"

Just as Jenny asked, Halaya returned from the kitchen with a pitcher of cool tea, two cups, and a small bowl of dried jahara fruit.

"Yes. Twelve days," she answered.

Jenny was certain that Halaya repeated the number for a reason, but she didn't know what its significance might be.

"You realize that after twelve days, there will be very little left for me to work with."

"Yes, I understand that. Have you decided to take the work?"

"I'm still thinking about it. However, if I do decide to accept it, I'll have to be paid."

"Of course. What do you normally ask?"

Jenny got up and walked to the shelves in the corner of the living room where Kierst's work was displayed. She picked up a small carving of a tr'yan. The bird seemed almost alive in her hand it was so well realized.

Tr'yans were symbolic of wisdom earned through careful observation, followed by swift and decisive action. The tr'yan in the carving was soaring on the desert thermals, its wings extended above the dihedral.

"If I'm successful, I'll accept this as payment. If not, I'll have to insist on return passage home and twenty credits a day for my time."

The carving was probably worth quite a bit, but it seemed a fair trade for several days of her professional services. Insisting on return passage home and twenty credits a day if she failed was about the same as asking for nothing. The arrangement was a necessary formality. She wasn't family or a guest, and work required fair payment.

"Agreed."

Halaya poured tea for them and left the room. Jenny put the carving back on the shelf and rejoined David on the couch.

"Jenny, if Curran's not dead, then he's not sick or hurt either, is he?"

"No."

"I've camped with him in the mountains at home in Montana. He can take care of himself. So if he's not hurt and he's not sick, why is she so worried about him? What's going on?"

"She knows he can take care of himself as well as you do, and if she thought he was sick or injured, she would have asked a local tracker and a local healer to help, so that's not it either."

"Then what *is*, and why *you*, and why is she insisting that he's dead?"

"I don't know. Maybe so neither of us has to take responsibility for interfering where we're not wanted. Curran didn't ask for help. Maybe none of us are supposed to be involved in whatever it is he's doing."

They passed the next hour talking about other things. When the sun started to set, and it began to cool off a little outside, Jenny went for a walk, returning in time for the evening meal. The three of them ate outside under the ramada, visiting comfortably together into the evening, talking about local politics, the arts, and the growing popularity of Kierst's work. Then Halaya asked Jenny if she'd like to see Kierst's studio, and when she said yes, Halaya led them across the courtyard to it.

The studio was cluttered with piles of driftwood gathered from the river after flash floods, collections of animal bones, dried plants and seeds, rusted machine parts, and carvings and projects in all stages of completion. Without even meeting him, Jenny liked the man who worked there.

By the time they left the studio, it was late. Jenny asked Halaya to show her Curran's room, and the three of them went there together.

Until she saw the room, Jenny hadn't thought about where she'd be sleeping, assuming she'd be given a guest room across the courtyard. She had only wanted to see his room to look for clues and partially to satisfy her curiosity, but sometime during the day, Halaya had taken her duffel bag to Curran's room and left it on his bed for her. Now she would be sleeping in Curran's bed, without Curran. She felt an aching tenderness for him coupled with a sick, empty feeling in the pit of her stomach.

Halaya was about to leave when Jenny asked her if there was a teacher of the Arak'Kaz in town.

"Yes, of course. There are several."

"Do you know the name of Curran's teacher?"

"Yes."

"Please write down the others for me."

Halaya wrote down the names for her, and where they lived, then she excused herself, leaving the two of them alone to look around the room together.

"How well do you know this room, David, and Curran's things?"

"Pretty well. I've slept here a couple of times when they've had guests."

"Is anything missing? Moved? Changed?"

"Well, there's the photograph, for one thing."

He picked up the photograph from the small table next to the bed and handed it to her.

The photograph had been taken at Red Deer's the night of the dance. It looked to Jenny like the work of the annual phantom photographer—the same person who'd taken the photograph of her and Kristen that Curran had seen in her bedroom.

Jenny remembered the exact moment the picture was taken. She'd been more than a little drunk that night. She had just kissed Curran, and he'd stopped dancing and returned the kiss. In the instant after the kiss, she'd looked up at him, and it was that moment the photographer had captured. There was no mistaking the love and wanting in her eyes, or the warmth and pleasure in his. The moment the photographer had captured was so intimate, she was almost embarrassed, knowing David and Halaya had both seen it.

"You know, there's something very odd about this photograph," she said to David.

"Yeah. That it's here at all. It's so intimate I'm amazed he would allow anyone to see it, let alone display it here like this."

She returned the photograph to its place on the table.

"Anything else?"

David looked around carefully.

The bedroom was spare yet tranquil and soothing. Except for a beautifully designed rug hanging on the wall across from Curran's bed, the walls were bare. There were small driftwood tables on either side of the bed and a meditation area in the corner by the window, consisting of a knee-high wooden bench with a hand-woven prayer rug in front of it. A vase of dried grasses rested on the bench.

David opened the closet door. Curran's clothing hung neatly from the rack.

"I think he's taken a knife with him. It used to hang on the inside of the closet door. And there's a small medallion missing from the meditation bench. It has a silver tr'yan on it inlaid in a piece of polished stone."

Jenny had seen medallions like the one David described. Only those who had survived the Arak'Kaz earned the right to wear them.

"What kind of knife? A tool, a weapon, a ceremonial knife...?"

"Definitely not a tool. Double-edged, like some kinds of fighting knives, but with a beautifully engraved blade."

"Anything else?"

"No." He looked at her hopefully. "Are you ready to tell me what's going on yet?"

"I'm still working on it."

"Alright. Well, I'll see you in the morning. I'm going to bed. I'll be right next door if you need me."

"Okay. Thanks, David."

***

Jenny tossed and turned for several hours, doing a lot more thinking than sleeping, and finally, just before first light, she decided she needed to talk to David. She dressed and went to his room.

David's door was slightly ajar. She opened it further and stepped in.

"David?" she said tentatively.

When he didn't answer, she walked to his bed and knelt beside him, touching him lightly on the shoulder.

"David, wake up. I need to talk to you."

She shook him gently, and he came awake with a start.

"Jenny? What's the matter? Has anything happened?"

"I'm sorry, David, I didn't mean to startle you. I've been doing a lot of thinking, and I need to talk to you. I'll meet you in the kitchen, okay?"

"Okay. I'll get dressed and be there in a couple minutes."

"You won't fall asleep again?"

"No. I'm awake. Put on some coffee, will you? It's on the counter in the canister closest to the sink."

"Okay."

By the time David got to the kitchen, Jenny had the coffee brewed.

"Let's take the pot and some food out to the ramada," he said.

The sun was just coming up, and it was still cool. Everything was covered in heavy dew, and the foliage of the jahara trees glistened in the soft sunlight. They toweled off the table and chairs and sat down. David poured a cup of coffee for each of them and broke a loaf of *theica* bread.

"David, I want to know what happened on Thaetar. I want you to tell me everything you know about it, because whatever happened to Curran there has everything to do with what's happening here now."

David told Jenny as much as he knew about what had happened on Thaetar and all of what had happened in Sick Bay after Curran was returned to the *Defender*.

"He touched them, didn't he?" she said. "He touched minds with two people who couldn't direct what he saw or shield themselves from the touch, and it went very deep, and then they both died violently."

"At the time, it never occurred to me that he might have touched minds with them, but I think now that's what happened."

They were quiet for some time before Jenny spoke again.

"Did you know that he came to see me before he came here?" she said softly, looking down at her hands on the table.

"He did? What was he like?"

"Distant. Troubled."

"Angry outbursts? Moodiness? Sleep disturbances? Anxiety? Avoidance of intimacy?" He ticked off the symptoms.

She nodded. "All of it. Nightmares and flashbacks, too."

"How do you know that? Did he tell you about them?" he asked anxiously.

"No. I felt them."

David studied the dark liquid in his cup while Jenny told him what she'd seen and felt through Curran.

"I should have considered the possibility of something like this happening after that outburst in Sick Bay, but when there weren't any further symptoms, I let it go. The brecia waves had stopped, or at least I thought they had.

"When brecia waves stop, the healing process is supposed to be complete, but when it's interrupted or suspended as it was in Curran's case, the incident that caused the trauma is subconsciously denied or buried. As a result, the patient gradually begins to feel less and less until eventually, he feels nothing at all. But even nothing is better than continually re-experiencing the pain that caused the trauma. At first, the feelings will keep resurfacing so they can be worked through, but once they're buried, and the patient begins to deaden himself emotionally, it's usually too late to help.

"According to the literature, where he is now is called the Borderland. From what I've read, it's hard for anyone who hasn't been there to even imagine it. He's standing at the edge of an endless abyss. For the patient, stepping out into that endless darkness inside himself feels like a total annihilation of the self, but that's where he'll have to go if he's ever going to find his way back.

"In the condition he must have been in when he came to see you again, all he would have needed was a little added stress to bring on active symptoms. Did something happen between you?"

"Yes."

When she didn't offer anything more, he didn't ask.

"David, can you get today off?"

"I already have."

"Will you go with me to the family altar tomorrow?"

"Yes, of course."

"When Halaya gets up, please ask her for topographical maps and aerial photographs of TaZarin's land and of the land surrounding it."

"Do you know what he's doing yet?"

"I think so. I need to see someone first."

"A teacher of the Arak'Kaz?

"Yes. With any luck, I'll be back by late afternoon."

CHAPTER 11

There were four names on the list Halaya had given her—two men from House Kei'heila, a woman from TaZarin, and a man from House Havarr. She eliminated the woman from TaZarin since she might know Curran personally and chose the man from Havarr at random from the remaining names.

Jenny walked to his house and stood outside the courtyard gate, resting her head against its ironwork tr'yan as she tried to slow her breathing and calm herself. When she felt she had her fear under control, she opened the gate and walked through the courtyard to the door. She took the wooden mallet from the alcove, struck the chimes four times, and waited.

At length, a man came to the door. He stood almost six feet tall, tall for a Deniban. He was slightly beyond middle age, perhaps about seventy-five or eighty, and had the typical high cheekbones, copper-colored skin, and green eyes of people from Deniba's interior deserts. His thick black hair was graying slightly at the temples, and a neatly trimmed beard followed his jaw line. He was wearing the traditional loose-fitting pants and belted tunic of a Warrior-Teacher. The man's expression was emotionally neutral, yet Jenny still thought she saw a hint of merriment around his eyes.

"Yes?"

"Master Havarr, I have a question. May I ask?" she said in her Sixtos-accented Deniban.

In answer, he struck her squarely in the solar plexus with the heel of his hand.

It seemed to Jenny as though he'd barely touched her, yet he'd sent her sprawling. She blacked out for a few seconds, then lay on the ground with her knees drawn up to her chest, waiting for what seemed like an eternity for her lungs to fill again. She'd even been half-expecting the blow, but he'd executed it with such speed she still hadn't seen it coming.

When her head cleared and she could breathe again, she got up and went back to the door.

It was shut.

She knocked softly, and this time he answered at once.

"Master, allow me to ask. It's important."

"Important? In what way is it important? To whom?" he asked dispassionately.

"It's of no consequence to you, but—"

"How can it be of no consequence to me?" he roared back at her. "If you speak to me of this thing, you will involve me in the workings of it. You will entangle my life with yours." He looked at her sharply. "This is not a small thing to ask. Now leave before I'm forced to remove you."

Then he slammed the door in her face.

Jenny stood at the door, considering her situation. He'd told her to leave, but he'd answered the door when she knocked the second time. He didn't have to. By speaking to her the second time, he had given her permission to stay, but she didn't know how long it might be before he would see her and let her ask her question. For a Deniban student coming to seek out a teacher, this waiting could take days. Jenny didn't have days.

It was still early in the morning, but the temperature was already well into the eighties. The sky was blue and cloudless, and the sun was burning hot. Jenny looked around the courtyard.

The area between the gate and the door was still shaded, but the shade wouldn't last for more than another two or three hours. She picked out the place that would remain shaded the longest, took off her boots, and sat in meditation, her mind holding fast to the image of the pool of still water. She had only hours before the sun and the heat would end her vigil, but she wasn't leaving without the answers she'd come for. She didn't have time to go shopping for another teacher. She would stay until he saw her. She just hoped it would happen before they had to take her away in an ambulance.

***

He watched the woman from the window by the door.

He could make a prospective Deniban student wait in the courtyard for days, having someone bring them a little food and water at the end of each day. For a Deniban, that kind of treatment wasn't life-threatening, just harsh and unpleasant and sometimes frightening. Thirst and hunger, discomfort and uncertainty tested the student's discipline and resolve, and the weak ones went away. However, this woman wasn't Deniban, and she hadn't come to him as a student. She'd come because she needed his help. Nevertheless, those who came to him for help had to earn it. A teacher did not offer assistance to someone who lacked the strength to return it. He left the window and went back to his work.

Four hours later, he opened the door and walked out into the courtyard.

"*Frangai!*"

Jenny didn't hear him.

"Stupid frangai!" he yelled. "Will you sit there in the sun all day?"

***

Jenny looked up and saw him walk into the house, leaving the door open behind him. Now that she wasn't meditating, she felt hot and feverish. She tried to stand up but couldn't. She'd been sitting in the same position for almost four hours. She slowly untangled her legs and stretched them until they moved normally, then she slipped her boots on without tightening the laces, shuffled unsteadily to the door, and stood in the entrance hall in front of him.

"Your clothing," he demanded, his eyes never leaving hers.

Without embarrassment or hesitation, she undressed and handed him her clothes.

"Bathe."

He pointed down the hall.

Jenny walked down the hall to the bathing room and showered. She got out feeling somewhat refreshed, if not exactly well. She toweled off, used the lotion that someone had left for her by the towel, and slipped into a caftan they'd also left.

She was exceedingly thirsty but didn't drink. Only a frangai would drink water from the bathing room. Water for washing was filtered and reused over and over again to prevent waste. It was perfectly safe to drink, but long-standing custom forbade it, and no one did.

She stepped out into the hallway.

"This way, frangai," the master's voice boomed from down the hall.

She followed his voice to the kitchen. He was sitting at the table and motioned for her to sit down across from him. She seated herself in the chair indicated and waited.

***

He'd been expecting the woman to launch into an explanation of why she'd come to see him as soon as he invited her to sit, but she didn't. Instead, she remained silent, waiting.

At the door when she'd first arrived, he'd felt The Code of Right Conduct in her mind, the words repeated as a mantra to calm herself before she spoke to him. While she sat in meditation in the courtyard, he'd felt the image of the still pool in her mind.

The woman displayed few of the erratic thinking patterns and emotions he had come to expect from humans, and he had to admit that her knowledge of Deniban customs and tradition intrigued him. A human who knew the Mind Disciplines and the Way and practiced them was certainly a curiosity.

He poured a cup of water and offered it to her.

"Thank you."

He watched as she drank it slowly, savoring it, setting the cup down between sips. She must have been terribly thirsty, but she didn't behave like a frangai.

When she finished the first cup, he poured another. This she drank more slowly than the first.

"Why are you here, frangai?" he asked, not unkindly.

"My name is Jenny Black Wolf, and I'm an off-worlder, not a barbarian."

He lashed out with his right hand, intending to grip the nerve center in her shoulder, but she'd already shifted her weight slightly, anticipating what her insistence on being recognized as a full person might provoke. As she parried the attack with her forearm, he saw the amusement in her eyes. There was no anger in her at his attack and no arrogance at having stopped it. She knew he'd let her.

'I am also Deniban,' she said in Speech.

He had not expected Speech from a human.

"An interesting claim, frangai."

After her insistence on being fully recognized, his words were a deliberate slight, but she didn't react to it.

"Why have you come here?"

"I need to understand some things before I can track a man."

He felt her on the verge of telling him that the man's family had asked her to search for him, but she stopped herself, taking responsibility for being here on herself, not putting it off on someone else.

"I believe his life is in danger."

"The rest," he said, and waited for an answer.

"The truth! All of it!" he yelled when she hesitated. "What is this man to you?"

"We're mind-linked," she said quietly. "We've been bonded for over a year."

"Yet, the two of you are unmarried."

"Yes. I'm also in love with him."

He accepted this last bit of information as he had accepted the first, but without comprehension.

"The man's name."

"I've given you *my* name. It will have to do. I won't give you his. I know you can take it from my mind, perhaps you already have, but it won't be given."

The woman knew he could take whatever he wanted from her mind whenever he wished. If she tried to stop him or withhold the truth, he possessed the power to literally tear her mind apart, looking. That frightened most people, and he sensed her fear, but he also sensed her openness.

"Master, ask anything about me you want. I'll answer as honestly as I know how. I also accept the obligation to you that my request for help will incur, but I will not tell you anything about this man that isn't necessary, and I will not pass my debt to you on to him."

He looked at her intently. She didn't flinch from the intense contact.

"Agreed." Then, "You have been married before," he said.

"Yes."

"And what of your husband? You've left him for the man you're looking for?"

"My husband is dead. I've lived alone for three years."

"And this man. You share his bed?"

"No. I'd like to, but no."

"He doesn't want it?"

"He does, but he's not shal'tan, and neither am I."

"How do I know this?"

141

***

His questions were proof that he had taken nothing more from her mind than what he could sense on the surface, only now, Jenny almost wished he had looked more deeply. He was respecting her privacy, and she appreciated that, but how could he know what was true?

She knew what he must be feeling through her. She knew he wouldn't understand it, and words would never get to the heart of it. If she were shal'tan, the last thing he would want to do would be to help her find a man who might be trying to save himself from her.

She decided to take a chance. She put her hand on his, deepening the mind touch with the physical contact, and reached out to touch his mind with hers.

***

He opened himself to her touch. Almost immediately, he felt her desire for the man and the intensity of their bond. He saw the two of them lying together in the grass in a moonlit alien landscape, the scene presented with the man's face hidden from him, and again in a violent and passionate sexual embrace at the door of an alien home. Then she showed them simply reading together on a couch during a summer rain. He felt such a strange mix of emotions through her. Emotions he couldn't name and didn't fully understand. Emotions he had never felt before. Perhaps the combination of caring, commitment, and sexuality he felt through her was what humans called *love*. That word and what it meant had always been a mystery to him before. Now because of her, he was beginning to see what love might feel like. He also thought the sexuality seemed similar to what he experienced with his wife during fall, heightened perhaps, and not limited to only one season, but still normal and in her control.

He found himself measuring her by the courage it had taken to show him her heart without comment or explanation and then leaving it to him to understand as best he could. She knew it was possible he wouldn't understand and had accepted the risk that he would reject her because of what he saw, yet she had taken the chance and done it anyway. He also saw her choice as a gift, and he accepted it as such.

"My name is Shaia, of House Havarr," he said quietly.

The woman looked at him in amazement, understanding what it meant to be allowed the use of his personal name. Her hand shook slightly as she moved it away from his, picked up the cup of water, and finished it.

"More?" he asked.

"Yes. Thank you."

"What brings you here to me, Jenny Black Wolf?" he asked.

"I'm not sure I know what questions to ask, Master Havarr," she answered, continuing to address him with the respect due him. "It's something I've only heard about."

"Ask."

"It's something I don't believe is done often. Maybe it's not done at all anymore. Something someone in terrible pain might choose as a last resort to heal himself. I know it isn't a part of the training of the Arak'Kaz, but it couldn't be attempted or even considered by someone who didn't have the training."

She hesitated before saying the words.

"The *Boitan a'She'Shan*," she said in Sixtos.

"*Boitan a'Sha'Skan*," he corrected in homeworld Deniban. "This is something that is rarely spoken of."

He looked at her again, judging, weighing.

"You cannot possibly know what it is you are about to involve yourself in," he said.

The knowledge of the Boitan was for the few and closely guarded. How could she, an off-worlder, even know of its existence? Yet her knowledge of the Way showed in everything she said and did. All of her behavior bespoke the training she had received, yet who would have trained her?

"Who was this man who was your husband?" he asked.

In answer, the woman moved her left hand across the table toward him and turned it over, palm up. He took it gently in his and looked at the long thin scar across the base of the palm.

He had seen the shield of Kei'heila on her shirt and assumed it was nothing more than an affectation. Now he knew he was mistaken. Her husband had been Deniban. The scar of the marriage ritual was the undeniable evidence.

"He was my teacher."

He understood now how she had come to know Deniban custom and tradition with a depth few off-worlders ever achieved. His respect for her grew, and his compassion. Her husband was dead, and now she was involved with a man who had undertaken a very serious venture, one that could well take his life. This young woman had already experienced the pain of a broken bond. Now there would be more suffering to come.

"What gives you the right to interfere in this matter?"

"I don't know that I have any right," she answered. "That's part of why I've come to you. I *do* know that he's alive, and I want to be with him. He's already made his choice. I won't try to keep him from acting on it. I just want to be there with him. I understand that a person who takes this path has the right to a second if he chooses."

"Did he tell you what he intended to do or ask you to be his second?"

"I think he tried in his own way to ask me for help, but I didn't understand what was happening to him. Now that I do, I've come to ask you to teach me what I need to know. I don't want him to have to go through this alone."

"Alone or not alone, that is his choice to make," he answered. "However, if you feel that he tried in some way to ask for your help and you've only come to understand it now, you have the right to ask him. If he refuses, you will have to leave."

"Master, I don't know anything more about the Boitan than the name and some ancient stories."

"If I explain this to you and you're able to find him, have you the courage to leave him if that's what he wants?"

She looked away from him to hide the tears that filled eyes.

"I don't know," she answered.

Then she met his eyes and said it again.

"I don't know."

If she had lied to him, he would have sent her away immediately, but she hadn't. She'd told him the truth. He brought her another cup of water and began to teach her what she needed to know.

Toward the end of their conversation, Shaia's wife came in with Jenny's freshly laundered clothes. She changed into them while his wife served bread and tea and joined them at the table.

"Remember this, Jenny. It isn't only whether or not you have the courage to leave if he asks. If he accepts you, do you have the courage to stay? If, at any time while he's in the past, he asks for your help, your presence with him obligates you to do anything he asks. *Anything.* Once you've chosen to involve yourself in this, there is no turning back. Do not make this decision lightly.

"Also, you need to be very careful about touching his mind, and in your case, even about touching him physically. Because of the nature of your sexuality, you'll reach him more quickly through your touch than through anything else you might choose to do, and there may be no warning before it happens. If he takes you with him, neither of you may come back."

He felt a wave of fear course through her body.

"You're right to be afraid, Jenny. Let your fear temper your courage with caution."

When they finished their tea, he walked Jenny to the door.

"There is one more thing for you to know, Jenny Black Wolf. To be mind-linked as deeply and for as long as you and this man have been is in itself a dangerous thing. If you live, the two of you will have to decide whether to marry or to end the relationship. There is no other way. You cannot remain together as you are. The two of you will destroy each other."

She nodded and stepped outside.

"Thank you for your kindness, Master, and for your help. And please thank your wife for the clean clothes and the tea."

"I will."

"I'll be back to see you again. I pay my debts."

"I'll be looking forward to it."

CHAPTER 12

Jenny stopped to buy some supplies on her way back to Halaya's. It was near dusk by the time she returned. Halaya was still at work, and David was in the kitchen, preparing the evening meal.

"Well, what happened?" he asked, turning to face her.

"I found out what I needed to know," she said as she leaned against the door frame, still feeling the effects of four hours in the Deniban sun and her visit with Shaia.

"And...?"

"Remember that abyss you were talking about this morning? It looks like Curran is about to take a few steps over the edge."

"That doesn't sound good. What's he doing?"

"He's preparing himself for a ritual called the Boitan a'Sha'Skan, The Gateway to the Ancestors. It consists of four, four-day-long vigils at four different sites. The first is always at the House altar; the others are at places of the person's own choosing."

She stopped and asked him for a drink of water.

He turned away to draw a cup of water for her and added some of the vitamin and electrolyte replacer he used himself.

"Between each place of vigil, when he's traveling, the searcher is allowed to eat and rest. But at each place of vigil, he's supposed to fast and meditate to ready himself for the final phase of the ritual."

"And what exactly is that?" he asked, handing her the cup. "What's he trying to do?"

"You have to try to understand this place the way Curran sees it, David," she said as she took the cup and sat down at the table. "He lives on land that's been held continuously by TaZarin for almost a thousand years. He grew up in a house that's eight hundred years old. His heritage, the traditions of this House and its history are a large part of who he is and how he thinks of himself. And through the use of his Arak'Kaz training, he has access to ancestral memories. Under certain circumstances and with certain techniques, those memories can actually be tapped, searched, literally remembered and lived."

"You're telling me that he's going to go back into ancestral memory to look for an answer for himself? What kind of answer can he find like that?"

"I don't know. The teacher said it's different for each person who tries it."

"So how did you figure all this out, and why *you*? What have *you* got to do with it?"

"I began to see it when Halaya repeated that he'd already been gone for twelve days. When he spent four days at the family altar, I'm sure she didn't think anything of it. Lots of things here are done in fours. Four is a mystical number. It represents the unity of all things within the Mind of the Universe. But when he wasn't back after six days, and she realized he'd taken the ceremonial knife and the medallion with him, she must have begun to suspect what he might be trying to do.

"She wanted me here not just because I'm a tracker, but because Curran and I are mind-linked. A person who chooses the Boitan has the right to have a close friend or a family member with him as a second. The second isn't allowed to interfere in what happens, but his presence can give the person a lifeline, a contact with reality that can help him find his way back. That contact is strongest with someone they're mind-linked with." It was also the most dangerous, Shaia had said, but she didn't tell David that.

"What are you talking about? 'Find his way back?'"

David had stopped working and was giving her his full attention.

"A lot of people who try this solution never come back."

"What the hell does that mean?"

She saw him starting to get worried, and his worry was showing itself as anger.

"They don't come back. They become lost in the past somewhere, reliving other lives, and they don't come back. They go into a kind of coma and are eventually allowed to die."

"And you're going out there after him? You can't be serious! If you felt his nightmares and his flashbacks when he was trying to control himself, what do you think *this* is going to be like? No wonder you're not supposed to interfere. If he touches you, he can take you with him. You're as crazy as he is!"

She looked away from him, suddenly feeling tired and drained and very alone. She hadn't wanted to start an argument or lose his company.

"I'm tired, David. I've got to rest for a while. And I'm not hungry. If you want to go with me in the morning, I'd still like you to come."

She went to Curran's room, closed the door, and was asleep almost as soon as she lay down. When she woke, it was dark, and she was hungry. She opened her door to go to the kitchen and saw that David had left a tray of food for her by the door.

***

Jenny was up at first light. David and Halaya had already made breakfast. The three of them ate together at the table while Jenny studied the maps Halaya had gotten for her.

House TaZarin Shirraz'At held over fifty thousand *ria* of land, the equivalent of over eighty square miles. Not all of the land was contiguous, and the boundaries were irregular, with tracts held by other Houses or given in trust to the government interspersed. Except for the fields and grazing lands near Shirraz'At, much of the land was essentially wilderness.

The maps showed several places of historical interest, along with a few of the ancient settlements. An open square on the map indicated an abandoned but still-standing building of some kind. A darkened square indicated one that was still lived-in. There were very few darkened squares outside of the Zuhar basin itself.

The old places were a part of Curran's landscape and Curran's memory, but not hers. He would know every foot of TaZarin land and the land around it. He would know historically what had happened at any given place and when. He would know where there had been ancient settlements or homes, old roads, wells, and waterholes. Curran knew the psychic terrain of TaZarin, and she did not. Where he would go and where he would make his final stand would be determined by that landscape and by the ancestral memories that land held for him.

After breakfast, Jenny packed the few things she was taking with her in the light backpack she'd bought the day before. David packed his day bag. They met at the door where Halaya was waiting for them.

"I've decided that I don't want to work while I'm here," she told Halaya. "I'm going for a walk. I'll be back in a few days."

Halaya acknowledged Jenny's statement with a nod. She took a thin silver chain from around her neck and placed it around Jenny's. A clear quartz crystal with a smoky black tip hung at the bottom of the chain.

"It was my mother's. Now it's yours. Keep it safe," she said.

"I will, Lady."

"See that you do, daughter."

Jenny's eyes widen in astonishment as she went down on one knee before Lady Halaya, her head bowed in deference.

"Come back to us safe, Jenny Black Wolf," she said, offering Jenny her hand.

Jenny took Halaya's hand and rose, but couldn't speak. She turned away from the door and walked into the courtyard with David following. She saw David about to ask her what was going on, but she raised her hand, silently asking him not to. She was too overcome to talk.

They left the house and took public transportation as far east as it went, then started walking across country. David led the way. During the heat of the afternoon, they found a sheltered place to rest and arrived at the altar about an hour before sunset.

The altar itself was just a simple wrought iron dish set on a short pedestal mounted on a six-foot square platform of cut stone. David had told her earlier that the altar had been maintained in the same place for almost a thousand years.

About a quarter-mile east of it, at the top of a boulder-covered ridge, there was an oval-shaped opening in the tallest of the rocks. At first light, the morning sun would thread the opening like thread through a needle and cast its light directly on the altar, crossing it from one end to the other as the sun rose higher in the sky.

About a hundred feet north of the altar, a spring trickled from a fault in the rocks. A small area was set aside near it for camping. Faint signs of Halaya and David's visit remained, but none of Curran's.

David and Jenny laid out their ground clothes and lightweight insulated blankets, gathered twigs and deadwood from around the spring, and built a small fire to heat water for tea. They ate the food Halaya had packed for them, and as the sun went down and the temperature began to fall, they sipped the hot tea and watched the sun set.

"I'm sorry I got so angry with you yesterday," David said.

"I ate your peace offering," Jenny joked.

"Yeah, I saw that," he laughed.

"Actually, you seem a lot less angry in general than you used to be," Jenny said. "More relaxed and at ease with yourself, too. Is it just being away from the *Defender* and all that responsibility?"

The David Rawlins she'd met on the *Defender* was hot-tempered and quick to anger as well as compassionate and kind.

"No. I've been changing. Things don't get to me the way they used to."

"How come?"

"Curran's been teaching me."

Jenny laughed out loud with delight. "So, that's why he kept asking me all those questions."

"Pretty funny, isn't it? *Me* of all people."

"I'm glad for you, David. I really am."

Jenny absently stirred the fire with a stick and added a little more wood.

"David, have you and Curran ever camped together on TaZarin land or anywhere around here?"

"No. He's never invited me to come home with him. I was really surprised when he asked Halaya if I could stay with them while I was here."

"Did he ever tell you about any special places he wanted to show you, anything like that?"

David pointed to the mountains east of them. The sun was low enough now that the mountains were just dark silhouettes against a darkening sky, only the crests remained illuminated.

"He told me once about a place in the Kazzarin Mountains east of here. He said there was a barely passable trail through the mountains at a place called Red Wall. I don't remember why he brought it up anymore, but I got the impression that the place was important to him."

Red Wall was on her topographical map.

"There's nothing left to go on around here. I'll cut for sign farther out tomorrow, but I doubt that I'll find anything. If I can't, I'll go to Red Wall first. It may be where he started the second vigil. At least it's worth a try."

"This isn't going to be easy, is it?" David asked, perhaps

realizing for the first time what she'd known from the start; that she might not be able to find Curran at all.

"No, it won't be easy."

David poured another cup of tea for them and sat holding his cup in his hands, thinking.

"Jenny, do you remember the photograph of the two of you in Curran's room?"

"Sure."

"Do you think it was his way of asking for you? Do you suppose his inviting me to stay with his parents could have been part of some plan? I mean, how else would Halaya have found out who the woman in the photograph was?"

"I don't know. Maybe..."

"Because he gave me some things—some images—several weeks before I came here, as part of an exercise we were practicing. I've been thinking about them ever since you told me about the four vigils. I think you should have them. I think that even back then, when he showed them to me, some part of him knew he would be doing this."

"Can you describe them to me?"

"I'm pretty sure I can *show* them to you. At least I want to try."

"Okay."

He took her hand, and they both put themselves in a relaxed, meditative state. Then David concentrated, carefully visualizing each image, and as she opened her mind to his, the images slowly formed. First, a thin golden ribbon of a trail along a barren mountainside. Next, a panoramic view of a broad, rolling plain with a rugged butte in the foreground and many others in the distance. Then a small but exquisitely beautiful waterhole with a hanging garden growing on the rock walls above it. Jenny thought she would be able to recognize all of them if she saw them, but there was no indication of where they were in relation to each other or how to get from one to the next.

"How did it work?" David asked.

"I got all of them. I'll know them if I see them. I think the second one may be the view from the top of the cliffs at Red Wall. That's definitely where I'll be going tomorrow."

As the twilight deepened and one of the two Deniban moons began to rise, Jenny took the crystal Halaya had given her from around her neck and held it in her hand.

"What is that she gave you?" David asked.

"It's called a moon crystal. Only women wear them. They're usually passed from mother to daughter, but sometimes when there's no daughter to pass it on to, it's given to someone else."

"Quite a gift," David said.

"She gave me a place in the Household, David. A daughter's place. With or without Curran."

"Will you accept it?"

"Not if Curran dies. My place is still with Kristen's family and House Kei'heila."

Jenny left the fire, hung the crystal from a branch of a small tree near the spring where it would be exposed to the moonlight, and returned to the fire.

"The crystal needs to be recharged by the moonlight once in a while or it will lose its power," she said.

"And you believe that?"

"Even if the potency of the crystal is only in the knowledge of all the other women through all the generations of TaZarin who've worn it before me, that in itself is a powerful thing and the ritual of recharging it keeps the awareness and respect for that power alive."

David sat quietly watching the fire with her before he spoke again.

"Jenny, did you know that Curran asked me once if I would be his brother; if I would look after you if he died?"

"No, I didn't. He never told me. When was this? Before he came here this time?"

"No. Almost a year ago. After he saw you at Starbase

Fourteen."

"You've been honored, David, but you'd better think about it very carefully before you decide. It isn't just a symbolic gesture. It carries serious rights and obligations. Once you swear the oath, you'll be bound by it for life. Not just to him, but to the rest of his Household as well."

He looked at her uncertainly.

"Curran didn't explain any of this to you?"

"No. He just asked me to think about it and never brought it up again."

"Every culture has its way of providing for a woman and her children, David. Here, the Household takes care of its own. There are no social welfare programs here, no life insurance, no government intervention of any kind in the Household's private affairs.

"If a married man dies, his wife and children remain in his mother's Household, under the care and protection of his eldest brother or closest male relative. If the brother's family can't afford to care for them, the financial burden is shared by other families within the House. A woman and her children are never left without food or a home or family. It doesn't necessarily mean that everyone will be happy with the arrangement, but it works. There is very little poverty here and almost no homelessness. If Curran and I marry and he dies, his brother would become my protector and father to our children.

"I guess Curran must believe that his brother would have a problem accepting me. Or perhaps he thought I would prefer you. Having never met his brother, I really couldn't say," she joked.

"If he went as far as asking me to consider acting as his brother, why haven't the two of you married?" David asked.

"David, how well do you understand Deniban sexuality?"

"Medically, quite well. Psychologically, reasonably well."

"Do you understand shal'tan?"

"I understand that the word is used occasionally as an

obscenity. I also understand that it's an almost untreatable mental illness. I understand the nature of the illness. In fact, I understand it better now than I did before I came here this time. A Deniban physician friend recommended that I read *The Shal'tan Poems* by Drakara when I told him there were things I didn't understand about it."

"He must think a lot of you, David. Those poems are considered to be some of the greatest literature ever produced on this planet, but they're rarely shown to outsiders."

"I can understand why."

The Deniban people had a long and honored tradition of erotic poetry. The poems touched on everything from the most sublime and spiritual feelings of the marriage ritual to the ripe eroticism of the time of mating. Much of the poetry would not be understood as erotic by a human, but some of it, and especially Drakara's *Shal'tan Poems*, were so violent in imagery and spirit that they went far beyond what any healthy person, Deniban or human, would consider erotic. They were horrifying and tragic—an appallingly graphic journal of a man's descent into the insanity of shal'tan.

"You can always read his *Poems of the Kotaho* if you want to understand what it's like for normal people. He wrote them before he went mad."

"Don't try to evade the question, Jenny. You started this. Now, where are we going?"

"To Curran, I'm shal'tan."

"That's ridiculous. You're a normal, healthy woman. And you're in control of your sexual impulses. A shal'tan isn't."

She didn't tell him that it wasn't entirely true and that so far, she and Curran had been lucky.

"But that's not how it feels to him," she said. "He experiences things with me that he probably wouldn't feel with a Deniban woman even during the time of mating. If he feels things with me that a shal'tan would feel and he doesn't want to give me up, what kind of man does that make him, David? And what if the marriage ritual fails, which it does sometimes, what then?"

David stirred the fire, and they sat watching the flames, wrapped in their own thoughts.

"I don't know about you," he said finally, "but I'm about ready for another cup of tea, and then I'm going to turn in," he said.

"I'll share the tea with you, but I think I'll stay up a little longer."

***

David woke with a start and looked across the dying embers of their fire to where he thought Jenny would be. When he didn't see her there, he got up to look for her. She was standing at the edge of their camp, looking across the grasslands at the dark forms of the Kazzarin Mountains east of them. He walked up to her, careful to make enough noise not to startle her.

"Jenny, are you all right?"

"No."

"Can't sleep?"

"Haven't tried."

She turned to face him, and in the soft moonlight, he could see the pain in her eyes.

"The night Kristen died was like this," she said softly, turning away from him to look back toward the mountains. "Very bright, with two moons in the Calderan sky. When he didn't come back to camp that night, I sat up waiting for him. When I felt him die, it was as though someone had driven a knife into my heart. When the bond died, a part of me died with it."

David enfolded her gently in his arms. She was shivering.

"I'm scared, David. I don't want him to die. If he doesn't want me, I can learn to live with that, but I don't want to lose him like this. I feel as though I'm just waiting here for someone to drive that same knife into my heart. I can't go through that again, David. I can't."

David held her close, gently stroking her hair.

157

"Jenny, come to bed. You need to get some sleep. We can share the blankets if you'd like."

"Thanks, David," she said at length.

She lay in his arms for an hour, trembling as if she would never be warm again, before she finally fell asleep.

***

Jenny woke the next morning before David. The sun was just coming up over the mountains, and the light touched the tops of the peaks with orange while everything else lay in shadow.

She retrieved the moonstone and put it on, then gathered wood and laid a small fire in the wrought-iron altar. When she was ready, she went to get David.

"David, I need you to be my witness."

David wrapped himself in his blanket and followed her. She asked him to sit a short distance east of the altar platform, facing her. As the sun rose and began to thread the eye of the stone needle, she stepped onto the platform and knelt before the altar. She lit the tinder, using the flint and fire steel from the strike-a-light-pouch she wore on her belt, and added some wood.

When it was flaming, she drew her knife from its sheath and, with the point of the blade toward the fire, placed it on a piece of scarlet cloth she'd taken from her shirt pocket. Beside it, she laid a small bundle of cut grasses tied with a thin red cord. Then she held her hands above the flames, waiting for the life force of the Ancestors to enter through them as she opened herself to the Mind of the Universe.

"'My name is Jenny Black Wolf, Old Ones. I am not of TaZarin, but I am here to make my offering nevertheless. All I ask is that it be accepted.'"

She picked up her knife and cut the palm of her right hand. Bright blood welled up from the wound. She took the small bundle of dried grass into her cut hand, closed her fingers around it, and held it tight. Then she placed it in the flames. The fire flared brightly as it consumed the dry grass, watered with her blood.

"'I join my blood to this land and ask acceptance, Old Ones, for we are all one in the Mind of the Universe.'"

After the words, Jenny emptied a tiny packet of medicinal herbs on the wound, wrapped her hand in the scarlet-colored cloth, and prayed silently for several minutes.

***

David sat quietly, cloaked in his blanket, watching her, listening as she both Spoke the words and said them aloud. It seemed to him that a subtle energy emanated from the altar, enfolding them both. He opened himself to it and thanked the Ancestors for their presence.

When the fire in the altar burned out, Jenny came to him and thanked him.

"Thank you for asking me," he replied. Then he asked to see her hand.

"It's fine, David. Don't worry about it. It will be healed by tomorrow."

When he insisted, Jenny unwrapped the red cloth and let him see. The thin line of the cut was clearly visible beneath the layer of powdered herbs, but there was no bleeding.

"Do you want to eat before you go? I can build a fire," he offered, trying to forestall the inevitable.

"No. I need to be going while it's still cool."

They broke camp quickly, and when they were done, Jenny checked the maps again.

"How far is Red Wall?" he asked.

"About fifteen miles. I think I can make it there by dark."

Neither of them knew what to say to the other, and Jenny needed to leave. They shared a quick wordless embrace, then Jenny stepped away from him, shouldered her pack, and walked away.

David watched her for a minute or two before starting back to Shirraz'At. He didn't want to stay and watch her disappear into the distance, knowing that he might never see her again.

CHAPTER 13

Two miles from the altar, Jenny stopped to take a look at her topographical map. In front of her the country opened out onto a broad, gently rolling plain, ending at the base of the Kazzarin Mountains. The map showed the Kazzarins running in a southeasterly arc for almost twenty miles. The cliffs at Red Wall were near the midpoint of the arc. On the other side of the cliffs, the mountains sloped gently down onto a high plateau.

In the distance, Jenny could see the narrow band of trees and brush that lined the banks of the Citana River. The topographical map showed the Citana as a thin blue line, paralleled by broken blue lines that approximated its summer conditions. It was the only year-round stream anywhere close, and the map showed only intermittent pools of water in it during summer. The trees along its banks lived on water that ran beneath the surface. Sometimes a person could dig down to the water. Sometimes it was too deep.

Jenny folded the map and walked down the long slope in front of her into a fine stand of widely spaced, mature cacholo trees, their gnarled, twisted trunks covered with a shaggy, bristling bark.

Like most Deniban desert trees, cacholos had leaves, not needles, but small ones, and were continually adjusting how they presented them to the sun, showing them edge-on during the heat of the day and more fully during the early morning and late afternoon.

Dense bunches of low-growing grasses, each surrounded by a thin covering of dead leaves and stems from years of earlier growth, protected the otherwise bare ground from erosion. Without it, the short, violent summer thunderstorms would wash the soil away, leaving nothing but stones and gravel behind. All of the grasses were summer dormant and dry.

By mid-morning, Jenny had intersected the remains of the old Brayenta to Kosin'A road. Neither of the towns had existed for over four hundred years, but the road had been paved with stone and built to last, and was still shown on her map. The part she had intersected was in remarkably good condition.

As she followed the road, she began to see more camaranth trees interspersed among the cacholos. Camaranths grew in any fold or depression that would hold even a modest amount of water after a storm or during the winter. The trees were about fifteen to twenty feet tall at maturity, their long trailing branches covered with small oval leaves. The branches tended to lie over on the ground, creating a dense shade that all kinds of birds and animals used for shelter from the heat of the day.

She followed the road for several miles before she began looking for a place to stop and rest during the afternoon heat. About a quarter-mile ahead and just off the road, she saw the remains of an old stone house. She cleared a place for herself in the shade near the base of the south wall, carefully moving aside the rubble with her foot to make sure no one was living under it that might object.

She spread her ground cloth in the shade and slept through the midday heat. When she woke, she ate a handful of dried fruit and *watapa* seeds and began looking around the old home site for the well. There had to be one. No one would have built a dwelling here if there hadn't been water.

On Deniba, a ranch or farm's house and outbuildings could be gone for centuries, but water was so important that the old wells were maintained by the House that owned the land whether anyone was living nearby to use it or not. Even on land ceded to the government during the Restoration, wells were generally still maintained by the House that ceded the land.

She found the old hand-dug well on the far side of the house. It was in good repair, complete with a tight-fitting wooden lid weighted down with rocks. She filled her water bottles, then dragged the old enameled watering pan with the rock in the bottom of it to keep it from blowing away over to the well so she could fill it, too. Travelers who used wells like this one were expected to fill whatever wildlife waterer was left near it. This one had been empty for a long time. It had a thick layer of dust in the bottom and no tracks around it.

She moved on, leaving the old road when it turned away from her route and continued east. By nightfall, she was within a mile of Red Wall.

***

Jenny was up before dawn, awakened by the cold. The morning air was heavy with the sharp, biting scent of camaranth. She wrapped herself in her blanket, ate a quick breakfast of watapa seeds and dried fruit, and walked to the first of the two places her topographical map showed as possible routes to the top of Red Wall.

When she got there, it looked like it might have been a maintained trail once, but the narrow gap leading to the top was choked with rocks and boulders that had broken away from the cliff wall and by brush and trees, washed into it by years of storm run-off. The climb wasn't especially steep, but it was going to be slow and possibly dangerous if she wasn't careful. By mid-morning, when she was less than halfway to the top, the passage was in full sun, and the rocks were so hot she could barely stand to touch them.

She crawled into the deep shade of some fallen rocks and took off her pack. She opened one of the side pockets, found a single-dose packet of vitamin and electrolyte replacer, and poured it into her water bottle. Too tired and queasy to eat, Jenny drank the water, crawled deeper into the shade, and slept.

***

It was early evening by the time she completed the climb. From the top of the cliffs and looking west, she could see the rough rolling hills of the entire Dal Plateau and all of the country she'd already crossed. With so little humidity in the air, the landscape had a chiseled, hard-edged look. To the east, where she was headed, were the Banded Buttes. Although they were widely separated, the buttes were all part of the eroded remains of the same geological formation, and all of them shared the same bands of color in the same order and spacing.

Jenny left the top of the cliff and started looking for signs of Curran's presence. She thought Curran had been here about the same day Halaya asked David to contact her. Whatever sign she might find of him here would be at least seven days old.

Jenny also needed water. She knew Curran had been here for four days, so there had to be water nearby. Even a Deniban couldn't live exposed to the sun and wind for more than a day and a half without water.

She walked south along the ridgeline, searching for the place where he'd made his vigil and found it about a half-mile from where she'd reached the top. The spot had been swept clear of brush, and a square of stones was placed in the center, oriented to the four directions. Curran had left the place only a few times using two lightly traveled game trails. Jenny took the one to the southeast first, knowing it wouldn't lead to water, but curious about where it *did* go.

She found a small grove of watapa trees growing in a hollow just below the ridgeline where dirt and debris had collected over the centuries, giving the trees a place to take hold. Watapas were summer dormant and shed their leaves in the dry season to conserve water. The trees bore umbels of sweet-smelling orange flowers in the late winter, and by early summer, produced hundreds of small, leathery seed pods, each carrying four large seeds. Watapa trees had been domesticated for centuries and were often planted in groves.

All of the trees in the little grove had been heavily browsed to the height a full-grown *haraq* buck could reach, standing on its hind legs. Higher up, there were still plenty of seed pods that a man could get at, and in the loose dirt at the edge of the nearest trees, she saw Curran's tracks. Judging by the more recent tracks of insects and animals that had crossed them, Curran's tracks were about eight days old.

Jenny climbed one of the nearest trees and knocked down as many seed pods as she could reach. She shelled several handfuls, ate a few, shelled some more and added them to the bag in her pack, then went back to the place where Curran made his vigil and took the other trail. It led down a shallow incline to a place where a thin trickle of water ran from a seam in the rocks. She drank her fill from the tiny pool at the bottom, washed her face and hands in the cold water, filled her water bottles, and began looking for the place where Curran had left Red Wall, finding it just before dark.

She returned to the spring, laid out her ground cloth and blanket, and went to sleep. In the morning, she went back to the place where Curran had left the ridge, following the game trail he'd taken onto the plateau and toward the nearest of the banded buttes. When the heat of the day became too intense, she stopped at a small cacholo, draped her blanket over a branch, and laid down in the shade to rest until it cooled off.

Shortly after she started again, she found herself following the tracks of a small herd of *ben'thar*. Both males and females had horns, and seeing an animal with a three-foot-wide span wasn't unusual. Ben'thar were as fast as a good horse and unpredictable.

A person could walk through a grazing herd and be ignored, then do the same thing an hour later, and be attacked.

The herd had been grazing in the area for a while. Their tracks crossed and recrossed the trail Jenny was on several times. Then they began walking in a single-file, for the most part staying on or near the trail.

Ben'thar scattered out when they grazed, but when they were traveling toward water, they moved in a line behind a single dominant female. If the herd was already at the waterhole and hadn't moved on by the time she got there, Jenny would have to wait them out. She needed the water.

When she arrived, the animals were spread out for over a quarter of a mile, and six or seven of them were still near the waterhole. The herd seemed to be drifting slowly to the north, but they could just as easily decide to drift back again for another drink before they left. Closer to her, about thirty feet west of the waterhole, near a group of cacholos, Jenny could see the blackened embers of Curran's campfire.

She sat in the shade of a small camaranth and waited for the animals to leave, watching as thunderheads built up on the other side of the buttes. When the herd finally moved away, she went down to the place where Curran had camped and found the tiny spring he'd used nearby. After gathering some dry wood, she built a small fire where he had, boiled some water, dumped in two handfuls of theica and some dried fruit, and cooked it into a thick cereal.

She ate the cereal and watched the sun drop below the horizon in a blaze of reds and oranges. It turned the grasses a deep ruddy bronze, outlined the buttes in a dazzling orange light, and brilliantly illuminated the thunderheads she'd been watching.

Far to her east, distant thunder rumbled across the plateau. In the fading light, Jenny could see the rain coming down in torrents on the far side of the buttes, but overhead the night sky was filled with stars.

***

Early the next morning, Jenny rounded the south side of the nearest butte and got her first look at the Barrens. When she'd been to Deniba the last time, she had gone to look at another barren about a hundred and eighty miles west of here, but it hadn't prepared her for what she saw now. At the other barren, some attempt had been made at restoration. None had been made here. Ahead of her, the land sloped gently down into a basin surrounded by low mountains. Past a short, well-defined transition zone, there was little vegetation of any kind.

To Jenny, the Deniban desert landscape was austere but beautiful. This land was stark and heartbreaking. Widely spaced bunches of needlegrass, one of the poorer common grasses that grew as a minor species on good grassland, grew in relative abundance here, along with rip-gut. On good range, rip-gut was a common forb, but small mammals and browsers kept it eaten down short. However, once it matured, nothing would eat it, and it eventually took over a stand of grass and destroyed it.

The transition zone quickly faded behind her, and the ground became harder to read. It didn't carry a track well, and it was much more difficult to figure out where Curran had gone.

About mid-morning, she took a short break, stopping beside a cacholo so stunted it provided almost no shade at all. Above her, a *dikeeno* wheeled and soared on the wind, set its wings, and disappeared behind a low rise. When it rose again, it had a snake in its talons.

She got up and walked for almost another hour looking for a place to spend the hottest part of the day, but nothing presented itself. She was so dry that the membranes in her nose and sinuses had started burning. She'd been wearing a bandana over her nose, trying to recover some of the moisture from her breath. Now she wet the bandana and pulled it over her nose again so she could breathe the moist, damp air. Finally, about a mile further on, she saw a camaranth growing in a small depression that had once been a good-sized waterhole.

As she left Curran's trail and walked to the camaranth, she saw dozens of paths leading into and out of it. The camaranth was the only sizable shrub or tree Jenny had seen in miles, and it was supporting a whole community by itself.

She circled the tree at a reasonable distance. Fresh ta'taka tracks led into the cover of the camaranth's branches. Ta'takas were predators and would fight if pressed. Jenny didn't want trouble, but she needed the shade.

As she walked, she began to sing softly to herself. She wanted the ta'taka to know where she was and that she wasn't leaving. At the end of the song, she started talking to it, asking how the hunting had been, discussing the weather. Then she crouched down next to the camaranth's draping branches on the opposite side of the trunk from where she knew the ta'taka was resting. There was no answering snarl, and the animal didn't try to leave. She took off her pack, drew her knife and pushed the pack in ahead of her, then crawled in behind it through the thick tangle of branches.

Slightly to her right, a small, iridescent, blue snake lay coiled on a branch. The snake raised its head lazily and flicked its tongue to get her scent. Satisfied that she wasn't going to give it any trouble, it went back to its nap. Above her in the leaves, a bird flew in carrying food for its nestlings. To her left and about eight feet away on the other side of the trunk, the ta'taka eyed her cautiously. It was a lean, rangy animal with a tawny coat, green eyes, tufted ears, and a long bushy tail, and probably weighed about forty-five pounds. It gave her a low warning growl and waited to see what would happen.

She lay down on her side of the tree, and the two of them watched each other for several minutes before the ta'taka lost interest. It wasn't cornered, and it wasn't looking for a fight, just a place to get out of the sun, like she was. It put its head on its paws and appeared to go back to sleep, but its ears were still cocked toward her, listening. After a few more minutes, it stopped the surveillance and began to snore softly.

Late in the afternoon, she woke to the sound of rustling branches as the ta'taka got up and left for work. Jenny got up, too. She left the comfort of the camaranth a few minutes later and went back to work herself. It was slow and painstaking, and by dark, she had only made another two or three miles.

***

Early the next morning, while the dew was still on the ground, Jenny found the next place Curran had camped. There was a clear impression of his body where he'd slept and the remains of a fire where he'd cooked a small *ra'han*. The rodent's charred bones were lying in the burned-out coals.

By midday, she had also lost Curran's trail. Two days before, while Jenny was at the waterhole watching the storms, it had been raining here. There were no tracks more than two days old. The rain had erased everything else.

She stopped walking and sited along her back trail, then turned toward the direction Curran had been traveling and looked at her topo map. She had no idea where he was going or what his destination might be, and nothing on the map seemed to help.

She kept walking, hoping to pass through the area the storm had touched and picked up Curran's trail on the other side, but by the time she'd finally crossed it, she had gone almost two miles and seen no sign of him, even after she'd walked for a mile both north and south of where she'd stopped.

Jenny hadn't been especially worried before. She'd had a plan, and she'd carried it out. But the plan hadn't worked, and now she was tired and thirsty and out of ideas except to go back to the last place Curran had camped and start over from there the next morning. She made a shelter for herself using her ground cloth, blanket, and the fallen trunk of a cacholo tree, and sweltered in the minimal shade it provided until late afternoon. Then she started back.

Jenny was halfway back when she started feeling sick and vaguely disoriented. She hadn't had much water since early afternoon, and it had been hot and windy. She happened to be looking down when she noticed a clump of dried out crumpled leaves. She had walked past them without recognizing them, then stopped and walked back.

Using a sharp stone, Jenny started digging until she uncovered enough of the *ca'pron's* root to be able to work it out of the ground. She dusted it off, set the root on a flat rock with her bandana under it, and began grating it with her knife. She closed her bandana around the pulp, picked it up carefully, and squeezed the water into her mouth. The liquid tasted faintly acidic and slightly sweet. She grated more, drank what she needed, and put the rest of the root in her pack to take with her. She used the spent pulp to wash her face and hands.

When Jenny arrived back at Curran's last camp, dusk had turned to dark. She knew Curran was only two or three days walk ahead of her, but it could just as well have been two or three years. She had nothing to go on and no idea what to try next. Too tired to think about it, she rolled out her ground cloth and blanket in the same place Curran had chosen and fell into an exhausted dreamless sleep.

***

She was awake at first light. Water was now the most important thing she had in common with Curran at this place. He'd been without water here himself. She studied the map, noting every spring and waterhole within a day's walk of this spot. There were three, but only one in the direction Curran had been going, and it was over a day and a half away. Jenny grated the rest of the ca'pron, drank the liquid, ate a breakfast of watapa seeds and dried fruit, and watched the sunrise. She had no idea what to do next.

As she watched the sun begin to light the mountains, a winding pathway through a notch between two low peaks four or five miles north of where she'd stopped the day before began to show itself. The tops of the mountains were bright, the pathway a long golden ribbon of light traversing the shoulder of the mountain, the rest still deep in shadow.

She looked away for a time, watching other parts of the landscape as the first rays of morning light touched them, but her eyes kept returning to the mountain with the ribbon of light along its side. She ate another handful of seeds and slowly munched a piece of dried fruit as the scene in front of her began to correspond to an image in her mind.

With growing excitement, Jenny realized this was one of the places David had shown her. She was seeing it from a different perspective, but it was definitely one of the places. She ate the rest of her breakfast, packed her things, and started walking.

By early afternoon, she was at the bottom of the trail where the ribbon of golden light had been. She found good water in a spring nearby and by evening had reached the top of the pass and found where Curran began his third vigil in the ruins of an ancient city built along the edge of what was now a dry river bed.

Sparse grass grew in the ancient rubble-strewn streets. Parts of some of the stone buildings were still standing, but buildings that had been made of mud-brick were nothing more than eroded mounds of dirt covered with rip-gut.

Curran had been here for four days. Four days spent contemplating ruin. It was impossible not to think about it. Ruin was the single overwhelming aspect of this place; the ruin of an ancient civilization with obvious spiritual and cultural ties to what existed now, and the ruin of the land, which had resulted in the end of this city. There wasn't even a dot on the map to show where the city had been.

She followed Curran to what remained of the temple. The cornerstones and parts of the north and west walls were still intact. He had placed a small offering of watapa seeds on the altar and left along the road leading east. She took water from the temple spring, filled her water bottles, and placed an offering of dried fruit on the altar beside his. She spent the night in the protection of the atrium wall and left at daybreak, following the road east. Nothing remained of the road once it left the city except for the stone marker cairns that had been built along it. Some appeared to have survived on their own, but someone was clearly maintaining the others.

Several miles outside of the city, Curran left the road. His trail led down into a narrow rocky canyon that eventually widened, opening onto a broad expanse of grassland. As soon as Jenny reached the mouth of the canyon, the look of the country changed. The Barrens were behind her. The long, rolling, grassy hills ahead seemed wonderfully rich to her, and she felt energized and hopeful.

She followed Curran's trail for several miles to where it led down a shallow embankment and into a stony river bed. A thin stream of clear water flowed over the rocks. Jenny lay down in the middle of the stream and drank. When her thirst was satisfied, she filled her water bottles and crossed the river where she saw that Curran had and scrambled up the other side. It was easy to follow the tracks he'd left in the loose dirt, and they were no more than three days old. She went back to the stream and waited out the afternoon heat in the shade of its banks, certain her search would end today at the spring David had shown her.

CHAPTER 14

Jenny found Curran's camp at the edge of a small grove of watapa trees on a bench above the spring David had shown her. She watched him as he sat in meditation, unaware of her presence. Then she walked to the edge of the trees and stopped. When she was sure he'd become aware of her, she entered his camp.

"I was in the neighborhood and thought I'd stop by," she said. "If you don't want me to stay, say so now, before I get comfortable."

When he didn't answer, she took his silence for permission to stay. She was about to walk past him to the spring when she felt something so strongly in his thoughts that she couldn't just let it pass.

"I'm here because you asked me, Curran, and because I love you. What's so hard to understand about that?"

"After what I did to you?" he said bitterly.

"What are you talking about?"

"Why didn't you stop me?"

"Stop you from what? What are you talking about?"

"Why did you let me take you like that?"

She could feel the turmoil he was attempting to suppress come boiling to the surface. He was trying to believe he hadn't forced her; that their last few minutes together at her house hadn't been a brutal attack for which he could never be forgiven.

"I wanted it as much as you did," she said simply.

When he didn't say anything in reply, she spoke again.

"This is crazy, Curran. Why would I lie to you about it?"

"Human women often stay with men who mistreat them."

"You know me well enough to know I wouldn't."

She was about to say that he knew *himself* well enough to know he wasn't that kind of man, but that was part of the problem. He *didn't* know anymore.

"Curran, *mei kei'thara. Kei'thara ayala.*"

In Deniban culture, the words were almost sacred, having been spoken between two Deniban culture heroes, Rawlian and Lissa, and passed down through the generations for over two hundred years. Translated, they meant, 'My treasured one. Treasured sharer of my bed.'

He looked at her in disbelief.

"You've heard me say them before, Curran. When you held me in your arms after I came."

"I heard nothing more than the pounding of the blood in my head."

"I will never believe that."

"If it was what you wanted, why were you crying?"

"Because I needed the release you gave me so badly and—"

"If that was all you needed, any man could have given it to you."

"—and because I love you so much, Curran, and I was afraid I would never see you again."

He wouldn't meet her eyes, and she didn't see any point in continuing the conversation. She walked past him and laid out her ground cloth in the shade of one of the boulders closer to the spring. She took the *a'kia* root she'd found the day before from her pack and walked slowly down the path to the spring pool.

At the bottom of the trail, an emerald green pool of water surrounded on three sides by steep rock walls sparkled in the sunlight. Above the pool, water spilled down over a series of stony ledges. Every seam and crack in the wall seemed to have something growing from it, and desert orchids, flowers so rare they grew only in a few isolated locations where the conditions were exactly right, grew in profusion from pieces of decaying bark and wood.

Jenny lay down in the grass at the edge of the spring and satisfied her thirst. She splashed water over her head and neck, then sat up, letting the water run down her back, enjoying the feel of it against her skin. The chill took her out of her thinking mind and transferred her attention to her body, away from the turmoil she was feeling through Curran. She'd said what she could. He would believe what he wanted to believe. More words wouldn't change what he thought or felt. Only he could do that.

She unwrapped the a'kia root and pounded it against a flat rock with another stone, pulverizing it into a thick gel with a faint lemony odor. She took off her clothes and washed them with the soap she'd made, using a stick to beat them clean. As she worked, a small bird landed in the water on one of the ledges above her, splashing and bathing, then settling itself deeper into the water to soak. With its breast feathers saturated, it flew off to its nest, bringing water to its nestlings in its feathers.

When she finished the washing, she wrung the water out of her clothes, laid them on the grass to dry, and waded into the pool to wash the dirt and grit of six days of hard travel from her body. Besides being a good soap, the a'kia gel was also a mild astringent, and by the time she finished bathing, her skin was not only clean, but tingling.

Jenny stretched out in the water and floated on her back, watching the birds fly back and forth above her to their nesting places in the rocks. She was so relaxed she almost dozed off.

When she finally forced herself to get out of the water, she slipped her bare feet into her unlaced boots, picked up her clothes, and walked back toward Curran's camp. She hung the clothes on the nearest watapa, stretched out on her ground cloth and blanket, and was asleep in minutes.

***

Curran watched the play of sunlight and shadow on Jenny's body as she lay asleep under the watapa tree. He hadn't expected her to come, and now that she had, he wasn't sure he wanted her here. He'd had second thoughts about it almost as soon as he began to realize what he'd been doing to bring her.

He watched the stillness of her body as she slept.

He watched her wet hair gleaming in the sunlight.

He watched her objectively, as if he were examining a fine painting or a piece of sculpture, trying to feel nothing for her, but couldn't.

Through meditation and fasting, he had reached an extraordinary level of clarity, but now that Jenny was here with him, it didn't feel nearly so substantial. He didn't want to lose his hard-won clarity because he couldn't control his feelings for her, and more importantly, because he knew if he couldn't control them, those feelings could put them both at even greater risk. Those feelings might also be the only thing that could save them.

***

When Jenny woke, the sun had already been up for an hour, and she was wondering why the early morning cold hadn't awakened her. Then she realized she was wrapped in both her blankets and Curran's and saw that Curran had built a small fire next to her bed with a rock reflector behind it. The embers and the reflector were still giving off heat. A small ra'han was spitted on a stick over the fire. Curran had eaten half of it and left the rest for her.

Her clothes were folded neatly on the ground beside her. Resting on a stone next to the head of her bed was a desert orchid. He hadn't simply picked the flower and left it for her. He had taken the whole plant, bark, roots and all, and placed it next to her bed, knowing she would return it to the spring before she left.

Jenny stayed under the blankets a few more minutes, then dressed and ate a leisurely meal, enjoying the cool morning air. There was no hurry this morning. The Boitan was begun alone by both participants.

After she'd eaten, she went to return the orchid to the spring. She set it on a protected ledge and sat down in the grass to meditate and prepare herself. When she felt she was ready, she left to find Curran.

She followed his trail through a series of mound-shaped hills, across a dry stream bed and into a valley perhaps a half-mile across at its widest. The valley was lovely and peaceful, the grass thick and golden in the sunlight. Overhead, a tr'yan soared on the thermals, systematically working the valley floor. In the distance, she could see a small herd of haraq grazing, and there were signs that a good-sized group of ben'thar had been through the valley the day before.

Even though she'd never been anywhere near this place, it felt familiar, and the feeling kept nagging at her. She knew she'd never seen the valley before, but still felt certain that she had.

It was early evening when she found Curran five or six miles from the spring in a place where the valley narrowed slightly. He was lying on a woven prayer rug laid out toward the middle of the valley floor in direct sunlight and had apparently been there most of the day.

She knelt beside him. His pulse and respiration were slow, but she'd expected that. He'd slowed them himself. His skin was feverishly hot and almost dry, but she'd expected that as well.

Although Denibans normally sweated lightly, the Deniban body was designed to store heat. A Deniban's normal body temperature was just over one hundred degrees. During a hot day, it could rise to over a hundred and six. While a human body had to burn calories to keep warm when the temperature dropped at night, Denibans used their stored body heat. Without it, especially with his metabolism slowed, Curran could die of

177

exposure.

Next to him on the ground, there was an almost empty water bottle. He'd been able to come to consciousness during the day to drink. Jenny left one of her full bottles in its place and went to look for water, following the single-file tracks of the ben'thar to a muddy waterhole, its banks lined with a rank growth of grass and brush. From under the roots of a very old camaranth tree, she saw a slight current where a small spring fed into the pool. She filled the water bottles, walked back to Curran, and sat down in the grass beside him.

The temperature dropped fast as night came. Jenny wrapped herself in her blanket and ground cloth and sat quietly, watching him, waiting. She tried to stay open to any impressions that might come, but it wasn't easy. She didn't know what to expect or what he might ask of her, and she was afraid of what could happen to them if she wasn't quick enough to recognize danger. She wanted to touch him, but Shaia's warning kept her from it. She slept very little during the night, trying to stay awake and aware of him as much as possible in case he needed her.

In the morning, she built a lean-to near him made of fallen branches and brush she'd collected at the waterhole, covered it with her ground cloth and blanket, and moved in. She kept Curran's ground cloth and blanket rolled up beside her pack. The finished project wasn't going to win any prizes for architecture, but it did provide a modest amount of shade. She needed it. The heat was terrible, much worse than any of the days before, and the sky was cloudless.

Late in the day, when the animals began to come out to forage, Jenny made a throwing stick and went hunting. She came back with a ra'han and a couple handfuls of berries, dried so hard they were inedible. She cooked the ra'han and soaked the berries in water until they were soft enough to eat and had them for dessert. When she finished, she took Curran's ground cloth and blanket with her and lay down closer to him, waking at intervals to check on him.

In the hours before dawn, when most of his stored body heat had been spent, she moved the blankets next to him and careful not to touch him, covered them both. He was so far away, so deep within himself, she felt nothing from him at all. Even when he'd come back to drink during the day, she hadn't been aware of his presence. He seemed to be able to sense when she was gone and wait until then to surface.

The third day started much the same as the one before—trips to the spring for water, hours spent watching over Curran, a late afternoon foraging trip. It was the same except that on the third day, Curran didn't come to consciousness to drink, and for the first time, Jenny was truly frightened. She didn't know how long he could live without water in his present condition, but she didn't think it could be more than another day.

Despite Shaia's warning, that night, when she was awake, she lay beside him, their bodies touching. She moved away to sleep. She hoped her touch would give him enough contact with reality to keep him from going any further away than he already was, but she had no way of knowing if it did. His body was so still he hardly seemed alive.

By noon of the fourth day, the heat was incredible. It seemed to have taken on a life of its own. Waves of brutally hot air shimmered and writhed above the dry grasslands. A scorching wind rumbled and roared past her ears as it swept across the valley floor.

Deniban legends said that when the heat became this intense, it had a sound, and that sound had spirit power. Jenny heard the sound of heat and felt its power. It hummed and throbbed in her head. It beat deep inside her body like a pulse. It was the power of that sound that gave her the courage to open herself completely to Curran, without reservation. If she felt anything from him at all now, she would touch him in any way she could to try to bring him back.

She sat in the appalling heat, asking the Old Ones and the Mind of the Universe to help her when a tr'yan called out from across the valley. The sound of its clear, piercing voice shot through her like a bolt from a crossbow. In that instant, she knew why the valley was so familiar. Anyone who knew anything about Deniban history would know this place. She had read detailed descriptions of it many times and even seen photographs and holograms of it.

Two hundred years ago, something happened in this valley that had changed the direction of Deniban history, something so terrible and so sublime that it affected the collective mind of an entire people. House TaZarin had been intimately involved in that event.

TaZarin Shirraz'At had almost been destroyed here.

***

TaZarin Shirraz'At had asked for a meeting at this place with the Households of the western division of TaZarin to discuss joining in support of Charik and the new ways. Most of TaZarin Shirraz'At was already firmly committed to Charik and the practice of the Warrior's Way and the Restoration, but the people of the western Households were still undecided. The two hundred and eighty-seven members of TaZarin Shirraz'At who decided to come to the meetings had arrived several days early to conduct House business and prepare for their guests.

The day before the others were to arrive, scouts reported several large parties of armed and mounted men gathering at the south end of the valley, preparing to move on the camp. Men from Havarr, Le'ara, Graz, and several other Houses, all opposed to Charik and threatened by the new ways and the Restoration and well-aware that if TaZarin could be destroyed, some of Charik's strongest advocates would be destroyed with it.

The men of TaZarin met in a council of war and decided to send the women and children away to safety with an armed escort. The rest would remain to face the enemy. They would attempt to talk with them if possible, but if a confrontation became unavoidable, they would not give ground, and they would not fight.

When the decision was announced, the women refused to leave, as did all of the children old enough to understand what was happening and make a responsible decision. All of them practiced the Warrior's Way themselves, and all of them had sworn themselves to the same ideals the men had.

An escort of ten of TaZarin's best warriors left the valley with only the pregnant and nursing women and the small children. Those who remained formed ranks, laid their weapons on the ground in front of them, and waited as the council leaders stepped forward to meet the enemy.

The attackers ignored the council leaders as they signaled for a parlay and rode down TaZarin without hesitation or mercy. Of the two hundred thirty-eight men, women, and children who stayed behind in the valley, not one picked up a weapon or broke ranks, and only seven survived.

The attack was the beginning of the end for the ruling Houses. There had been other attacks against Houses that supported Charik, but the victims had always tried to fight back. The wholesale slaughter of these unarmed men, women, and children, who fought with nothing but the strength of their beliefs, roused feelings of outrage even among those who opposed Charik. And for the first time, there were prosecutions. The men who instigated and participated in the massacre were hunted down and turned over to the regional council for trial.

Although the ruling Houses tried to stop the trials, the local outcry was so great that it couldn't be done without causing outright rebellion. In the end, the trials had gone on, and they had helped spread Charik's ideas. The attack broke the hold of the ruling Houses forever and made the Warrior's Way an unstoppable force in Deniban life.

***

Jenny suddenly returned to the present, jarred into awareness by a change in the quality of the wind. It had shifted direction suddenly, and now it carried the smell of dust. The temperature was dropping fast as huge roiling clouds of dust and debris appeared above the east end of the valley. Within seconds the clouds had reached a height of eight thousand feet and began to march down the valley like an advancing army, turning the bright midday sky as dark as night. The wind whipped around them, pelting her and Curran with grit and gravel as the wall of wind and debris that was a shirraz bore down on them.

Jenny got up, ripped the ground cloth off the lean-to, and looped it under Curran's arms, creating a sort of make-shift harness to drag him with. She had to get them to shelter before the full force of the storm broke over them. A shirraz could drive gravel through a tree. It could scour deadwood to the color and texture of polished bone. It could flay the flesh off an unprotected person's body in seconds.

She headed for the shelter of some boulders she knew were about a hundred feet away, dragging Curran behind her. The air was so thick with dust she could barely breathe. Visibility was no more than a few feet. The wind was pitched at a low rumbling roar with an eerie wailing at the heart of it. Jenny could hardly stand against it much less move forward.

Suddenly a dead branch crashed into the back of her legs. She went down hard, bruising her ribs against a rock, got to her feet and staggered on, realizing that she wasn't going to make it to the rocks in time. Instead, she dragged Curran into a shallow gully she'd remembered seeing a few yards to her left. She stuffed one side of the ground cloth under his body, lay down beside him, and pulled the other side over them and under her own body, hoping that between the gully and the ground cloth, there would be enough protection to keep them alive.

As the storm bore down on them, Curran's body seemed to come alive beside her. Perhaps the stirring was nothing more than the instinct of an animal to survive, but something was drawing him closer to the world outside himself. Then, with no warning at all, she was pulled deep into psychic contact with him.

She began to see the battle develop through the eyes and heart of the man Curran had become.

***

The man stood in the middle ranks of the formation, his wife on one side, and his almost-grown daughter on the other. He was fighting an overpowering urge to pick up his weapon and fight, not so much to defend his own life, but to save the lives of his wife and child. His heart was pounding, and he was afraid, but he had no second thoughts about what they were doing. He stood silently beside his wife and child, waiting for death to come to them, and Jenny could feel the extraordinary strength of their feeling for each other.

Through his eyes, Jenny saw the enemy begin to advance. She knew that of the seven survivors, only three were men. If this man wasn't one of them and Curran lived the event with him, Curran would never come back, and if she were still in such intense contact with him, neither would she.

The battle line advanced down the valley to the front ranks of TaZarin, and the slaughter began.

***

'Curran, turn away now while you still have a choice. Michael and Katherine are dead. This won't bring them back.'

Nothing.

'This man died for a purpose, Curran. What purpose will be served if you die with him? Michael and Katherine are dead! Let them go!'

'I can't!' came his anguished answer.

'They're dead, Curran! No matter how long you hold them with you, you will never bring them back. No one ever promised you that life was going to be fair or even that it would make sense. You lived, and they died, and that's how it is. There is nothing you can do about it, and your dying isn't going to fix it!'

***

The man Curran had become was deadly calm. There was no fear in him now and no desire to fight, just his certain knowledge that what he and his wife and daughter were doing was right and necessary. Seen through his eyes, the battlefield had become strangely silent. The sounds of hooves, the squeak of leather, the screams and the sounds of weapons, very distant. The sounds faded into complete silence as he withdrew into himself, touching minds with his wife and daughter.

***

Jenny broke into a cold sweat. The sound of her own ragged breathing seemed extraordinarily loud to her, almost drowning out the screaming of the wind as the full force of the storm broke over them. She was hardly aware of the stones and debris pounding against her back as she covered Curran's body with her own and tried to protect him.

'Curran, let them go! I'll help you. I'll stand with you while you sing the words for the dead for them. It's time to let them go.'

She had to find a way to take him with her to another place, one where he would be safe. The place she chose was the cliffs at Red Wall.

At the top of the cliffs, where it felt as if a person could see the entire world, Jenny placed the bodies of Katherine Ryerson and Michael Collins beside two burial scaffolds, each covered by a beautifully woven funeral rug.

Jenny knew the power of the vision in Curran's mind was more compelling than hers, but she thought he could be drawn to it through her emotional warmth and the comfort she offered him, and he was.

He came to her and carried Michael and Katherine's bodies to their burial scaffolds, setting them down as gently as if they were still living. Jenny stood by and watched as he tied flight feathers from a tr'yan's wing at the head of each scaffold and fastened bright sky-blue prayer flags to the corners. The feathers would help carry their spirits to the Ancestors. The prayer flags would carry his prayers and those of their friends and families to the Mind of the Universe. As she joined him in singing the words for the dead for them, she finally felt him let Katherine and Michael go.

'Come with me now, Curran. Come home.'

He had to come back with her *now*. The effort of sustaining the vision for him was taking everything she had, and she couldn't sustain it much longer.

Suddenly a heavy limb hit her in the back. It struck hard, dragged across the length of her body, and was blown free, but for those few seconds of pain and surprise, Jenny had been shocked into the present, and when she returned to Red Wall, Curran was gone. He had returned to the slaughter in the valley.

She was able to see the man and his wife through him, but she didn't have the strength left to look any deeper, to know why Curran had returned, or to influence what he did. All she knew was that an answer he desperately needed still eluded him, and it was something he wanted so badly he was willing to die to find it. Whatever it was, only seconds remained before it would be too late to matter.

Near exhaustion, Jenny's mind began to drift and by the time she was able to focus again, the man's daughter was dead, and his wife lay at his feet dying. The man roared in rage and pain as he was slashed across the chest and ridden down by the same man who had just murdered his wife.

Jenny was spent. The vision faded and blurred, returned, and then was gone altogether, and she couldn't bring it back. She had nothing left to fight with and no way of knowing what was happening to Curran. All she had left was her love and her fierce determination not to give him up.

She touched her lips lightly to his. The sense of aliveness she'd felt move through his body just a few minutes earlier was gone now, and a chill of fear passed through her. He was so still and unresponsive she was afraid he might already be unreachable, but she tried anyway.

'Curran, do you remember the night we spent together when I told you I loved you? Do you remember how you felt? I remember how I felt, Curran. I remember everything about that night. I remember the taste of your kisses, the feel of your breath against my cheek, your hands on my body. I remember all of it.'

She let herself re-experience everything she'd felt with him that night, holding it in her mind, giving him a place to come to. She kissed his face, his mouth, dragged her fingernails across his flank, trying to reach him in the only way she had left.

She felt him slowly become aware of her body against his, her touch, and the sound of her voice in his mind.

'It's not a dream, Curran. I'm real, and I'm right here.'

'Jenny..."

'I'm right here, Curran.'

'Jenny, don't leave me here. Please. Don't leave me in this place.'

She pulled the ground cloth away from them. The shirraz had passed, and sunlight streamed all around them. She was about to kiss him at the place where his torn collar had fallen open and exposed his shoulder, but instead, she bit him. Hard. His body shuddered under hers, and she bit him again.

His breath came in deep, wracking gasps as he moved his hands just far enough to put them on her back. She held him loosely in her arms as he lay beneath her crying.

***

The next day the two of them returned to the spring. They bathed and washed their clothes and lay in the shade to rest, sharing the ground cloth and blanket they'd been able to save after the shirraz. Jenny's body was covered with bruises from the storm, she ached everywhere, and they were both exhausted. They had hardly spoken to each other during the day, but the silence had been comfortable and healing.

In the evening, they walked to the spring to listen to the night birds singing.

"Curran...?"

He took her hand in his and kissed her palm.

"What is it, Jenny?"

"Did you find any answers? Did you find what you went back to the valley for, or has all of this been for nothing?"

***

"There were answers," he said, a soft smile on his lips. "They didn't come as I'd expected, but there were answers. *You* showed me a way to free Katherine and Michael. The man and his wife showed me the rest. It wasn't an answer I'd come here looking for, but I found that I couldn't leave without it."

The man and his wife were kotaho and kotahan to each other. They had married at a time when marriage was new and untried, but it had been the only choice open to them other than to part.

If he left Jenny, he knew the bond could be allowed to atrophy. It would be painful, but it wasn't too late. But would that choice make him a better man? Give him a richer life? Perhaps he and Jenny would have children together, perhaps not, but he would have *her*. He was as inextricably bound to her as he was to his House and land. She was as much a part of who he was as they were, and of who he would become.

He held her hand tenderly in his and began to recite from Drakara's *Poems of the Kotaho*.

> "Woman of flesh, woman of spirit
> Together we stand at the flashpoint
> about to ignite,
> To be welded together as one in the heat
> of our marriage night.
>
> "As I lay in your arms completed
> I cannot tell where your body ends and mine begins.
> We are as different as earth and sky,

And as inseparable."

The smile Jenny gave him in exchange for the two verses opened his heart and filled him with feeling. He took her gently in his arms and kissed her. It was a soft, slow, languorous kiss, and he felt Jenny's passion rise almost immediately, but for the first time in many months, he was not afraid.

TURN THE PAGE TO BEGIN THE NEXT

Jenny Black Wolf - Curran TaZarin story

IN THE FORESTS OF CARACOR

CHAPTER 1

"Curran, are you sure you want me to keep reading this?" David asked, looking up from his desk.

Curran TaZarin, the *Defender's* Deniban first officer, had just handed him three letters, all of them from Jenny Black Wolf, and then retreated to the doorway of David's office, waiting for him to read them. David had started the first one. The letter was so intimate he could hardly believe Curran had let him see it.

"I'm sure," Curran answered. "You need to know."

"I *already* know. I've known since the day you came back to the ship from leave."

Curran had returned to the ship a haunted man. He worked until he was exhausted, then escaped into sleep. He ate ravenously, yet still lost weight. David, the ship's doctor, had known from the minute he'd seen him that Curran and Jenny Black Wolf, the woman Curran was mind-linked with and would have married, had become *shal'tan*.

David looked across the room at his friend. Curran's coarse jet black hair was brushed back away from his face. His mustache and the beard that followed his jaw line were neatly trimmed, although now, instead of emphasizing his high cheekbones, they highlighted the hollowed-out look of his face. Ten pounds lost from an already lean, medium-framed man couldn't be hidden.

Curran's skin had finally lost its unhealthy yellowish cast and returned to its normal copper color, and his green Deniban eyes were clear and alert, but for the first time since his return, Curran allowed David to see the pain in them.

"Please, David, just read. Then we'll talk."

David looked at Jenny's simple, unadorned handwriting on the page and began reading the letter again from the beginning. It had been sent from Caracor and was dated about a month after Curran returned to the ship. All three letters had arrived together yesterday in the only shipment of mail they'd received during the entire cruise.

> *Dear Curran,*
>
> *It's been a month now with no word from you. I'm worried about you. Even if it's no more than to say that you're all right, please write. I don't blame you for what happened. I hope you don't blame yourself. I wanted it as much as you did.*
>
> *I will always regret some of the things I said to you, most especially telling you to stop while I begged you in every other way not to. I knew what would happen when I touched the liqueur to your lips, and I knew what was going to happen in the courtyard of the hotel. When it was over, I went back to your room with you willingly. I could have run from you then, but I didn't.*
>
> *I feel well again, Curran, and I want to see you. Just to talk, if nothing else.*
>
> *I won't lie to you and tell you I'm not afraid. I don't know what will happen to us if we see each other again. I also don't know if we can recover what we had, but I want to try. I do know that I love you and that I continue to feel your presence with me, so something must remain of what you once felt.*
>
> *Please write, Curran. I miss you and I want to know*

how you are.

Jenny

"Are you going to answer this?" David asked.

"No."

"Why not?"

"How can I? What can I say?"

"She's worried about you. You could start by saying you're all right."

"Do I look like a well man to you?"

"No, not really," David conceded.

David set the letter on his desk beside the other two and ran his hands through his unruly brown hair. He had known Curran for almost seven years, since the *Defender's* first cruise as a research and exploration ship.

David was forty-two, tall and well-built, with hazel eyes and an open, friendly face. Curran was six years older, but in terms of the Deniban life span, they were essentially the same age.

They had both met Jenny almost two years ago when she'd come aboard the *Defender* to help with a search and rescue mission on Caldera. Until then, neither of them had known a human could learn the Mind Disciplines—the thinking skills and techniques Denibans learned in order to use and control their psychic abilities—but Jenny had learned them from her husband Kristen, who'd died in an accident four years earlier.

Shortly after Jenny left the ship, David had asked Curran if he thought he could teach the Mind Disciplines to *him*, or at least the thinking skills. David thought learning them would be useful, considering his quick-tempered, often volatile nature and Curran's calm, self-possession.

David remembered the first thing Curran said to him once he'd decided to teach him.

'The mind is a reservoir of information and a means for solving problems, David, but the emotions are the true source of a person's knowledge about the physical world, the world as sensed and experienced. They reside in the body, not the mind. They are to be experienced directly and immediately, then dealt with and discharged.

'The first of the thinking skills is observation. You learn to observe your mind, watching the thoughts and emotions that pass through it, allowing them to leave without judgment or attachment. Non-reaction is a choice. So are your habitual reactions. Observation allows you to change your choices. Reaction is learned. It can be unlearned.'

It didn't take a genius to see that Curran's current mental state didn't exactly match the paradigm. David waited quietly for Curran to continue.

***

"She came to my hotel room," Curran said, looking directly at David and thinking how strange his voice sounded, so distant and unreal.

The *Defender* had just returned to Starbase Fourteen, her home port, for a refit and six months of leave for her crew. He and Jenny had made plans to meet there, then travel to Deniba to enact the marriage ritual and later, to spend time with his family.

Jenny had been radiant, her pleasure at seeing him again after so many months of separation, obvious and unguarded. She'd come to his door wearing the same simple black dress she'd worn the first time they'd met at the base, and he remembered smiling to himself, aware that the black dress was the only dress Jenny owned.

"She was standing in the doorway, and before she'd even stepped into the room, I told her the crew had been recalled to the ship."

A border dispute had broken out near the Alliance's treaty boundary with the Karghan Federation, and the crew had been recalled. His six months of leave had turned into the two days he had remaining before the ship left to join other elements of the

Sixth Fleet on patrol.

Jenny had stood in the doorway in stunned disbelief, the sexual tension between them suddenly so intense it felt as if the air had been charged with an explosive fuel just waiting for the spark that would ignite it.

"She said she thought it would be best if she left for a while. She needed some time alone to collect herself. I told her I wanted her to stay.

"She said, 'We both know what will happen if I stay.'"

Except for the time of mating in fall, sexual contact between Denibans was without urgency, slow-paced, and often infrequent. Adapting to Jenny's human sexuality hadn't been easy for him. He and Jenny had spent a year on a knife's edge between what he thought of as the normal sexual play between seasons and the place they'd arrived at when he told her he had to return to the ship in two days. That place was one misstep away from shal'tan.

'Stay with me, Jenny,' he'd said in Speech.

He'd seen the shock in her eyes as his Spoken words resonated inside her mind. She would have stayed with him in any case, but using Speech to influence her had been an unforgivable cruelty.

'Please, Curran. Don't do this.'

It was like a prayer, and all the while, he'd watched her trembling with need.

Without the linking bond, Deniban couples had no interest in staying together once the mating season was over. Under normal circumstances, Deniban partners had to know each other well before a linking bond even began to form, if it formed at all, yet he and Jenny had barely known each other when they'd become mind-linked. The psychic bond they shared had been created suddenly, by accident, and it had gone very deep. Sexual contact of any kind deepened a bond, and although a Deniban woman was always free to choose a new partner or partners each season, a mind-linked pair returned to each other.

He and Jenny had been sexual together, but they hadn't mated.

Even so, the intensity of their bond put them at risk. Shal'tan came only to couples who were mind-linked, and it came to all of them eventually if they didn't marry. It was the profound psychological changes created by the marriage ritual that allowed a mind-linked pair to stay together without becoming shal'tan. However, marriage was a choice not made lightly, and it was one many Denibans refused because the bond of marriage was exclusive, irrevocable, and for life.

"Curran?" David prompted gently.

"She stayed," he said evenly. "It was so gentle, David, and so sad."

"Sad?" David asked.

"It was as if both of us were filled with remorse for something that hadn't even happened yet."

He was trying to maintain some level of emotional neutrality, but once he'd said the words, he knew by David's reaction that he was failing. David broke eye contact with him and turned away, giving him a few seconds to recover.

"We slept for a time afterward," he continued. "When we woke, we both felt fine. Nothing had happened to us, and besides, we only had to survive for two days and then I'd be gone."

He and Jenny had gotten up, showered together, and gone to dinner.

"There was a kind of timelessness to what happened next," he said.

He believed now that he should have recognized that feeling as the first indication of what was to come, but he hadn't. He and Jenny both enjoyed the meal and the pleasant unimportant things they'd talked about—people they knew, things they'd done together. All of it verged on the almost-normal, except for the timelessness.

"After dinner, I ordered two glasses of *ja'har*," he said as he crossed the office and sat down in one of the chairs in front of David's desk.

The fiery red liqueur played a part in the marriage ritual and in each reenactment of it. On every other occasion in Deniban life, ja'har was meant to be savored slowly, but on the wedding night, it was meant to be consumed in one swallow.

Curran remembered losing himself for a moment in the glow of the liquid in the tiny liqueur glass. The deeper he'd looked toward the stem of the glass, the richer the color became, from ruby red at the top to a deep, ripe, reddish-purple at the bottom.

He remembered looking up and seeing Jenny dip her fingertips into the liqueur in her glass and reach across the table to touch her fingertips to his lips. He'd licked the ja'har from her fingers and watched her tremble with need and anticipation. Then he'd raised his glass to his lips, his hand shaking, and drained it in one swallow. Liquid flame shot through his body. It blazed from his belly into the center of his chest and from there into his arms and shoulders.

Then he'd watched as Jenny picked up her glass, slowly rolling the stem between her thumb and fingers, her eyes never leaving his, and drank down the ja'har in one swallow. She gasped as it reached her belly, and he'd seen the tenderness leave her eyes, replaced by a kind of feverish glittering.

It was the same thing he knew she was seeing in *his* eyes.

"We drank the ja'har, and then I took her hand and led her from the table into the hotel courtyard," he said, looking away, unable to meet David's eyes.

It had rained earlier in the evening, and the air was heavy with the scent of flowers, blooming in the courtyard gardens. He wanted her so badly he could hardly breathe. His legs seemed to move without his volition as he pulled her into the shadows under the trees at the south side of the building. In a few seconds, he was rooted as deep in her as a tree in earth.

"We didn't even get as far as my room," he said, finally looking directly into David's eyes.

"She didn't try to stop you?" David asked.

"By then? No, not exactly."

He would never forget the sound of Jenny's voice or what she'd said when he'd tried to stop.

'Don't you quit on me now, you son of a bitch. I'll kill you if you stop.'

"My God, Curran, if the two of you had been caught, you would have lost everything you've ever worked for."

It would have resulted in a medical discharge. Deniban personnel who were actively shal'tan were discharged immediately, with no recourse.

"Don't you think I know that, David? It didn't matter. Nothing mattered."

Nothing mattered but the two of them and the need that tied them to each other. He still didn't know how they'd gotten back to his room, but the courtyard had just been the beginning. The more they had of each other, the more they wanted.

"At first, I thought if we stayed together, the need might burn itself out, but of course, it didn't."

It only grew worse. What Jenny told him had taken months to happen to her and Kristen, happened to them in just a few hours. They were both insatiable. The physical act became more compelling each time yet more unsatisfying.

Toward morning, Jenny's body had begun to feel strange under his hands, and when he touched her, flashes of color and patterned light danced in his head as he started to hallucinate. The coupling continued all that day and into the next evening until they both fell into an exhausted sleep, unsatisfied and close to violence. They couldn't even talk to each other without fighting.

"It was almost dark when she woke," he said. "I'd been awake for a while, resting next to her in a sort of daze, pretending to sleep. The violence of the feelings between us was terrifying. It seemed to me that if I so much as tried to speak to her, she might murder me, but at the same time, I knew if I touched her, she would come into my arms, and it would start again. I found myself silently praying she would leave the bed, but I would have killed to keep her there. When I realized she was going to try to leave, it took everything I had not to stop her."

Jenny had gotten out of the bed as quietly as she could, but she was so spent she couldn't stand. When she'd tried to walk away from the bed, her knees had buckled under her, and she'd lain on the floor, silently sobbing with the effort it took not to go back to him. He'd watched as she dragged herself across the floor to her clothes, struggled into them, and left the room.

"It was astonishingly painful to be apart from her, David. I felt as though everything inside me had been ripped out, and I was nothing without her."

Alone in the bed he'd shared with her, he began to shiver in an icy fever. He'd pressed his face into her pillow, taken in her scent, and wept inconsolably, certain he would never see her again.

***

In the silence that followed, David found himself thinking about Drakara's *Shal'tan Poems*. About the violence of the imagery and how far the poems went beyond anything a healthy person, Deniban or human, would consider erotic. They were horrifying and tragic, an appallingly graphic account of a man's descent into the insanity of shal'tan. Then he thought about Curran. About how the hormonal alterations of shal'tan were still affecting him, keeping his body in overdrive like an engine running without a governor.

David knew as a doctor that the feelings shal'tan partners experienced were like those of the time of mating only more intense, more powerful, and like a drug, they became addictive. Eventually, the relationship would turn violent and abusive as the couple became increasingly unable to satisfy themselves physically or emotionally. Yet the need to re-experience the heightened physical pleasure in the early stages of the cycle was only part of it. The shal'tan experience was so overwhelming that when it stopped, the partners felt nothing. It was the need to fill the terrible emptiness Curran had just described, that was perhaps the most destructive aspect of the experience. Even if they were able to separate and recover their health, the shal'tan experience often drew the couple back to each other to repeat the cycle until it either killed them or brought on permanent insanity.

David couldn't deny the risks involved if Curran and Jenny were to see each other again. The cycle could renew itself, and the descent deepen, or they might be able to salvage what they had and go on. He didn't know. If Jenny was speaking as a shal'tan, David knew her wanting to see Curran again was need, not love. If she was well, it was an act of courage.

"After everything that's happened, Curran, she says she still loves you and wants to see you. You owe her some kind of answer even if you don't plan to see her again."

***

Curran sat quietly, having barely heard what David said. He hadn't intended to say nearly as much as he had. He ached to see Jenny again. He was also afraid. Ironically, he thought that all things considered, the fear was probably a good sign.

Curran picked up Jenny's second letter from David's desk and held it.

"I used to look forward to getting these," he said. "Seeing Jenny's words on paper, having something from her I could hold."

At first, the letters had seemed quaint to him. Except for packages, most people used electronic mail, but the idea of exchanging letters had grown on him, and Curran began to write, too. Despite the extra time it took for the letters to reach him and the considerable expense of sending them, the waiting made receiving them all the more special.

He handed the letter to David, and David opened it. It was dated almost a month after the first.

> *Dear Curran,*
> *My work here on Caracor is going well, and I*

should have it completed on time. Other than that, there's not much news.

Please write, Curran. I'm worried about you, and I miss you. I miss your company, the sound of your voice, your touch. I realize now, since it's been so long, that you've probably decided not to see me again, but I still feel your presence with me. I don't want to let you go, Curran, but I need to get on with my life, without you if I have to. If I don't hear from you in a month, I'll assume it's over. If you do decide to write, use the electronic mail address I gave you before you left on patrol.

I love you, Curran, and I want to see you, but I won't ask again.

Jenny

David put the second letter back in its envelope, picked up the third, and opened it. It was dated just a few days after the second one. The first two letters carried a franking stamp from the territorial capitol of Caracor, and both had return addresses. The third was smudged and had a well-worn look, as if it had been carried in someone's pocket for some time. Postage for it had been paid for at a public machine on Seora.

Curran,

I have to see you. I know the Defender is returning to her homeport within the month. Please, if you have any feeling left for me, meet me at Starbase Fourteen when the ship goes into space dock.

Please don't start your leave until I have a chance to talk to you. If you can, bring David with you. Don't use the electronic mail address I gave you, and don't try to answer this note. Just meet me in the bar at the Parma Hotel. If you don't come, I'll understand.

There was no signature and no return address.

The ship was only a few hours from port, and David hadn't made any plans for his leave that couldn't be canceled.

"I'll wait with you, Curran."

CHAPTER 2

David and Curran sat at a small table toward the back of the Parma Hotel's bar. They'd been waiting there each night for the last seven nights and had long since given up looking every time someone new entered the room.

The bar was pleasantly dark, and tonight it was fairly busy. Earlier in the evening, they had talked again briefly about Jenny, and then the conversation had turned to David's wife, or more accurately, David's ex-wife.

David and Janet had married the year after he started medical school. The marriage lasted almost seven years, but it was a part of his life he and Curran had never talked about. David knew he would never fully understand shal'tan since he would never experience it, but he understood the agony of wanting a woman he couldn't have. It had been that way with him and his wife once, only by then it was too late to matter. Janet had already left him.

"David, when Janet left—"

"She did the right thing, Curran. I wasn't much of a husband. I was too busy working and too self-involved."

David hesitated before going on. After all this time, it still hurt to remember.

"It wasn't as though she didn't try to talk to me about how she felt. I just didn't want to hear it. I was as dissatisfied with our life together as she was, but unlike her, I didn't want to deal with it. Fixing what was wrong would have meant having to change, and I didn't want to be bothered."

"Was there another man?"

"No. I accused her of being unfaithful, but she wasn't, and I knew it. She didn't leave me for someone else. She left *me*. It just hurt too much to admit it. As long as I could believe there was someone else, I could deny my share of the responsibility for the mess our marriage was in. It took me a long time to accept it, but the divorce was the best thing for both of us. It set Janet free, and it forced me to grow. Sometimes I wish I could see her again, though, just to talk."

"You never see her?" Curran asked.

"No, but I heard she married again a few years ago. They have a little girl."

David stretched lazily, looked around the bar, and took another sip of his Thaetan beer. He'd been nursing the same beer for almost an hour. Curran had been drinking *cama*, a kind of fermented tea popular on Deniba, made from the roots and bark of the desert *camaranth*. David thought the stuff was awful, but Curran had been drinking a considerable amount of it lately. The brew was mildly intoxicating to Denibans, but Curran had left most of it untouched tonight. The teapot was cold, and Curran was getting ready to take it to the bar and ask the bartender to warm it for him when David saw him tense.

He didn't even have to look to know that Jenny had just arrived. The expression on Curran's face was enough. When he *did* look, he saw a trim, well-muscled woman of medium height with short light-brown hair, dark brown eyes, and Caucasian facial features, standing just inside the doorway, looking for them. She was wearing a pair of faded jeans, an old denim work shirt, badly scuffed hiking boots, and a beat-up leather jacket. She carried a small duffel bag in her right hand with a lever-action carbine lying across the top, the saddle scabbard underneath it.

Jenny was a second-generation native of Gavalon. She'd told David once that when she was seventeen her parents' ranch had failed and they'd decided to leave Gavalon. She'd refused to leave with them, choosing instead to stay with the Lakota Sioux family she'd been living with.

Curran struggled to free himself from his chair and stand up, and just as David was about to make a joke about it, he smelled an unusual spicy musk in the air. He was astonished and then mortified for his friend. The release of a Deniban man's sexual scent was an involuntary response to deep arousal, an invitation to pleasure. It was a very private thing and a terrible humiliation for it to happen in public.

Curran seemed oblivious.

David recovered himself and waved to Jenny. She waved back and started toward them.

***

Jenny was just a few steps from their table when she was brought up short by Curran's scent. Her face went white as she fought to gain control of herself. She stood beside their table spellbound, remembering the scent of Curran's spice on her skin when she'd left his bed and the almost unbearable stimulation of her dress against her body as she'd left his room.

She'd gone to a hotel across town and then stood in the shower for an hour, trying to wash his scent from her body, from her hair. It was impossible. His scent had become imprinted on her brain. Every time she thought of him, it returned. The remembrance of that scent and of the sensations that came with it had taken weeks to fade.

***

"Jenny, may I get you something to drink?" Curran managed.

The tension between the two of them was like another presence at the table.

"Juice. Some fruit juice would be good, Curran. Thank you."

205

David thought she looked terrible, tired, and ill. He wasn't sure Curran had noticed.

"David?" Curran asked.

"Just coffee," he answered, his eyes never leaving Jenny.

Curran left to go to the bar, and David walked around the table to offer Jenny a seat, noting that it hurt her to move her left arm.

Jenny put her arms around his waist and lay against him. He felt her sob once in his arms before she regained enough composure to speak.

"I'm so glad to see you, David. Thank you. Thank you for coming."

"It's alright, Jenny," David said softly. "Whatever it is, it'll be alright now."

Curran returned from the bar and stood watching the two of them in each other's arms. He set their drinks on the table and sat down. Jenny and David joined him, Jenny having chosen the chair that faced the door where she could watch anyone entering or leaving the room.

"Don't you need a permit to carry that thing around?" David asked, referring to the rifle that lay on top of her duffel bag. He was hoping a little small talk might give Curran some time to settle down.

"Only if you're carrying a concealed weapon. I've kept the rifle in plain sight. It's the handgun that's concealed."

David was startled, but didn't ask.

"I've already had four offers on the rifle. Everyone seems to think it's an antique."

"It isn't?"

"No."

"Is it loaded?"

"Yes," she answered as she scanned the room for the third time.

"What the hell is going on here?" David asked. "This isn't about you and Curran, is it?"

"No."

"Well, what then?" David said, revealing his growing anxiety through the sudden self protective anger that even Curran's lessons had not been able to eradicate entirely. "Your second letter said your work on Caracor was going well, and you were almost finished. What's happened since then?"

Jenny looked at David and then at Curran, realizing that if David had seen the second letter, he'd surely seen the others, too. For the first time, she smiled at Curran, acknowledging his decision to tell David everything and the courage it had taken to make it.

"'Since then' is only the aftermath, David. It's the work that's the problem."

Jenny had taken several sips of the juice Curran brought her and was starting to look a little better before David realized the "juice" was actually *linsit*, a fruit-based drink Denibans often gave to people who were ill.

"Jenny, can I get you something to eat?" Curran asked.

"Thank you, Curran, but I'm not feeling very hungry."

David thought the truth was that she probably couldn't keep anything down.

"So, what kind of work were you doing?" David asked.

"The work was actually started sixty years ago, David, before the planet was opened for settlement. It's a continuing study mandated by the Alliance Territorial Charter. The part of it I'm involved with was established to create a baseline terrestrial plant and animal database for reference and then to update it every five years.

"Twelve years ago, when I started working for Dalt-Ex Survey and Exploration, one of my first jobs was on a survey crew doing a five-year follow-up inventory in the *makonen* forests near Capitol. When I became an independent contractor, I bid the contracts myself for the last two inventories."

"What sorts of things do you do for an inventory?" David asked.

"Record species types and abundance, tree heights and diameters, site conditions, kinds and condition of seedlings, mortality rates, growth rates, rates of overall change in forest composition. That sort of thing."

"Well, it doesn't sound like a person could get in much trouble doing that," David said.

"That's what I thought until someone tried to kill me."

"What!? What did you find?"

"That's just it, David. I don't know."

"How can you not know?"

"I really don't, David, but I intend to figure it out because they've pushed me about as far as I'm going to be pushed."

"What does that mean?"

"It means I'm going back. I've been running for six weeks. I'm not running any further."

David watched as Curran nodded, but remained silent. It wasn't as though Curran hadn't been listening, David thought. It was more that he didn't trust himself to speak and was waiting until he felt more sure of himself.

"I'm also angrier than I think I've ever been in my life," Jenny continued, "and there's something else, too. Whoever did this stole something from me, and even though I know that no matter what happens, I may never get it back, I'm not going to stop until I know why."

"What was stolen?" David asked.

"David, you know I've taken dangerous jobs before—jobs where I could have been killed— but they were always of my own choosing. This isn't the same. This time I was happily minding my own business, and someone tried to kill me."

David listened, recognizing that what had been stolen from her, and what Jenny's anger was covering, was her sense of being safe in the world and in control of her life

"I don't understand, Jenny," Curran said. He spoke quietly, his gaze steady and calm. "What did you find in the woods? Why would anyone want to kill you for whatever it is?"

"Curran, things are happening in the makonen forests. I've seen changes in species composition and abundance, radical changes in makonen mortality and growth rates—"

She stopped abruptly, seeing David's blank expression and realizing that he and Curran didn't have any framework to hang the information on.

"Maybe I should start at the beginning here," she said.

"On the main continent of Caracor west of Capitol and anywhere in the temperate zone below an elevation of sixty-five hundred feet, makonen and *arrakt* are the predominant species. These trees are living fossils. A hundred million years ago, even before the grasses had evolved, there were precursors to modern makonen tree in existence.

"This forest type, in more or less its present form, has been stable for almost thirty thousand years. There were several brief periods of glaciation when the makonen forest receded from the northern part of its range and colonized land to the south usually inhabited by a different forest type, but when the glacial periods ended, the makonen-arrakt forest re-established itself in its original range.

"There's nothing like this type of forest on Deniba, Curran. The closest thing is maybe the mixed pine and hardwood forests on Earth, but while it takes two hundred years for that kind of forest to grow from establishment to maturity, it takes about seventy to eighty years on Caracor. Changes happen fast and are observable on a human time scale. What I've been seeing has become so obvious that anyone who knows these woods at all can see the difference. The trends started to show up ten years ago, but no one gave it much attention, waiting to see what the next inventory would show. Five years ago, they were becoming clearer. Now there's even more evidence that something serious is happening."

Jenny paused briefly to finish the linsit. When she returned the glass to the table, Curran reached out to take it so he could go back to the bar and bring her a refill. Without thinking, Jenny put her hand on his to stop him. David saw Curran's eyes widen at the sudden shock of her touch and watched as he withdrew his hand.

"Does anyone have any idea what's causing it?" Curran asked, recovering himself.

"No, not really. The changes may be perfectly normal fluctuations caused by some sort of interaction we haven't seen before and don't understand yet. Still, a lot of people on Caracor are getting worried, and there's been quite a bit of complaining to the government about what's happening.

"Lots of the animals that live in these forests are extremely dependent on makonen nuts and arrakt seeds for food. Beyond that, the planet as a whole needs them because of how important they are to its hydrological and oxygen cycles. And then there's the value of the forests themselves as a potential source of pharmaceuticals and for raw materials."

"Did you make your findings public?" David wanted to know.

"I wrote up the report and submitted it along with the field data to the chief administrator's forestry advisor, plus I had the data entered into the Forest Inventory Database at the Institute of Forestry in Capitol."

"Anything else?"

"I granted an interview to an investigative reporter from the Territorial News. We talked for several hours about the work and the direction things seemed to be going. She wanted to know if I had the evidence to back up what I was saying and when I said I did, she asked me to give her copies of all my data."

"Did you?"

"Yes."

"What did she write?"

"I don't know. I never saw the finished article, but all of the information I gave her is a matter of public record. Once it's entered into the central database at the Institute, anyone can access the public side of it and see what's there."

"Was it?" Curran asked.

"Was it what?"

"Entered in the central database?"

"Well, sure it was," she said. Then she thought about it. "I guess it's possible that it wasn't. I mean, I didn't do it personally. I just turned everything in at the Institute, as required. All they needed to do was upload it."

"Is it possible that by giving the interview, you inadvertently made yourself a target?" David asked.

"Maybe, although I can't see how."

"What kinds of trends did you report that could make someone want to keep you quiet?" Curran asked.

"The kind of stuff I was just telling you about; changes in populations, growth rates—"

"That doesn't sound like anything to get that excited about," David said skeptically.

"Just to say there's a change in species composition and abundance doesn't even begin to convey the complexity of what's happening there now or what may happen if this continues, David. It doesn't stop with just one thing. One change leads to another and then another, rippling through the whole system until it becomes an avalanche of things.

"For example: makonen trees grow in dense groves along the stream banks. They're the dominant tree in the stream bottoms and on north and east-facing slopes. They provide protection from erosion and shade for the fish that spawn in the shallows. When the trees die and fall into the streams, their bodies provide cover where smaller fish can hide. Without the fallen trees, smaller fish become easy targets for the bigger fish that eat them, and their numbers decline. With the shade gone, the water temperature goes up. Lots of fish are sensitive to changes in water temperature. Besides that, warmer water carries less oxygen. Some fish are very sensitive to lowered levels of dissolved oxygen in the water."

"Like trout, on Earth," David said.

"Exactly, David. Also, without the trees and the other plants that grow in association with them, stream bank erosion increases. That leads to siltation in the rivers. That lowers oxygen levels further, and with more sediment suspended in the water, less sunlight gets through. That affects the growth of the tiny water plants that fish at the bottom of the food chain depend on."

Jenny stopped to take a drink from David's water glass. Her face was shining with a light sweat. Even sick with fever, her eyes were alight with excitement as she talked about the woods.

"Next, without enough of the fish that normally feed on them, insect populations take off. Then the population of insect-eating birds and the other birds and animals that feed on them goes up, too. The increased population of birds leads to heavier competition for food, cover, and nesting sites. When the insect population crashes due to increased feeding pressure, the birds leave or starve, and so do the animals that feed on them. Then insect populations explode, only this time, there's nothing much left to control them. Insects are a vector for introducing disease into the trees. They're always present, and there's always some disease, but without the birds and fish to control them, disease becomes rampant."

"I'm beginning to get the picture."

"David, I'm just hitting the highlights here, but you can see the effect of what seems like just a minor change in the system."

"How far into the cascade have things progressed in these forests?" Curran asked.

"In some areas, nothing seems to be happening at all. But where the changes are the most pronounced, the rate of change seems to be accelerating. No one knows how far this can go before the system breaks down and can't recover."

"So you gave this interview, and then someone tried to kill you," David said. "Where did it happen?"

David noticed that Jenny had stopped scanning the room as

she'd become more involved in teaching, but he'd also noticed that Curran was watching the room, looking for anyone who seemed out of place or was acting suspiciously. David found himself doing it too.

"I was at the government-built bunkhouse in the study area. I was outside on the roof, getting ready to do some repairs when it happened."

"You were alone?"

"Yes. Most of the inventory sites are pretty remote, so during an inventory, the field crews are based at bunkhouses and live there when they're not in the woods. At my sites, we'd completed the fieldwork, and I'd finished the reports and handed them in. I'd only gone back to the house to take care of the roof and spend a few days by myself before closing it down and going home to Gavalon."

"Did you see who it was?"

"No. I slid off the roof when he shot me and ran."

For a few minutes, while she'd been talking about the woods, Jenny had looked almost well. Now she looked exhausted.

"I hid in the woods, stayed quiet, and watched the house. I saw him come out of the woods by the back porch. He found the place where I'd run into the woods but didn't follow me. Then he searched the house. I didn't have much there, but he took it."

"Would you recognize him?" David asked.

"No, I was too far away, but while he was busy at the house, I walked up the ridge behind the house and looked around until I found the place where he'd taken the shot. The man is about six feet tall, one hundred and sixty or seventy pounds, left-handed, and walks on the inside of his left heel. I'd know his tracks anywhere."

"What happened next?" Curran asked.

"I walked across country to a friend's cabin and stayed there for a few days. Then he took me to Capitol, where I discovered I'd become a non-person."

"A 'non-person'?" Curran asked.

"I went to the bank to get some cash and close out my account only to find I didn't have an account anymore. No documents, either. Then just for the hell of it, I went to a store and tried to use my credit card to buy some clothes. I got out just ahead of the police. The card hadn't just been canceled; it had been red-tagged. I was afraid to use it again after that. I was afraid of being arrested or simply made to disappear."

"Don't you think you're getting a little paranoid?"

"No, I don't, David," she snapped. "Someone wanted to deliver the message that if by some chance I hadn't died in the woods, I wasn't wanted on Caracor. I got the message.

"I eventually made it to the spaceport outside the capitol and hung around for a week until I could get work."

"You got work without having any papers?"

"The ship was hauling livestock, some of it illegal, I think. They needed someone to take care of the animals. When I told them I could and that I wouldn't ask if they didn't, they hired me. So now I'm here, but I'm not going to be staying. I'm going back into the makonen forests to look for whatever it is I didn't see before, and I need your help."

"What can *we* do?" David protested. "I don't know anything about the ecology of a makonen forest than what you've just told us."

"Yes, but you know about animals."

Jenny knew that David had briefly considered becoming a wildlife biologist before he'd entered medical school, and his interest in the subject hadn't changed. He'd also been raised on a Montana ranch and had doctored sick animals since he was a boy.

"David, the Institute of Forestry is part of a huge botanical and zoological research station at Capitol, sponsored by the territorial government. If you could gain access to it, pass yourself off as a veterinarian or a wildlife biologist, anything that would allow you to gain access to their database, it would help a lot. The animal studies for my area were done last year. All the data for them and the ones before are on file there. I need to know what's in those files, and I need someone who can interpret them. Maybe something in the animal population is affecting the forests. I need Curran to help me in the woods."

"I can probably fake my way through the work with some study, but how can I pass myself off as a vet or a wildlife biologist? I don't have any credentials."

"I have friends in low places. They can make you anything you want to be."

"What kind of 'friends' might that be?" David asked.

"Ship strippers."

Ship strippers were illegal salvage operators, often little more than thieves. David looked at her half in reproach and half in disbelief.

"Those people were good to me, David. They took me in when I was sick and hungry and never asked me for anything. Now, they're willing to help. Are you?"

"Yes," he answered.

"David, take some time to think about it first. Someone tried to kill me. They could try to do the same to you."

"I'm in," David said. "And so is Curran," he added.

There had never been any question in Jenny's mind about Curran. When she'd seen him waiting in the bar, she knew he'd already made his decision.

Curran took Jenny's hand in his, seemingly unaffected by the shock of their previous contact.

"Thank you, Curran," she said, smiling softly, looking down at the table. "Thank you both."

Then she looked at David. "David, can I stay with you tonight?"

David glanced at Curran, a little uncomfortable with the idea until he saw Curran's hand tighten around Jenny's in reassurance and acceptance. She couldn't stay with Curran, that much was certain.

"Yes, of course."

"Then I'd like to go now. I'm very tired."

Curran got up and paid their bill, then the three of them walked to David's room, where Curran excused himself and continued down the hall to his.

CHAPTER 3

David closed the door to his room and locked it behind them. Jenny stood by the bed and took off her jacket and shirt. With the shirt off, David could see the stained dressing around the upper part of her left arm below her shoulder. He went to the closet and got the corpsman's medical bag he'd taken with him from the ship, just in case it might be needed.

She winced as he cut away the makeshift dressing and exposed the wound. The bullet had passed through the fleshy part of her upper arm. The wound was partially closed and badly infected, and the infection had become systemic.

"God, what a mess," he grumbled under his breath. "How long has it been like this?"

"The infection? About ten days."

"And the fever?"

"About a week. The wound was starting to heal fairly well before I left Caracor, but it's gotten worse since then."

"No kidding. Have you seen a doctor?"

"How am I supposed to see a doctor, David? I'm a fugitive. Any responsible doctor would report treating a gunshot wound.

"No offense," she added.

"None taken. Are you taking anything for the infection?"

"Talinox."

It was a common broad-spectrum antibiotic used in both humans and animals.

"It stopped keeping up with the infection, and I was afraid to increase the dosage."

"You've been dosing yourself by following the directions for animals, by body weight?"

"Yes."

"What are you taking for the pain?"

"Bentazadine."

"Are you crazy?! Bentazadine's not approved for use in humans. Just animals."

"It worked better than some of the other stuff I tried. It controls the pain, but still leaves your mind sharp."

"Wonderful," he said irritably.

He had her sit down on the bed while he prepared and administered two injections, both to deal with the infection, plus a muscle relaxer and a local anesthetic.

"I can't work on you here on the bed, Jenny. Just lie down and rest for a few minutes while I do some rearranging."

"Okay," she said lazily as the drugs began to take effect.

The room had a large desk attached to the wall across from the bed. David covered it with clean bath towels. Then he pulled out the desk's center draw and lined it with a hand towel so he could use it as an instrument tray. He adjusted the wall lamp above the desk so it would illuminate the work area and then moved the floor lamp from the corner of the room to the desk where it would provide some additional light. When he finished, he returned to the bed and sat down beside her.

"Are you feeling any numbing yet?"

"Yes."

"Okay. We'll give it a few more minutes. In the meantime, you can lie down on the desk," he said, helping her up.

She lay down on the desk, and David clipped a pulse-oximeter onto her index finger to monitor her pulse and oxygen saturation levels.

"Jenny, there's no point in pretending. First, I've done as much for the pain as I dare without knowing how much bentazadine is in your system. Second, if there are any bone chips or debris in the wound and I can remove them safely with the instruments I've got here, I'll do it. If not, you're going to have to take your chances with a local doctor."

"It's okay, David. At least the wound will be clean, and the infection will be under control. That's way ahead of where I am right now."

Jenny grit her teeth as he began to flush the wound with antiseptic.

"It hurts?"

"Stings a little." Then a second later, "...more than a little."

He pulled on the headband of the medical scanner and snapped the visor down into position. The scanner allowed him to monitor the instrument readouts as well as view the video images from the probe as they were projected onto the inside of the visor. Then he sanitized his hands and put on a pair of surgical gloves.

"How does it feel now, Jenny?" he asked, flushing the wound again.

"Numb. Doesn't hurt."

"Good."

He opened the entrance wound and inserted the probe, watching the images it reported to the visor as he carefully cleaned the wound track. There were no bone chips and no debris. He closed the entrance and exit wounds, sprayed on a flexskin dressing, and took off the visor.

"You'll need to lay still a while longer, Jenny, just until the flexskin sets up. As soon as it does, I'll help you undress and get in bed so you can get some sleep."

"David, I'm supposed to meet a man tomorrow at midday."

"Your friend in low places?" he asked.

"Will you meet him for me?"

"I will, Jenny, but right now, I want you to get undressed and get in bed," he said, helping her off the desk.

As they walked slowly to the bed, Jenny stopped, dug into the right-hand pocket of her jeans, and took out a ring.

"Give him this ring and the packet of papers in my duffel bag. He'll work with you if you have the ring."

"Jenny, you need to sleep," he said as he took the ring from her hand and put it in his pocket. "We'll talk about it again in the morning."

He helped her undress and get into bed. When he was sure she was comfortable, he picked up the bloodied towels, rolled them up tightly, and hid them in his baggage. He'd have to find a way to dispose of them tomorrow. Then he straightened up the room, took the extra blanket from the closet and the other pillow from the bed.

"What are you doing?" Jenny asked, her words slurred by exhaustion.

"I'm going to sleep on the floor over there."

"Don't be ridiculous. Get in."

"You need to sleep. I don't want to disturb you."

"Nothing is going to disturb me tonight, David, but if you really think the floor is a better place to sleep than the bed, I'll be happy to join you there. I wouldn't want to miss out on a good thing."

She was already trying to get out of bed.

"Okay, okay. I give up," he said in exasperation. "Just stay put."

He replaced the spare blanket in the closet, tossed the pillow on the bed, and got in beside her.

"You'll thank me in the morning when your back doesn't hurt," she said, already half-asleep.

"You're probably right," he said, rechecking the flexskin dressing.

"Are you in any pain?" he asked.

"No."

"If you get uncomfortable, wake me up so I can give you something. Your body doesn't need to waste energy fighting pain. You need to sleep."

"Okay," she mumbled.

"So, you'll wake me if you're in pain, right?" he said, going over it again to assure himself she'd understood him.

"I promise, David. Honest."

"That's better. Now sleep," he said and turned out the light.

He stretched out on his back and closed his eyes. A few seconds later, he felt Jenny's hand in his.

"Thank you, David," she said softly.

Jenny was asleep in minutes, but David couldn't rest. He felt drained, but he also felt wired and restless. He rolled onto his side and put his arm around Jenny's waist. He was lying in bed with Curran's woman. It filled him with sadness. It was Curran's place to be here with her now, not his. At least, he thought, Jenny had someone to comfort her tonight. Curran had no one.

***

The next morning when David woke, Jenny was still sleeping soundly. He checked her vital signs, gave her something for the pain, and a light sedative to keep her sleeping. Then he removed the flexskin dressing to make sure the wound was healing cleanly and sprayed on a fresh one. Finally, he left her a note telling her he would be back soon and walked down the hall to Curran's room. The two men left the hotel and walked to a cafe they both liked about a half-mile away. Little was said on the way.

Once they'd ordered their meals, the silence returned, although David noted that Curran had ordered enough food to feed himself and two other people.

"Curran, I'm uncomfortable about this, so I'm just going to say it."

"There's no need to say anything, David. I assumed you would sleep with her, and I'm glad. I'm glad she had you with her."

"It should have been you."

"We both know that's not possible."

The waiter brought David's coffee and Curran's cama and left.

"How badly infected was it, David?"

"You know about that?"

"I knew she was sick, and I could smell the infection. My sense of smell is more acute than yours."

"It was a mess, but the fever broke sometime last night, and the wound is healing well. She's incredibly lucky the bullet didn't do more damage, although she's still going to have to deal with the scar tissue."

"A bullet," Curran mused, turning it over in his mind.

"Strange, huh? That's what I thought, too. Why would someone who was probably sent to kill her use a weapon like that? Why not a neural pulser or a disruptor? Something untraceable."

"So when the body was found, it might look like a hunting accident and not be investigated?" Curran speculated.

"That's a thought."

When their food arrived, Curran ate ravenously. He didn't stop to talk again until he'd finished everything he'd ordered.

"Did you know, David, that she's a fugitive?" Curran said as he finished his cama. He'd spent part of the morning doing some unauthorized research into the police files for Caracor and the sector.

"She mentioned it," David said, sipping his coffee.

"The warrant isn't limited to Caracor. They're looking for her off-world, too."

"What?! That can't be right, can it?"

"It says she's wanted for questioning."

"Someone is going to a lot of trouble and expense just to find her for questioning. Isn't it usually just violent or career criminals they look for off-world?"

"Exactly."

"What has she gotten herself into?"

"I don't know," Curran replied, clearly worried.

"Jenny gave me this ring and this packet of papers and asked me to keep an appointment for her today," David said, setting the ring and the packet of papers on the table between them.

"With who?"

"Her friend in low places."

"Have you looked at what's in the packet?"

"No," David answered as he finished the last of his breakfast. He put down his fork and opened the packet. There was a folded note, sealed with tape, on top. He showed the note to Curran but didn't open it. Then he leafed through the papers. "It's a list of equipment and supplies and some transfer co-ordinates," he said, handing them to Curran. "How does she plan to pay for all this? The analyzer would cost me a year's pay all by itself."

"Good question," Curran said as he finished looking through the papers and handed them back to David.

"Let's go back to my room, see how she's doing and ask her."

***

They arrived at David's room to find that Jenny had already gotten up, showered, and was sitting up in bed, watching the news. Her hair was still wet, and she smelled faintly of soap and shampoo.

"Anything interesting going on?" David asked.

"No, same old stuff. The biggest story seems to be a major drug bust near Thaetar. They seized a whole shipload of *sengata*."

"I wish someone would put those people out of business forever," David said. "That stuff kills people."

Sengata had arrived on the drug scene about ten years earlier and had since grown enormously in popularity. The drug had little or no effect on humans. In Denibans, it produced a pleasant but short-lived euphoria, followed by extremely unpleasant auditory and tactile hallucinations. The drug was rarely used by either species. In Thaetans, however, the intense euphoria was accompanied by colorful and evocative visual hallucinations. Music was supposed to be an entirely new experience when heard under the influence of sengata. The drug was also highly addictive in Thaetans, and after continued usage, its action became unpredictable, often producing terrifying hallucinations, drug-induced fevers, paranoia, convulsions, and eventually death. Although dozens of arrests and seizures had been made, no one knew where the drug came from or what was used to make it.

"How are you feeling?" David asked his patient.

"Pretty good. Mostly tired and achy."

"Are you ready to eat something?"

"I am. I'm hungry."

"Good. I'll order something. On second thought, I'll go get something," he said, not wanting anyone to see the room or Jenny. He looked at Curran. "Is that all right?"

"Yes, David. We'll be fine."

David left, and Curran locked the door behind him.

"You're looking better this morning," he said, sitting down in the chair across the room from her.

"I feel a lot better," she said. "Thank you for being here, Curran. I thought you would come, but when you didn't write, I wasn't sure."

"I've not been well."

"Yes," she said, "but how are you now?"

"Last night, when I first saw you, it was difficult. But strangely enough, I feel better now than I have in a long time. I'm not sure whether that's a good sign or not. Perhaps it's just a prelude to another round of shal'tan—the first dose of the drug, so to speak."

"Perhaps it's a sign of our bond renewing itself and of the comfort we feel in each other's company."

"I would like to think so," he said.

"Curran, I've recovered emotionally."

"Yes, I can feel that."

"So you'll understand that when I tell you I still want this relationship, it's not just some shal'tan delusion."

"I know it's not, Jenny," he said, but his eyes never left hers as he waited for the rest.

"I'm as afraid as you are, Curran."

It was what he'd hoped to hear. It was a sign of sanity that she was still afraid of what could happen to them.

"It seems we both want the same thing," he said.

"Do you think we can live together on Caracor for a few months before we go to Deniba to be with your family and marry?"

"Yes, for a while. If David will help."

Jenny understood that he was referring to *anthrin*, a drug that suppressed the normal Deniban male sexual cycle.

"If things start to come apart for us, I can make arrangements to get you to Capitol, and you can help David, but for as long as we're able, I'd like your help in the woods."

"For as long as we're able," he promised.

There was a knock at the door, and Curran got up to let David in.

"Everything okay?" David asked as he stepped into the room.

"We're fine, David," Jenny answered.

"I'm glad to hear it. Now eat," he said, handing her the food he'd brought back.

"It smells good," she said, taking the lid off a bowl of soup and trying a spoonful. It was delicious but so hot that she decided to set it aside on the nightstand to cool for a few minutes.

"Jenny, tell us about the man you want us to meet," Curran asked.

"He's a friend. That's all you need to know. Don't bother asking him for his name or anything else about himself. If he wants you to know, he'll tell you. He also won't expect *your* names, but he'll figure them out. The two of us go back a long way."

"Can he really get you all this stuff?" David asked.

"He can, and he will. His homeworld is Caracor. He understands what's going on there. No matter what you think of him or how he acts when you meet him, he's a good man and honest in his own way. He'll do what he says, and he won't promise what he can't do."

"But where is all the money for all this coming from?"

"The food and supplies are being donated. The computers, the analyzers, and some of the other stuff, you don't want to know about."

"Ah," David said, beginning to grasp the origins of the "you don't want to know about" items.

"Where do we meet him?" Curran asked.

"The park pavilion at the east end of town at midday."

Curran knew the place. It was a rough neighborhood, but a lovely park.

"How will we know him?"

"Wear the ring, David. He'll know you."

***

The man in the park turned out to be a surprise. David didn't know exactly what he'd been expecting, but it wasn't what they saw. The man who met them was well-dressed and neat, a Thaetan, his thick mane of white hair brushed straight back away from his face. He'd been there when they arrived and must have seen the ring on David's finger almost at once, but he'd watched the two of them off and on for almost thirty minutes before approaching them.

"Who are you?" he asked David without preamble, the nictitating membranes over his blue-blue Thaetan eyes flickering in a mix of curiosity and suspicion.

"My name is David Rawlins. I'm Jenny's friend."

"If you're her friend, who is this one?" the man asked, looking at Curran.

"Jenny's bond-mate," David answered.

"It's good to meet you, David," the Thaetan said, offering his three-fingered hand, the vestigial webbing showing between the fingers, to David in a traditional human handshake. "And Curran. It's a pleasure. Let's go somewhere a little warmer and talk."

The Thaetan led them to a pleasant bar not far from the park where they sat down at a table in the back. When the bartender came for their order, the Thaetan instructed him to keep an eye on the door and watch who came and went. "We don't want to be disturbed," he said.

"Yes, Sir."

The bartender returned with their drinks and nodded toward the front of the bar. The Thaetan took a quick look and then sat back.

"Trouble?" David asked.

"No. Just a friend of mine helping out."

David recognized the man. He'd been in the park too, near the pavilion. Apparently, he was a bodyguard.

"Now, let's get down to business," the Thaetan said, holding his hand out to receive the papers he knew David was carrying.

"First, what do you know about what Jenny's gotten herself into," David asked.

"Not much. Just that something is happening to the makonen forests, and no one seems to know why. You people are lucky, maybe luckier than you know. The makonen forests are a wonder, and you may be among some of the last people to see what they look like before they disappear forever."

"Surely, it can't be that bad," David said.

"Some places it's not bad at all. There's been no change. Other places...

"I don't know what Jenny's told you, but in Jenny's area, the forests are changing so fast that in twenty more years, the woods I grew up in are going be unrecognizable.

"In the uplands, the forest gaps that form when the big trees fall would normally be filled by early colonizers like *helianthus* and *thuga*. Arrakts and makonens would follow them. Now only the helianthus and thuga come up. The makonens aren't replacing themselves, and the forest composition is changing because of it. A lot of what goes on in these forests isn't well understood, and no one knows the consequences of the kinds of changes that are happening now."

"You sound pretty knowledgeable about this," David said. "Are you a scientist?"

"No, I'm just Jenny's friend, but I've been educating myself. A lot of us have."

The Thaetan held out his hand again. "Now, to business."

David gave him Jenny's shopping list and watched him study it. "Tell her the food and supplies have already been arranged for and are going to be loaded tomorrow. I can get most of the rest of the equipment if she's willing to wait a few more days, but not all of it. Some of this I couldn't get no matter how long we waited."

"We'll wait the few extra days," David said. Jenny needed the time to rest.

The Thaetan began marking off the items he couldn't get. When he finished, he called the bartender over and asked him to make a copy of the list. Then he opened the folded note and read it.

"The false IDs and credentials you'll need are no problem, David. All I need to know is who you want to be.

"Setting up dummy bank accounts for you is no problem. Cash is no problem," he said, handing David an envelope filled with bills.

"We'll let you know about the IDs and credentials," David said, a little shocked at seeing the amount of money in the envelope.

"Good. I'll leave word for you here when my ship is ready to leave."

The Thaetan finished his drink in a swallow and abruptly left the building.

"David, let's go across the street to the park. We need to talk."

When they had arrived back at the pavilion, Curran stopped.

"David, I want you to give me anthrin."

"No." David was emphatic.

"Listen—"

"No! Absolutely not. And besides, I thought you two said you were fine."

"That part is true. For now. But I've checked. We'll be arriving on Caracor in mid-summer. The photoperiod in the area where we'll be working is the same on Caracor at that time of year as it is on Deniba in early fall."

"That's just great." The Deniban sexual cycle was keyed to the photoperiod. "Is there any other good news you'd like to share with me?"

"No. That's all," Curran said mildly.

"Have you ever had anthrin before?"

Curran was clearly hesitant to answer.

"Curran, don't lie to me about this. If you and Jenny want children, don't lie to me. Not about any of it."

The drug was effective, but it was also potentially dangerous. It could destroy a man's reproductive capacity permanently. In rare cases, it could even be life-threatening.

"Once. About twelve years ago."

"Were there any after-effects?"

"None."

"I won't promise. I'll do the blood work. Then we'll see."

"That's enough," Curran said, accepting David's terms.

They walked back to David's room at the hotel. Jenny was sleeping quietly.

David collected a blood sample from Curran and returned to the ship, where he still had some official business to finish up before he could begin his leave. He did the blood work for Curran and finished the last of his reports. Then he calculated the titration that would keep the anthrin dosage within safe limits for Curran, selected the tiny micropump he would implant on the inside of Curran's upper arm, and filled the reservoir with the drug. When he finished, he went back to his office to take a final look around before leaving the ship.

Within a few hours after David implanted the micropump, Curran was already looking better.

Within a day, he'd even started to eat normally again.

"How long will it last, David?" Curran had asked before David began the procedure.

"I don't have any way of knowing. Its effects will get weaker as the photoperiod shortens. I'm pretty sure of that. There's also the question of your proximity to the other half of this problem. I don't know what effect that might have."

"How long?" Curran insisted.

"Maybe three or four months, give or take."

***

By the end of the third day, Jenny was out of bed and had recovered some of her strength. She'd also recovered her eagerness for work, designing a reading program for David and Curran that would help them understand what was happening on Caracor. She didn't try to give them everything available or promote anyone's pet theories, just enough to get them both curious. She wanted them to be able to think without preconceptions, to see with new eyes.

Soon they were asking questions, and because she refused to answer them, hoping that finding their own answers might lead them down different paths than she'd been following herself, they were constantly looking up new material and discussing the evidence.

When word came the next day that the Thaetan's ship was ready to leave, the three of them packed up the few belongings they had with them and left for Caracor.

CHAPTER 4

Curran and Jenny arrived on Caracor at the edge of a small clearing. Behind them were the stacks of crates and boxes that held their supplies and equipment. Behind that was the cabin they would be living in together.

Curran stepped away from Jenny's side and entered the forest alone. It was cool and dark and shadowy after the intense direct sunlight in the clearing. The trees were enormous. His arms couldn't begin to encircle even a small one. The bark at the base of the oldest makonen trees was almost two feet thick and deeply ridged. The foliage was a rich green a little darker than the irises of his green Deniban eyes. The bigger trees were over a hundred and twenty feet tall, their tops forming a dense canopy above him. Sunlight filtered through the canopy in slivers and streaks and ribbons of shimmering light as the uppermost branches swayed gently in a light breeze. The arrakts were almost as tall, their reddish-brown bark forming thick scales, their dark green leaves drooping slightly in the afternoon heat. Helianthus and thuga dominated the understory. The forest floor was covered four inches deep with leaf litter and felt springy under his feet.

Every step he took into the forest seemed to carry him deeper into some vast, timeless space where everything around him would ultimately prove to be unknowable. As if, in the end, no amount of study or intellectual effort would ever fully capture the reality of what was there. Nothing like this existed anywhere on Deniba, or on any world Curran had seen.

Curran knelt on the thick carpet of makonen needles and decaying leaves. All around him, in the trees and on the ground, the woods were alive with the sounds of birds and animals. Above him on the nearest makonen, he could see a tree mouse running along a branch, stopping to feed on the tips of the makonen needles. To his left, he heard the whistles and barks of a makonen squirrel. Then he caught a glimpse of it. The squirrel was about eighteen inches long, but almost half of its length was tail. Its coat was a deep reddish-brown, the color of black coffee in a white cup. Two thin tan stripes ran down its back with eight ivory spots spaced between them. On the sun-dappled forest floor, a makonen squirrel would be nearly invisible unless it moved.

He brushed aside the leaf litter, dug his fingers into the soil beneath it, and brought up a handful of earth. He rolled the earth between his hands, pulverizing it, studying the feel of it, letting it fall through his fingers and back to the ground. The soil was damp and fecund, the scent sensual and mysterious.

Curran stood up and laid his body against the body of the nearest makonen tree, his arms outstretched, his cheek pressed against its rough bark. At length, he began to feel a subtle energy enter into his body. The energy brought with it the living awareness of a being hundreds of years old, a being that understood the world in a way he couldn't have imagined ten minutes earlier, yet he was experiencing it now—a deep, sustained knowing of this place and of the lives intertwined with its own.

Curran was taken by an overwhelming sense of his own smallness and of exhilaration as well. People were nothing in such a place. It had existed for eons before humanoids evolved. It would continue to exist long after they were gone.

***

Jenny watched Curran walk to the forest's edge, enter, and disappear within it. She wanted him to be able to experience the forest by himself the first time. When he'd been gone for several minutes, she walked a short distance into the forest and knelt down to study the leaf litter. The makonen needles, which took the longest time to decay, made up the bulk of the forest litter. The previous year's arrakt leaves had mostly decayed, a sign of healthy soil.

She dug into the loose soil under the leaf litter until her fingers came in contact with the first roots. The soil was so interpenetrated by so many roots it was like touching a piece of finely woven netting. She would have had to tear it apart to dig any deeper, although the soil itself was loose and friable.

The roots she touched were interwoven with the roots of hundreds of other trees and shrubs, but all of it made up only a tiny fraction of what was in the soil. Under her feet and for as far as she could see, and for hundreds of miles beyond, there was this dense mesh of interwoven roots. The intricacy of what was underground was vastly more complex than what was visible.

She scooped up a handful of the grayish tan soil. There were more living microscopic plants and animals in one square foot of forest soil than there were people living in Capitol. Those plants and animals were the foundation of everything. They determined what lived here. They determined if anything at all lived here. The soil was the beginning of everything, the sustainer of everything, the place where everything returned when it died. She breathed deep, taking in its rich, familiar musky sweetness.

Scientifically, it was possible to break down the handful of soil she held into its very atoms. She could know exactly what was in it. Every organic compound, every mineral, every yeast and mold and fungus, every microscopic plant and animal, and in what amounts they were present, yet by themselves, they were meaningless. It was only the whole that held the wisdom, the knowledge of how to grow things. The parts could be understood piece by piece, atom by atom, but the whole could never be fully comprehended, and it could never be recreated by humans.

The forest was the interaction of so many things—site, soil, water, weather, climate, fire, wind, all of the plants and animals that lived on it or in it. The idea that humans could control or direct something so complex—something that was always in motion, continually evolving in response to the things it experienced—had always seemed to Jenny to be both arrogant and naïve.

She had just gotten to her feet when Curran came to her side.

"This must never be lost," he said softly as he stopped beside her. *"Never."*

"This is why I had to come back."

Then she turned abruptly, and with Curran beside her, she walked back to the pile of equipment in the clearing.

"Well, there it is," she said, gesturing expansively toward the cabin. "Home."

"Home" was an old wildcrafter's shack.

He looked at the small cabin and then at her. "How long has it been since the last time you saw it?"

"About five years. A friend told me about it. I spent a few weeks here, after finishing work on my survey areas."

The cabin's squared logs were still sound, but the pile of flat rocks that held up the porch floor's right corner had collapsed. The porch floor was sagging, and so was the right side of its roof. The front door was hanging by one hinge and part of the roof had fallen in.

"Kind of a fixer-upper," she said.

Curran looked at her blankly, unfamiliar with the term.

"A handyman's special."

"A ruin?" he suggested.

"That about covers it," she agreed.

"I think we'd better take a quick look inside and evict whoever may be living there," Jenny said as a small fox-like animal ran out from under the sagging porch floor and into the woods.

"Good idea."

There were few animals on Caracor that would deliberately attack a person, but none of them were especially afraid of people either. They also didn't consider people to be food, but that didn't mean they wouldn't bite, sting, or claw if sufficiently threatened or provoked. Some of the bites could be dangerous.

They did a cautious inspection, carefully opening cupboards, looking under furniture, taking care not to startle anyone, and get bitten in the process. There were several abandoned nests, lots of droppings, but no permanent residents. The cabin was filthy, and it had been raining inside part of it for some time, but the building was basically sound. Even the floorboards under the hole in the roof were still sound. The boards were rough-sawn *zanthis*, which was extremely rot-resistant.

They went back outside to decide on a plan of action.

"I think it would be easiest to start by taking everything out of the cabin and seeing what's salvageable," Curran said. "After that, we can sweep down the whole house—walls, rafters, everything—and wash the floors and cabinets afterward."

"Most of the repairs look minor, and we've got all the tools and supplies we'll need," Jenny said.

"We don't have the materials to replace the roof," he pointed out.

"Everything we need is out there in the woods. Tomorrow we'll look for a dead thuga that's still standing. We can fell it, cut it into rounds, and I can rive shingles out of it. There should be a froe in the tools somewhere. The rafters look good and most of the purlins, too. The planks from the packing crates and that fallen-in shed out back should give us enough lumber for furniture."

"What about water?"

"There's a spring out back."

Jenny led him into the woods at the back of the cabin, then

down a narrow overgrown path along a rocky hillside. At the bottom of the path, there was a small pool of water in what remained of a rock-walled spring box. At one time, the spring box had a wooden cover over it, but the cover had rotted away and fallen into the pool, along with several years' worth of dirt and leaves. A tiny trickle of water ran out of the pool and into a small spring branch.

"That's it?" he said skeptically.

"It'll be fine. It just needs to be cleaned and dug out again. It used to run a lot of water."

"Let's go back to the house and break open the boxes of tools," he said. "I'll start on the house, and you can start here."

"Okay. Just be sure you wear gloves while you're working. There's no point in taking chances."

***

Jenny returned and started cleaning out the spring box. The water was icy cold, and within a few minutes, her fingers were numb and she was soaked and filthy, but she was enjoying the work—the feel of the sunlight as it filtered through the trees, and the sounds of the birds and animals around her. The animals were curious and unafraid, going about their business, occasionally stopping to watch her.

Jenny dug out the muck and rebuilt the rock walls. When she finished the job, she sat back against a tree and watched as the muddy water began to clear, and the little pool filled with water that spilled out over the rocks below and into the branch. The thin trickle of water she and Curran had found a few hours earlier was now a flow of several gallons per minute. She was tired, and her arm ached, but it was healing well, and on the trip to Caracor, David had given her exercises to help her deal with the scar tissue.

When Jenny got back to the cabin, Curran was sweeping the walls. He stopped to look at her as she stood under the hole in the roof, muddy and wet, with the fading sunlight streaming in on her. He took his time looking, and Jenny let him.

"Can we use the spring yet?" he asked.

"I was hoping to find a bucket so I can haul some water up here to the house."

"I found two five-gallon buckets while I was carrying everything out. They're outside by the edge of the porch, along with a few other things I thought were salvageable. However, you're not the one who's going to get the water. You shouldn't be carrying anything that heavy."

"Okay."

"When can we eat?" he asked. "I'm getting hungry. Are you?"

"I'll see what I can find."

By dark, they were sitting at the small cook fire Curran had built. Curran was baking some pan bread in a frying pan he'd found in one of the boxes of household supplies.

Jenny had made a pot of sweet-smelling tea from the roots of a small shrub she'd pulled up. It was steeping on a rock beside the fire. She'd also picked and cooked several kinds of greens and found some berries for dessert.

When the bread was done, Jenny watched Curran as he ate his share. He ate slowly and with pleasure. Since David had given him the anthrin, he'd even put on some weight. Neither of them spoke much during the meal, content simply to sit by the fire, listen to the night sounds and eat.

Her hunger sated, Jenny got up and opened the crates marked "Bedding and Household Goods." She dug around for their sleeping bags and ground cloths, dropped Curran's beside him, spread hers by the fire, and began to undress for bed, as unselfconscious about her body as any Deniban woman.

She felt Curran's eyes on her, but knew that although he might be enjoying the play of the firelight on her body, he felt no desire for her. She put on a clean T-shirt and slid into her sleeping bag.

Curran banked the fire, laid a few green helianthus branches on it to keep the insects away, undressed, and got into his sleeping bag. Jenny lay on her side, watching him. She was tired, but content, and happy to be in the forest again. She rolled onto her back and looked up at the small part of the night sky they could see from their little clearing. After a time, she closed her eyes.

"I love you, Curran."

The words were spoken softly, barely audible above the sound of the wind in the leaves and the singing of the insects, but loud enough for Curran to hear them plainly.

Curran didn't answer. She hadn't expected him to. Curran had never told her he loved her. He probably never would. He had never pretended to understand the word.

"Sleep well, Jenny, *mei'keithara*," he said.

Jenny smiled to herself at his reply. 'Jenny, my treasured one,' he'd said. He had never spoken those words to her before.

She watched the stars for a few more minutes, then closed her eyes and went to sleep.

CHAPTER 5

David walked up to the roof of the three-story building he would be living in while he was on Caracor. He'd left his duffel bag and corpsman's bag on the bed in his apartment and gone to the roof to get a better look at the city. He walked past the solar panels and rooftop gardens and looked out across the city to the rolling wooded hills that rose row after row away from the river bottom where the city was built. He'd read extensively about Capitol and seen movies and vids, but it wasn't anything like he'd imagined it to be.

Capitol wasn't so much a city surrounded by a forest as it was a forest with a city built within it. Even here, in the middle of the city, the smell of trees and earth and the sound of leaves were everywhere. Trees lined the streets, and small wooded parks and greens were spread throughout the city. People's yards, even the plazas and public areas of businesses and office buildings, were forested or filled with shrubs and flowers.

To the west of David's building, the Zanthis River meandered through town, a wide silvery ribbon of water with wooden bridges spanning it at irregular intervals. There were a few cars on the streets and some trucks, but most of the traffic consisted of cyclists and pedestrians. People gathered in the parks, fished off the bridges, visited in open-air cafes.

David was enthralled, already in love with the city. He knew it was a thoroughly modern city, yet it felt comfortable and intimate. Capitol was built on a human scale and in such a way that the inhabitants could interact with it and each other without losing their awareness and sense of participation in the environment in which they lived.

David walked downstairs to his apartment on the second floor, the one on the left side of the landing. The apartment was clean and sunny, the furnishings spare, but more than adequate. He unpacked the few belongings he'd brought with him, put them away, and walked out into the neighborhood to find a grocery store and a place where he could buy some sheets and towels and a few household items. He was back in an hour, cooking dinner.

In the evening after he'd eaten, David went back outside for a walk. He ended up at a sidewalk cafe, drinking Thaetan beer with the cafe's Thaetan owner and a couple of human customers who appeared to be regulars. It was a slow night with plenty of time for visiting.

"So, David, how do you like Capitol?" Rhiami, the café's owner, asked.

"I just got here, but I already like it."

"Do you have a job yet, or are you just starting to look?"

"I'm here on a grant from the Habragayre Foundation to study at the Institute of Forestry."

"Oh. What's your area of interest?" the owner asked.

"Wildlife biology."

David had enough forged documents and ID's to pass himself off as just about anything from a professor to a lab technician. Still, he'd decided just to be David Rawlins, a wildlife biologist visiting Caracor on a grant from a phony research foundation. He'd decided that being at the Institute on a grant would give him the greatest freedom of movement. All he needed was a workspace and access to the Institute's database and library. He had plenty of "grant" money, a résumé, all the credentials he needed to document his academic background, and a copy of the supposedly approved grant proposal. All he had to do now was convince Peter Carmichael, the Director of Research, that his grant was legitimate.

"I know Peter Carmichael. He's the Director of Research over at the Institute. He comes in here fairly regularly. Do you have an appointment to see him yet?"

"I'll be going over there first thing in the morning," David said. "Everything's already been arranged."

He was planning to see Peter Carmichael first thing in the morning, but there was no appointment, and he'd be playing it by ear.

"Well, tell him I said hello, and be sure to stop in here tomorrow and let me know what happened. We can have a beer to celebrate."

"Thanks. I'd like that," David said as he got up to pay his bill. "I'll see you tomorrow."

***

The next morning David took a free city-supplied bicycle from the rack in front of the neighborhood grocery store and rode to the research center across town. The city streets were shady and inviting and dappled with sunlight. With so little traffic noise, it was possible to hear the leaves rustling in the morning breeze and the songs of birds.

He parked the bike in front of the big two-story building, walked to the information desk in the lobby, and asked for directions to Peter Carmichael's office. When he got there, the door was open, and a secretary was working at the desk in the outer office.

"Hi," David said. "I'd like to see Director Carmichael."

"Do you have an appointment?"

"No, but I've got a grant to study here at the Institute for the next six months, and I was instructed to see the director as soon as I arrived."

"Your name, Sir?"

"David Rawlins."

"Well, I don't see your name on the list of our grant recipients," she said, looking over the list. She shuffled through some more papers on her desk and checked the computer. "There's no notation here about you either. That's funny."

"Not really. I'm not here on a grant from the Institute itself. I have a grant from the Habragayre Foundation. I was supposed to check in with Director Carmichael as soon as I arrived in Capitol. It's all been arranged."

The secretary took another look through the papers on her desk, but still couldn't find anything about a David Rawlins or a grant from the Habragayre Foundation.

"I'm really sorry about this, but I still can't find anything. However, Mr. Carmichael is in this morning. Maybe he can see you now, and we can get this straightened out."

She picked up the phone, buzzed the director, and explained the problem. Then she nodded, hung up, and waved David toward the inner office. "Go right in. He'll see you now."

"Thanks," he said.

As David walked into the office, the director got up and came around his desk to greet him.

"Hi, David. I'm Peter Carmichael. I hear we're supposed to be expecting you."

Carmichael was a small energetic man of about fifty. He had a firm handshake and a pleasant, unassuming manner. With a casual wave of his hand, he invited David to take a seat across the desk from him and then resumed his place behind it.

"What seems to be the problem?" he asked.

"I'm here on a grant from the Habragayre Foundation," David explained. "I'd been told by the people at the foundation that they'd made all the arrangements."

"Well, we don't seem to know anything about it," the director said with genuine concern, "but I'll recheck our records and see what we can find. The Habragayre Foundation, you say? I'm not familiar with them."

"Probably not. They're a small private foundation headquartered on Dalton's Planet," David extemporized. "Actually, I don't know if you'll have to bother with contacting them," he said, trying to keep the panic out of his voice, since it was unlikely Carmichael would ever reach anyone at the "Habragayre Foundation" except a computer voice instructing the caller to leave a message. "I've got a copy of the grant proposal right here, along with my credentials and a voucher for the funds. I'm here to study timber cats."

He handed Carmichael his credentials and the voucher and watched the man's eyebrows rise in amazement. The sum was substantial, more than enough to provide a research director at an institution chronically in need of funds with an incentive to make a place for David to do his research. Carmichael was so startled by the amount he didn't even ask to see the grant proposal, although he did look at the credentials and David's resume.

"They gave me a stipend to live on, so all of that is intended to go to the Institute to pay the costs of my being here. I know you haven't been able to make any plans to accommodate me, but really, all I need is a desk somewhere, library and database privileges, and access to the grounds. I guess if they're not available, I can call the foundation. God, I hope they don't decide to rescind the grant."

David could see from Carmichael's expression that he was hoping exactly the same thing and that he had no intention of risking the cancellation of such a substantial grant by calling its originators and telling them the Institute had no place for their recipient.

"Well, I don't see any real problem here," Carmichael assured David. "It's probably just an oversight. It happens. Let's see. I can put you in with Kate Timmons. The man she shares her office with is in the field right now. I'll take you over there and introduce you. Then if you can be back here in a couple of hours, we can have your paperwork processed and your ID's ready for you."

"That sounds great," David said earnestly, handing Carmichael a copy of the grant proposal, which theoretically should have already been on file. "I appreciate all your help, especially on such short notice. I'm sorry about all the confusion. I've never had a problem with the foundation before. They're usually very good about getting everything arranged."

"Don't worry about it, David. We'll have everything straightened out in no time."

Peter escorted David to the second floor, then down the hall on the building's south wing, and knocked on the door of the third office on the right before the end of the hall.

"Come in," said a pleasant, somewhat harried sounding voice.

"Hi, Kate," Carmichael said as they entered the room.

Kate Timmons was sitting at one of the two large desks in the room, rifling through a huge stack of papers, caught in the act of searching for something she'd apparently misplaced.

"This is David Rawlins," Carmichael began. "David is a wildlife biologist. He's here on a research grant from the Habragayre Foundation. And he'll be sharing your office for a while until we find him more permanent quarters for him? Okay?"

Peter was asking Kate's permission, not making a demand and expecting her to accept it whether she liked it or not.

"Sure. It's been too quiet around here with R'Etan gone," she said.

By her expression, it was clear that David's sudden arrival was a bit of an inconvenience, but she seemed willing to accept the situation gracefully.

"Thanks, Kate. You're a lifesaver. This is a real emergency. It seems that we've somehow managed to lose all of David's paperwork, and nothing has been arranged for him. If you'd refused to take him in, my next plan was to put him in a broom closet somewhere."

"Well, desperate measures for desperate times, right, Pete?" she joked, still somewhat distracted as she thumbed through another stack of papers.

"Something like that. Well, I'll leave you two on our own to get acquainted," Peter said as he left.

"So, what are you here to work on, David?" Kate asked, temporarily giving up the search.

"Population dynamics in timber cats."

Timber cats were a small predator with a varied diet that included everything from mice and squirrels to berries and carrion. He'd read enough about them to know they filled a niche similar to that of bobcats in the North American forests on Earth. He'd learned a lot about bobcats when he'd worked for a team of wildlife biologists during the summers before he started medical school. The pay was bad, but he'd loved being in the woods, doing the work.

"What do *you* do?" he asked.

"I'm a soil scientist."

That was certainly a bit of good fortune. She probably wouldn't know much about timber cats.

"Does this work of yours have any direct application for the people who gave you the grant?" Kate asked.

"Possibly. At least we think it might. A forest management company supports the foundation. They've been having a hard time maintaining predator-prey numbers in the forests they're trying to rehabilitate on Atalga. The predators keep losing ground, and as a result, they can't control the damage to the trees caused by an overabundance of what passes for mice and squirrels there. Maybe there's an answer here, in a forest that hasn't seen that kind of problem."

Kate held his gaze the entire time he was talking to her. He felt awkward with her looking at him so intently, but he also found himself engaged in a way that surprised him.

He thought Kate was probably in her late thirties. She had high cheekbones and almond-shaped eyes with an epicanthic fold. Her skin glowed with health. Her long black hair reached to the middle of her back and was tied loosely behind her neck. She was tall, almost as tall as he was, slim, and her bearing was regal without being intimidating. In fact, it was in direct contrast to how she dressed and how she spoke. She was wearing jeans, work boots, and a T-shirt with a makonen tree on it, and when she spoke, she was direct and without pretense. In spite of that, or perhaps because of it, David felt off-balance with her, not quite able to get his bearings.

"Do you suppose R'Etan would mind if I stacked up some of his papers and made a little room at his work station for myself?" he asked cautiously.

"What? Oh, of course not. I'll help. I know what we can move and to where."

Kate started making orderly stacks of the papers and books on R'Etan's desk and work area and carrying them to the closet where she laid them neatly on the shelves. There was nothing for David to do except to stay out of the way, so he roamed the office, looking around while she worked.

Pinned to the bulletin board on the wall above Kate's work station, he saw a copy of the article based on the interview Jenny had given. David was shocked to see it there, but he didn't comment on it, unsure of what to say without knowing Kate better and understanding how she felt about what was happening. Stopping at her desk, he picked up one of her holo-cubes.

"You're husband?" he asked.

Made in the USA
Middletown, DE
26 January 2021